The Garden O
And Peri

Bruce W. Perry

The world breaks everyone and afterward many are strong at the broken places.

A Farewell To Arms, Ernest Hemingway

I went to the Garden of Love,
And saw what I never had seen:
A Chapel was built in the midst,
Where I used to play on the green.

And the gates of this Chapel were shut,
And Thou shalt not. writ over the door;
So I turn'd to the Garden of Love,
That so many sweet flowers bore.

And I saw it was filled with graves,
And tomb-stones where flowers should be:
And Priests in black gowns, were walking their rounds,
And binding with briars, my joys & desires.

The Garden Of Love, William Blake

CHAPTER 1: Emma Blair Winslow, London, 2051

I ride my bike in Southwark, just a few blocks south of the sluggish green Thames and the London Tower Bridge. I go south of the Thames and let myself get lost on Bermondsey Street, making swirly patterns with thick tires on the leaf-covered road. It's empty with occasional cobblestones on the sidewalks. These blocks still give off an antique charm, subtle airs of the city's leftover flair. The neighborhood's slightly bohemian flavor.

My name is Emma Blair Winslow. I am 22 years old. My mum, Emma Wallace Blair, wouldn't recognize these neighborhoods, even though Southwark was one of her favorite districts. The streets are overgrown with full-leaved, thick-canopied trees and lush bushes in full blossom. They hide the old flats and pubs and boutiques that used to populate Bermondsey.

I hear the squeak of my bicycle as the sun drifts behind an empty building across the river. That's the City of London, proper, where the banksters and the smart set hung out. No more, those skyscrapers are largely empty. They are not of much use in this small world. The London of barely 10,000 people.

I get a little lost on Bermondsey. I have a pack with me. I know the city well, and I'll take a long route to where I'll meet Jason Hunter at a park off the Cut called Millennium Green. We keep one of our many gardens there, and it's time to pick some onions and tomatoes.

I speed up on the bike, the warm wind blowing through my long hair. I see no other cyclists or anyone on foot. People have pulled stuff into the street, like chairs, sofas, tables, even crude barricades to mark off neighborhoods. Can't suppress their territoriality. I ride around this stuff easily, as I'm used to it.

This is not hostile terrain, as far as I know, and my knowledge of the city is beyond good. There are a lot of places you should never go to, however, especially after dark. You wouldn't want to anyways, unless you had to.

I didn't know the London of Black Cabs and SUVs, and Teslas and Mercedes. Now it's bikes and walkers and electric carts and occasional motorcycles. Compared with the choked, bustling London of old, back in 2026 and before, the streets are often empty and silent. When you see a person, you hail them. It's fairly easy to detect intent with a quick look, and for most humans here, the intent is to survive and not to hurt or interfere.

Only a few people or families live on each block.

That's true of Bermondsey and most places. Guitars strumming, quiet chatter or boisterous laughter echoing off the discolored, vine-covered buildings. People tend their gardens, sew or clean clothes, make shoes and repair eyeglasses, and fashion neat little inventions, like effective water pumps for using the Thames.

I pass a small park; young men are playing basketball on the cracked pavement, and a football game goes on behind a beaten-up chain-link fence. Six on six. A few of them stop playing and hoot at me. I pick it up again, pedaling furiously, bending to the task of moving on to the next neighborhood.

The young men can be quite ratty; London toughs, that hasn't changed. Scrawny, tattooed arms with cut-off sweat-shirts, and a few or more missing teeth. They'll grab a girl once in a while, though the punishment for molesting, from the militia, or local neighborhood enforcers, will be harsh and uncompromising. I've heard rumors of lashes meted out and worse, but I haven't seen it myself.

I'm not a violent person. I don't condone it, which has been a source of debate with Jason.

Threats are still rare, and I don't believe this neighborhood poses one. Still, Jason worries when I bike alone. Which is a lot.

I play sports myself. Football, soccer as the Yanks used to call it (when there were lots of Yanks), still dominates. Funny how that works; must be part of the DNA, because no one is forced to play sports. I'd be bored otherwise. The London of 2051 is a fairly libertarian society, other than organized food production and the occasional mustering of the defense militia, majority women if you believe it.

As I mentioned, not everyone born into the New World has good intentions. Most do. If I had to put a percentage on it, I'd say 98.

It's a simple world with basic priorities: eat, drink, grow, harvest, pee, poo, help your neighbor, avoid accidents. Ones like falling off a bridge into the Thames, or squatting a skyscraper and falling down an unused elevator shaft. That happens.

At Bermondsey Square I take a right and head more directly toward Waterloo Millennium Green. I could use a coffee; there are a few shops. But I'll wait for Jason. He'll be pissed because I'm late.

There are no cellphones to notify people of your tardiness, or to harangue people with texts. Never actually used them, or even seen a working one, but Mum mentioned them as prominent in her diary. I have no use for them; I like freedom.

The streets are more like paths and some have turned to dirt, like this one. The Old London had plenty of parks, but was mostly made up of stone buildings and skyscrapers and narrow antique streets and Thames-side strolls. This London is forests and paths, with buildings hidden behind gobs of lush vegetation.

I ride my bike everywhere. Handy, still a great invention. The only place more popular than a coffee or grog shop is a bike repair place. Yeah, in case you wondered, people have figured out how to cultivate coffee beans, but they're also available via the many trade routes that have opened up.

My main position, my role in society if you must, is as nurse physician. Meaning, I can be both. Someone has to be around to patch people up, deal with feverish children, make recommendations about the ailments of older folks. You see, we have no organized, hi-tech hospitals. People give birth, live out their lives, and often die, at home. This is "primitive" compared with the way things used to be, but it's the only state of affairs I know.

So, the bloodied and the battered, at least nearby St. Paul's Cathedral, come to me. The Cathedral is where Mum Emma gave birth to me. Fitting, that it's where I tend to the sick and succor the dying.

CHAPTER 2

As I ride hard toward Millennium Green, I come upon more groups of people, some sitting at tables outside chatting and enjoying the good weather, others on their little scooters or bikes, headed for the Thames or wherever.

I smile quietly. It's a happy day. By necessity, I've learned to live in the moment, because expectations are somewhat narrow compared with what was going on in 2026, before the germs took over. When you could strive to be almost whatever you wanted to be. "Grab the brass ring" and all that. The horizons aren't as broad anymore, but they are expanding. You can go to different places, if properly prepared. Jason and I have been talking about the European mainland–he sees some opportunities.

As a nurse, I see everything. I work in the makeshift hospital we've set up in St. Paul's Cathedral. I've gotten very good at staunching blood flow and stitching up wounds. Boys are still boys. They still play in the London ruins and picrce the soles of their feet on errant nails.

This is no utopia I live in. Most of the population from before has died. We do what we can. The city is overgrown like an arboretum and often silent but for the breeze and the birds, which have returned and flocked to the ponds and the weeds and the tree canopies that flourish everywhere. It's a lost city, and a good place for me to grow up. I want for nothing. But *it's no utopia.*

I have, as a nurse, a lot of people die on me, but enough of that. At least we have no cigarettes (they were before my time), because it's only the pot smoking we do.

The pharmacies have long been looted out, so there are no manufactured medicines. No aspirin, NSAIDS like they used to call Tylenol, heavy pain killers, beyond booze, which is still copiously brewed and distilled. People are pissed, all the time, if you can believe it, more than in the Old London.

Vaccines don't exist. We practice "holistic natural immunology," such as purposely exposing young'uns to measles and chicken pox, so they don't get worse versions later.

In my entire lifetime, the Barmy Fever, the Great Forgetting, has faded out. We are wary of its return, however. Cannabis and its derivatives is widely cultivated and consumed. It's a known preventive and palliative.

We know the difference between the virus, the Barmy Fever as many call it, and the workings, or lack thereof, of an old person's brain. It's a world of difference, actually.

Sadly, because of the lack or total absence of modern

medicines, and because London citizens can't be hooked up to machines to keep them alive indefinitely, the super old folks, like nonagenarians and centenarians, have become rarities. We've got a few old folks that somehow survived the Fever 25 years ago, not too many of them past 85.

You see 'em now and then, strolling through the parks with a cane, dreamily recalling the Queen or Princess Diana, who's buried near me Mum.

Oh yeah, royalty. They're almost all gone. We didn't hang on to the royal institutions. It just doesn't make sense anymore to have posh men and women in their linens and Oxfords shacked up in Buckingham Palace, no longer ravenously pursued by paparazzi, with their brittle personal lives raked over the coals by the *Daily Mail* (which doesn't exist), sipping whisky, riding horses, and pinning medals on people.

We might bring back the Royal Marines, but doubtful on the royals.

Sheesh, during the plague, we were lucky to have humans, *period.*

I stand by my bike now, alongside the park, waiting for a Jason sighting. I see the old Shard in the distance, knifing into the blue, puffy clouds drifting past like stately ships.

It's warm. The air smells faintly of lilacs and roses, the green rot of leaves piled in the gutters. Then abruptly the floral scent is spoiled by the odor wafting by of piss. Life and its infinite variety.

A number of the trees we planted along the sides of these no-longer-city streets are fruit trees. Apple, cherry, peach, plum. That was on purpose, the planting done during my lifetime. This way, food of some sort is always growing, the wilder the plant the better, to keep people fed.

You can go to the parks and find raspberries, blackberries, tomatoes, carrots, even onions. Kids run around with fruit and tomatoes in their hands, some have little salt shakers in their pockets. They sprinkle it on the tomatoes.

Salt is mined elsewhere in the land and trained down to London. Yes, we have limited train service, as engineers like my late father got some of them working.

As I might have mentioned before, health among the young people has improved compared with before. No more buckets of sugary drinks, continuous pizza consumption, candy bars on demand. Only natural sugars from fruit, really; no factories around to refine it.

As the trade routes open up, we do have some honey, molasses, wheat, and corn. We have a bit of butter and cheese, done up in the artisanal way. All of this helps in the winter, when we lose the outdoor growth of fruit and veggies.

Greenhouses, where much of the cannabis is grown, make up for some of the vegetables lost to the winter.

It's mostly bartering to acquire things, but pound notes and coin are making a wan comeback. A lot of it is back in circulation.

Finally I see Jason, with his own bike. I recognize the mop of hair flying in the wind, the light denim coat with lapels, the black bicycle with its red reflectors. He makes his way through the park, then stops and straddles his bike, beckoning me to join him.

He's been after me for a long time. He's a great looking 24 y.o. who grew up a "London street boy"; an orphan like all of us. Got in more trouble than most of us. Broke a lot of windows once with a gang of other sketchy lads; he was rubber-stamped early on as a delinquent. That gave him a chip on his shoulder, "issues," but many of us who grew up in the urban ruins amidst the corpses of our parents, aunt, and uncles, have had to wrestle with our own dark emotions.

Jason has a machete strapped to his belt. Claims he always needs the protection, that the city is ceaselessly dangerous. He hates it when I don't carry a weapon. He keeps talking about Mum's axe and cricket bat, how I'm reluctant to inherit that part of her. Jason is pissed, tipsy, a bit of the time, and I'm irritated when he often brings up the necessity for violence. Such an alpha-male thing that I'm not into.

I've never had to use a weapon to protect myself in London. Not yet. I think I give off a comforting mojo that keeps any predators at bay, what bad lots we have here, which is not too many. Jason claims I subsist on complacency.

Most Londoners know me as a hospital lady. I'm an untouchable.

CHAPTER 3

Jason lives near me and across the Thames. He has a job at a distillery. His middle name is Stensrud and he fancies himself more Scandinavian than British. I see this as an egotism more than anything else; he says his reddish blond hair came from Danes invading a millennium ago.

He calls me his girlfriend. I'm not ready for that. I've only let him kiss me, indulge in a bit of fondling. We're more than friends though. We've become constant companions. He's a smart lad with an eager intelligence. It's possible I could fall in lust with him, if only he didn't act like he wants to shag me *all* the time.

I know it's only a natural drive, so I take pleasure in his attentions and don't blame him at all for being a randy lad.

He's only two years older than me, 24. I've known him since way back when he joined Harry, Jack, and

Max's gang. They used to bomb around emptied-out London, causing prepubescent trouble. When he was with Harry and that gang, they even disappeared for a week, floating away with a stolen boat on the Thames. It was around that time that Jason began following me around like a puppy-dog, but only lately have I truly enjoyed his company.

Jason has seasoned, he's no longer just a bloke who fancies pistols, crossbows, and getting pissed with friends (although a lot of that still happens). He'll read novels and poetry with me on languid Sunday afternoons in the park.

I pull my bike up next to his, offer a cheek. He kisses me, with a slight grimace at the formality. I don't sense the whiff of booze, however.

"How was the ride over?" he asks.

"Lovely." He touches my tires, scowls.

"A bit low. You know you get a flat in one of those neighborhoods in South London..."

"I know, I know. I have some bread and cheese." I pat the bag I've looped over my shoulder. "Let's pick some onions." The cheese is prized, merely a small piece of gamy Stilton.

We move into an area of the park that's more hidden and weedy. Recent rains have made everything a lush green. It gives a boost to the useless plants, the ones we can't eat. We trudge through the brush and the weeds up to our waists. Unlike others, we know where to look for the onions and tomatoes. We dig a few up and pick some red ones, wipe the dirt off them. I look up past the tops of the trees, watching the shadow of a cloud pass over the empty glass tower that resembles a misshapen pickle. That's 20 Fenchurch.

The afternoon's drowsiness comes over me. Suddenly the park's long lush grasses look inviting. I sit down cross-legged and begin cutting up an onion, handing the bread and a bit of cheese to Jason. He takes a seat beside me in the grass.

Not far away, large tomato plants spill over their cages. Jason picked a few more, now drops them into my bag.

"I might have a new client," he says proudly.

"Client?" I'm impressed by the corporate ring he gives it. He removes his machete and slowly slices up one of the tomatoes. The seed-laden juice drips down the blade; it makes me more hungry.

"Yeah. Fellow named Braden. Dr. Randolph Braden." I'd heard of him.

"What's he want?"

"A guided trip to the mainland." Jason has been trying to launch a guiding service for people who need to move beyond London and its outskirts. Even to Europe. Enough people are timid about travel to be willing to pay for help.

Jason doesn't like working at the distillery; the vapors and the mess he has to deal with.

He carves and chews the tomato, waiting for a reaction.

"Where, exactly, do they want to go?"

"Over to France, the mountains. The Alps."

"You don't say? When I think of France, I picture Paris. *La Rive Gauche*, cafes at night under torch-light, leaves blowing across the Champs-Élysées. The Alps must be empty. Why there? How can they grow food?"

"Not high up in the Alps, *amid* the mountains. On farmland, southeast of Nice. What used to be Nice..." Anywhere more than about 300 kilometers away from us was speculation, in terms of which cities and places had gotten back on their feet in an acceptable, safe way. Some places were still considered frontier, even, by rumor, barbaric.

"Nice, the Riviera. Sounds more like a holiday to me."

"Circa 2019, maybe. It's great land though, near a lake. He's got plans for it, the Braden guy."

"Dr. Randolph Braden," I say, skeptically.

"Know 'im?"

"Only by reputation. He pushes questionable home-brewed meds on people. Some people swear by them. He seems to have his spoon in a lot of pots."

"Well," Jason remarks buoyantly, more worldly. "He's made an offer, and he pays well."

Neither of us has been outside the U.K., but I've seen plenty of photos in dog-eared magazines printed back before the plague.

"Where'd you meet the doctor?" I ask.

"He saw one of my posters. He's an older guy, with a family. They have a house with acres of woods and farmland, over by Switzerland. Not like here, picking vegetables in a scraggly little park. We could grow real crops. Have a different life."

"We?"

"I thought you could come."

Silence. I remove a bread piece, tear off a chunk,

slowly chew. Since I probably can't go, Jason seems suddenly more desirable, with this possibility of losing him.

"What about my patients? I'm taking care of a ward-full of people right now. What about Max, Harry, and Jack?" I'm kind of a den mother to them. They're the only family I know.

"Elizabeth is pregnant, too."

"I know about all that," he says, faintly sullen. We've had enough veggies and bread. We stand back up and stroll to the bikes, which are never out of eyesight. For sure, the London street urchins will take stuff left unprotected.

Jason seems lost in thought. When we reach the bikes, he puts his arm around my waist.

"Think about it, okay?"

"Sure, I can think about it. But that doesn't do any good. Many people depend on me here. It's not like I can up, and abandon them."

London might be a former mega-city, from before the Barmy Fever, but now it's a small town. It must be that I'm also afraid of leaving the only hamlet I've known.

Jason seems bashful; the words not coming out too easily.

"It's not like I *want* to go away. It's a great opportunity that I don't want to let pass. When will I have another? Never?"

"Is this a 100 percent decision you've made, to leave?"

He shrugs. It seems awful risky to me. You leave everything behind, for some half-baked trek across the channel and into the unknowns. France isn't France anymore. It's a sprawling forest inhabited by tribes, hundreds of them living by the Seine and the Rhone. We know little about it.

Almost all of Europe has been reduced to a frontier, outside of the cities.

We throw our legs over the bikes and cast off. As we skirt the park, Jason stares off into a distant block.

"Do you see that?"

CHAPTER 4

"See what?"

"Over there! Those three blokes, running into an alley, naked as jaybirds."

I stop the bike, plant my feet on the ground, and look, see nothing.

"No, I don't see them. Rats, missed it."

"You didn't want to, believe me!"

"What's the fuss?"

"Just weird, that's all. Not a stitch of clothing, hairless, running hell bent...for nothing."

"Maybe running after whoever nicked their clothes." I start laughing, really hard. "Three nitwits with their bare white bottoms, running through London. Now that's funny! Ha ha!"

"You've got a strange sense of humor." He pushes off on his bike. Now I'm riding behind him. He slows when

I complain that I can't keep up with my bag of veggies on my back, then he pulls up alongside me.

"I didn't tell you about the footballers," I say. "One of them mooned me, I think. Never a dull moment around here."

"You mean you're *not* absolutely sure whether he mooned you? That's not something you can mistake for anything else."

We hear a distressed dog barking from the direction of the alley where the naked men ran, then silence.

"Weird, just weird," Jason says with high-minded disgust. "The city's going to pot." Then he looks at me with a quizzical fondness.

"When we go to the mainland, we'll need a medical professional."

"Planning on getting sick on the way, are we?"

"No, but I could charge more, if I had your services."

"They're needed here in Southwark. So why does this guy want to leave London in the first place?"

"Braden? He wants to make wine and cheese and wool and export them over the trade routes. Thinks there's a lot of money to be made. There's an opportunity there."

"He'll pay you in worthless Euros."

"No, pounds. It's in the contract."

"Contract? Written by whom? There are no lawyers. Or, merely self-appointed ones." I couldn't hide my skepticism, or was it resentment? "Why can't he just go by himself?"

We are out on Blackfriars Bridge, crossing the Thames, feeling the cool breeze off the heavy, sluggish waters below. A cross-breeze hits hard on the bike. We plan on taking a right, and making our way along Upper Thames St. I pedal harder, the wind buffeting me from the sides. The Thames is the same; a monumental flow of thick dark green water.

I notice a small vessel passing beneath the bridge. It has a few people on deck, hauling what looks like baskets of produce downstream.

Jason looks back at me, still steering his bike past the few other pedestrians on Blackfriars.

"The whole point is that this guy needs help with navigation and driving one of the Rovers."

"Rovers?" I shout.

"He has two old Range Rovers. And enough gas. At least enough for that trip. He wants to leave in two weeks. The destination is an old village on a lake, with lots of farmland next to it. Mountains above."

"How far is it?"

"Depends on the route I take...but it's going to be about a thousand kilometers."

"Jesus, wow."

"That's why I'm needed. Good opportunity with good pay. A real service." I'm not convinced, but I sort of simmer in silence. My gut feeling is ***you couldn't pay me enough for this trip.***

Randolph Braden gets the gas, I assume, in the form of biofuels. There are no available hydrocarbon fuels, because there are no refineries. The available fuel for gas-driven vehicles was purchased in 25-gallon drums for a high price.

I picture the Alps as scenic, crisp, dreamy. All I'd

known in my life was the Thames-side neighborhood, gray, wet, and bleak in the winter, the high buildings stained and crumbling in the clutch of a massive and encroaching forest. Sure, a change would be invigorating.

Then I think of Max, Jack, Harry, and Elizabeth. I'd break their hearts if I left. I know Max and Elizabeth; they'd be sure that they'd never see me again. A bit needy they are; Debby Downers. Jack would call me a fool, and Braden a swindler, and he'd be at least half correct.

As we turn into Upper Thames Street, I shoot a glance to the Thames again. The boat drifts aimlessly. It turns sidewise into the current. I watch it intently; it conks awkwardly against the concrete shoreline of the river on the Southwark side. The people on deck are either still, or they mill about uselessly.

I point over to the boat, calling out for Jason.

"Do you see that?"

"You mean the boat?"

"They're not doing anything to steer it. They're just adrift."

CHAPTER 5: Emma Wallace Blair, Edinburgh, September 2026

I finally stopped sobbing, pitying myself, in the middle of the New York-to-Edinburgh flight. Crying takes energy, which I needed to focus on more pragmatic matters, like what we were about to face in Scotland.

An Edinburgh airport tarmac and terminal crowded with the infected? Complete and utter chaos, like in New York City, which was in essence a giant wasp nest full of dying hornets?

The plane carried scientists and virology specialists. I was guilty about that. We'd been entitled to a ticket out, leaving thousands of families to the terror of an uncontrolled pandemic.

The flight was seven hours. We had no food, a little bottled water, limited communications as cellphone towers were gradually going down. Frankly, we were lucky to be in the air. People slept (like me), chatted nervously, or aimed frozen stares at their laptop screens, as if searching in vain for the answer for everything. We knew it was a virus, H7N11, that it was off-the-scale virulent, and that it presented as cognitive degeneration, but not much more than that.

It was like rabies, but the symptoms were instantaneous (rabies can incubate for weeks...). I didn't know which was better; I suppose, if you're going to get bad news, it's best to hear it quickly. But at least with rabies, there was a vaccine and a cure.

Some of the fellows staring at their laptops all through the trip were studying microscopic images of the virus itself, yet that could also be an assumption on my part. Many were gazing at photos of family members left behind.

I was lucky, in that way. At least I was returning to my homeland.

The pilot finally said, congenially, "Welcome to Scotland." Then we touched down. Yet his voice had a bit of sarc to the tone. Our introduction to the Northland was something I wasn't going to forget soon.

They let us out on the tarmac. All I had was a small rucksack, containing one change of clothes and a medical kit. In other words, all I could carry when I fled my downtown Manhattan apartment and leapt on a bicycle to JFK airport. To this small carry-on I added one bottled water and a few salty cracker packages, leftover snacks from back when the plane had paying holiday travelers.

Scottish soldiers toting rifles waved us along on the

tarmac. I was with two fellow scientists, Marie and Lennox. I believe their last names were Suarez and Williams. We were all in our 20s and shell-shocked, having abandoned our families and loved ones (Marie's were in L.A., Lennox's Brooklyn). But we were happy to be alive and uninfected with H7N11, so far at least.

I asked one of the stone-faced soldiers, "How's the airport? Can we get a cab into town?" I meant Edinburgh. He shook his head.

"The situation is unstable, dangerous Mum. Find a quiet place to hole up for awhile. That's all. Keep moving now."

Another soldier, ginger-haired, tall and lanky, quipped as we'd turned to go, "We're a day away from a shitstorm in Edinburgh. Maybe you should have stayed up in the air."

"Clam it, Temple," the first soldier said. "Stow the crappy attitude. Keep it t' yahself."

The guy kept talking, "Arm yourself. Get out to the country. Wait it out. That's what I say anyway." This wasn't reassuring, but I appreciated his candor.

There was a line when we got to the terminal. The soldiers here all had medical masks on. Personally, I didn't think their tactics made much of a difference if this virus was about. They were pointing handheld thermometers at our foreheads and shining flashlights in our eyes.

They dragged off to the side one woman ahead of me in the line. She staggered off with two masked soldiers on each arm.

"What's wrong with her?" I asked.

A guy turned to me, "Eyeballs dilated...fever..." I shook my head. In this chaos, it was one step at a time. They were making up the rules as they went along. Logic didn't reign.

I heard a loud crack behind me, resonating over the flat, dry tarmac. We all were startled and jerked around to look. About 300 yards away, a group of people ran full-tilt toward the plane and the line of disembarking passengers. They were barefoot, shirts mostly undone, like people fleeing a flood or an eruption. But something about their gaits and expressions spelled ***attack.***

I could make out the faces of the marauding people: bewildered, pained, ghastly. One of them had been shot and lay slumped on the concrete.

The first two soldiers raised rifles to shoulders and promptly opened fire, until seven more bodies were sprawled across the concrete, dead or mortally injured. No warning was given, no shots fired in the air over their heads. I was sickened and appalled. Then I understood it.

This was the new world, the new abnormal.

It was almost impossible to grasp; precisely what was unfolding in New York was happening here–more than three thousand miles and an ocean away.

Was there something about the number eight, or the group itself? I thought. I'd seen masses of the infected trucking down New York's wide avenues. I also remembered the one man in the Walgreens when all this started for me: confused, vacuous, harmless, alone with the virus. The polar opposite of those aggressors on the pavement.

This virus had a puzzling presentation, and the effort

itself of puzzling it out, for me the scientist, helped put the horror at a distance.

Airline travel spread the disease; maybe it wasn't quite so unbelievable. These people sprawled on the pavement were merely passengers like us, propagating the virus.

Then I thought, maybe we're lucky they're not just shooting us one by one as we leave the plane.

Officials were looking at passports outside, just past the medical check. How did I escape infection by this virus? I thought.

They let us into the terminal. Unlike J.F.K, it conveyed an unsettling silence and emptiness. Voices echoed. Soldiers stood at posts about every ten yards. They monitored their stations warily, suspicious of everything. How would we get to Edinburgh? I thought, sensing a frustrating helplessness.

Where would I sleep? Was it safe, as in reasonably so?...No place was as safe as it was merely days ago.

Lennox, a Black man of medium height, still in shirt-sleeves and a loosened tie, pointed to another scientist who was waving at us across the way. I expected there was a shuttle bus that would take us to "safe quarters" or a hotel. VIP treatment for scientists trying to save the world.

When I exited to the street through a door, we found a beat up, 20 y.o. Land Rover with three other nervous people sitting in the back. Any luggage was strapped to the roof rack. The vehicle was covered with brightly colored bumper stickers. Lennox got into the front seat, Marie and I hopped into the back, which was retrofitted with two separate back seats.

Edinburgh Old Town was only 20 minutes away.

We pulled away from the airport terminal. I looked back and saw a soldier smoking and fidgeting near the exit we had gone through. He waved at me, gave the thumbs up.

The skies were clear and empty. It appeared that airline travel had ground to a halt.

CHAPTER 6

We rode silently, as I gazed out the window. We were still exhausted by the flight from N.Y.C., and from witnessing the massacre on the airport tarmac.

I'd seen infected people hurling themselves off the Queensborough Bridge, and F-35 warplanes dropping bombs on residential neighborhoods in Queens, perhaps the supreme act of last-minute desperation. You don't get used to it, I thought. There are oft-repeated myths about becoming "numb" to the dead and dying. I can't become inured to death. Not yet.

When I find a beetle crawling across my trousers, I flick it off or release it into the breeze rather than squash it. All life is sacred–whenever I have a chance to treat it so.

We were passed by lines of cars fleeing from Edinburgh in the other direction. Clusters of bereft people wandered the highway, appearing purposeless, despondent, desperate. I saw tight gangs of grubby teens, itching for trouble. Maybe it was only my suspicious nature, but I expected to confront some social breakdown and collapse.

Urban areas aren't equipped to deal with a sudden, hard-hitting pandemic. Food and water runs out, within 48 to 72 hours.

Services are turned off. Inhabitants begin to riot and maraud. Living in the city, in normal times, is novel and dependent on a certain stability and prosperity. It's a life of charm, reflection, the distillation of small moments, urbanity, nightlife, and art, not rugged survival.

A modern city seems to run itself by magic. I find the skylines of New York, Paris, Barcelona, and Miami beautiful at night. But I always had a problem with the lights left on, especially in the evening.

When you exit a room at night, you always turn the lights off. Not so in contemporary cities. I used to gaze disapprovingly, but with curiosity, at the facades of empty, well-lit offices, which embodied the work life of whomever had just abandoned them. I marveled at the excess of these perpetually bright buildings.

During a pandemic or another kind of catastrophe, all of this shuts down. It's revealed for what it is, a flimsy facade. Life becomes not "Sex In The City" or vogue gatherings breathlessly covered by ***The Hollywood Reporter, TMZ,*** or Twitter, but a strenuous struggle for life's necessities.

Now Edinburgh was emptying out, at the same time we were coming in. I called out from the back seat,

"Where are we staying?"

"A community center," somebody in the know said from the end of the seat. "Attached to the hospital."

"What? Community center?"

"Basically, a big shelter full of bunk beds."

"They've got a bunk with your name on it," Lennox quipped.

"That doesn't sound safe," I said. As in, a recipe for viral spread.

"It's all they've got right now," the man down the end said. He was tall, with a lugubrious bearing and a prominent Adam's apple. To me, he seemed the very epitome of dorky scientist.

"We can do research in the hospital," he said. "Everything's nearby."

I didn't want to sound spoiled but...Edinburgh still had numerous hotels. In its previous life (a week and a half ago?), the city was a tourist haven. I thought of the place where I met Will, only a few years ago. It was a Marriott, on Princes Street, near Calton Hill, right in the center of everything.

The last place I wanted to lay down my head was a prison barracks. Some kind of ad hoc place assembled beside a stressed hospital wing.

"Well," the driver said, cheerfully. "You can camp out if you want, in the park, across the street from the statue of the Duke of Wellington. Arthur Wellesley. Defeated Napoleon at Waterloo in 1815. Did you know he was born in Dublin?"

"Why do they have a statue of him in Scotland?" Marie asked.

"The British love statues of men, especially those of military and heroic bearing. In case you haven't noticed. You know, Winston Churchill in Trafalgar Square. That's a tall one."

The driver had thinning, scraggly gray hair, a full beard, and a scarf that he wore above a plaid shirt. Ned was his name. He was the one who loved bumper stickers. One of them said, "Let's all spit at once and drown the bastards." He was incongruously chipper, given the dire circumstances.

I could see the ocean through the window, reflecting a placid sunlight. I liked talking to him.

"This your Rover, Ned?"

"Yeah, vintage 2006. It's been to India and back."

"India? Seriously?"

"I took a long tour of India in this very rig. Went through Eastern Europe and Turkey. Unforgettable trip."

"What were you doing here in Edinburgh? I mean, recently?"

"Well, I was driving a Black Cab in London. When it got really bad there, I had to abandon me flat and come north. I came with Meghan. She died, bless her soul. So I got another one."

"I'm really sorry to hear that," I answered, with a somber sympathy, but puzzled. He looked back at me with a half smile, then focused on the highway again.

"She was an 18 y.o. cat. Had a good long life. Found a stray and called her Meghan Too. That's T-o-o. It weren't hard to leave London," he spoke to the windshield, seeming to find relief in chatter. "Picked up a doctor on the road a few weeks ago. The bloke asks me to shuttle scientists back and forth to the airport. He'll keep me filled up with gasoline (Ned pronounced it *gazzoleen* like they do in the Australian films). They give me food and water, whatever I want."

Ned shot a glance back to me again, eager and proud of his new deal, the way he's set up during the apocalypse, as it were.

"I'm shacked up in an empty apartment in Old Town. Meghan Too and a dog, Hank. Took 'im in off the street. A spaniel, good dog. Everyone needs companions..." We were almost home, Old Town.

"You're generous to the pets," I said. "That's nice. How do you find Edinburgh?"

Ned laughed, because I'd put that like a naive greenhorn, overly pleasant given what had happened.

"Oh, the city's not badly hit. Yet. The businesses are mostly closed, though. Lots of residents fleeing to the country. Almost everyone who can, going to the very north of Scotland. Or taking boats and vessels to get away. I don't know where the boaters think they're going. Ibiza? Greece?" He chuckled quietly.

"What are the barracks like? Near the hospital."

"You want my honest opinion?"

"From you, I don't expect to get anything but."

"A pit, to be blunt."

The gawky scientist in back appeared unhappy with that remark. He crossed his arms and scowled. I didn't like him; snap judgements on demeanor are, unapologetically, in my nature.

"The community center suits our purposes fine," the

man said.

Ned shrugged. "Overcapacity, in my opinion. Getting a bit untidy, they are. Don't get me wrong, I'm not out to judge. I know these are weird times. Most new folks are squatting in apartments. Nothing wrong with that. They're there, they're empty. The hospital keeps the dead now stacked up in a skating rink next door. Wouldn't want to live next door, but my instructions are to take new arrivals there."

"Thank you for your honesty," I said, eyeing the scientist across the way. He grimaced out the window, where the city's neighborhoods as we neared the center had more people on the street.

I stared at the people, searching them for the tell-tale signs: aimlessness, vacuity, the 1000-yard stare. I saw no predatory groups of them so far, except for the airport; the vicious mobs like I'd seen in New York.

I still wasn't convinced that Edinburgh was the place where we could wait the plague out, if such a place ever existed. It was just a matter of time.

CHAPTER 7

Lennox listened carefully as I conversed and plotted with Ned. Lennox was a thoughtful, soft-spoken bloke. We'd stopped in traffic.

"Listen Ned, the hotels are closed, right?" he asked.

"Yeah, most. They locked 'em up. Management left."

"What about the Marriott?" I asked. "The one on Leith Street?" This was the place where I had met Will. It was near Calton Hill, which you could see through the window of my room. Will and I had spent a nice evening up on the hill, enjoying the view of sea and cityscape and the evening's airs.

They were great memories, full of regret and unrequited longing. For him, of course.

I was quite sure Will was gone, taken by the virus in New York.

There was nothing wrong with convincing Ned to

take us to the old hotel.

When society breaks down, I thought, make do with the best that you can find. Optimize, because you know the pickings are going to be slim most of the time. You'll be scrounging pitiably for any essential, so if you can find an uncommon comfort, a bonanza like an empty, four-star hotel, grab it. Go all in.

There are also practical considerations. The hotel is located next door to a pharmacy, I recalled, a short walk down Leith. Those were the supplies I cared about the most now. I wanted to keep enough propylene glycol around, as a disinfectant; bandages and gauze, surgical tape, higher quality vitamins and minerals, even leftover antibiotics. If I could find some that hadn't expired.

Pharmacies, up until this pandemic, were designed as "super stores," also carrying bottled water and cheap snacks.

I knew Edinburgh wasn't going to stay safe for long. This infection moved too quickly and its symptoms were instantaneous and crippling, for any community to try to stay ahead of it.

I sensed I was being selfish, but this was reality, coldly grasped. And ad hoc teams of scientists weren't going to solve this one in time. That was a pipe dream, however well-intentioned. In the best of times, it's difficult to come up with new vaccines and effective treatments for lethal germs. I wasn't going to mention this to the grim scientist with the big Adam's apple.

I thought, let's work with Ned, Marie, and Lennox, put one foot in front of the other, make a plan to survive. Get a good roof over our heads and solid provisions, ones that could, hopefully, be resupplied.

"So you can drop us off at the old Marriott?" I asked.

"That I can," Ned said, staring straight ahead.

"What if the hotel's closed?" Marie said. "Locked?" I realized then that I wasn't going to win her over.

"I want to go where they told us to go," she said quietly, with a touch of innocence.

"So I'll drop you's off there," Ned said, including our fellow passengers. "And then go on to the five-star digs."

"Four stars," I said, making an attempt to introduce some levity. "Given the fact that it's probably abandoned, you can lop off two more stars. That makes two total."

What I recalled about the hotel, other than meeting Will there for the first time at the elevator, was that you could look out the window and beyond Calton Hill, see the gorse-covered ridges of Holyrood Park. I remembered the lush yellow and green colors of the view.

We dropped off the lugubrious scientist, who seized his luggage off the roof brusquely and walked off toward the barracks.

Marie hesitated getting out of the car. I sensed she felt weird going in without me.

"Good luck getting into the hotel," she said. "Are you coming back here if you can't?"

"Probably."

"Be careful."

"You too." The door shut and Ned pulled quickly away from the curb. I thought they'd want to convene the scientists tomorrow, but I doubted I'd go unless I felt that I was properly set up. The city seemed to be under siege.

The sidewalk was empty when Ned dropped us off on Leith Street, just off of Princes, near the closed Marriott. I looked around the neighborhood and everything came back to me. Including the warm sensations of visiting an international city as a young lady, with a heady purpose, for the first time.

How utterly changed life seems after a pandemic. You dream of how life was before the disease throttled it, almost like an elderly person dreams of their careless youth.

A few people, moms with their kids or lone, older men, scuttled about the streets warily, looking unbathed with their slept-in clothes.

What were we doing here? I thought. Jet-lagged and having just stumbled off a plane. Escaping New York, that's what.

"Where do you live?" I asked Ned. I was standing on the sidewalk. I had the feeling I should pay and tip him, like the Black Cab driver he once was.

I wanted him as an ally from now on. He seemed the straight-forward, affable realist.

"Over there across the park," he nodded. He meant Queen Street Gardens. "It's called Northumberland St."

"What number?"

"1300, if you can keep it to yourself. Just knock."

"Okay. You know where to find me. Thanks for the ride. Do you know of any place cooking food around here?"

"No. Every business is closed up. Emma, right?"

"Yup, Emma."

"Incredible! I always forget names the first time around! Cheers," he said, rolling up the window. Then he pulled away from the curb. The Rover accelerated, heading downhill on Leith. No other cars moved on the street.

I watched him go, seeing the back of his head and curly gray hair. This one has some moxie, I thought, automatically differentiating him from the people who don't.

Then I turned toward the outdoor cafe, behind hedges in front of the Courtyard Marriott, and it all flowed back to me again, a previous life I lived as a single gal in New York. Imagining a return trip to Scotland, making the reservations online, packing, flying, meeting Will–it was a whirlwind. Not a care in the world, compared with this. This *thing,* this permanent threat, a shroud we live under.

Lennox was already at the hotel's front door, jerking and jimmying the latch. It was locked. I wandered through some hedges to the empty cafe. I instantly noted the table Will and I sat at, where I paused.

We ate and drank cold wine. We watched groups of happy people, city dwellers, stroll by, as the sun's rays flared from behind the chimney pots on the roofs across Leith Street.

I hadn't known Will 36 hours then. This was like returning home after many years, but the house has been torn down, I thought. I sensed waves of regret mingled with sadness and a raw sense of loss. I felt the passing of time, a happiness that has expired, due to circumstances far beyond my control. I could still embrace that memory though, and for a short time it made me happy.

In between two dried-up potted plants, I saw the door from the cafe to the interior space. I walked over and tried the knob but the door resisted. Then when I pushed the latch the door gave way and a relief flooded in. I entered the hotel, a palely lit room that made up the restaurant inside.

CHAPTER 8

This was the first time I'd breathed easier since I'd made the plane following the frenzy in JFK.

"Lennox!" I called out. "We're in!" I thought he'd made his way to the back of the building. I went inside.

I smelled food, if past its prime. I was starved. A room full of white linen-covered tables, still holding plates of food. Hastily left, which surprised me. I hadn't detected that level of alarm in the city's streets, yet. As in, just fleeing and leaving perfectly good food around.

The servings were moldy and spoiled, however, just when I considered settling down for a meal.

I called out twice, "Is anyone here?" Nothing but silence, not even the vibratory hum of HVAC. The building was turned off. That, I'd assumed. The building seemed empty, at least for now. I wanted it mostly for myself and Lennox. I didn't want to have to trust or depend on anyone else. My modus operandi for that moment: be skeptical of anyone's motivations, don't trust anyone I didn't know.

I made a cursory search of the room for anything edible, coming up only with a brown apple that was part of a toppled over centerpiece. I found a sizable chunk of hard bread crust. I scraped old yellow butter off a leftover plate, spread it on the crust. It hit the spot, tasting more like a piece of cake given my relative starvation.

I'll search the kitchen itself later, I thought. I'd planned to harvest boxed or bagged dry goods: flour, rice, oatmeal; corn starch, dried potatoes, salt. They might have a working freezer back there.

Lennox came in behind me.

"Let's choose rooms," I said.

"I'll take the honeymoon suite."

I found some circular, carpeted stairs. The elevator wasn't working. The Marriott wasn't a tall hotel, so I aimed for a room on the second floor. I wanted to sleep, take the edge off the stress I'd just suffered. But I knew the rooms were all going to be locked.

"Got any ideas for opening these rooms?" I said to Lennox behind me.

"Yeah. We look behind the front desk and find the keys. They're probably on one of those key displays on the wall. This is a European hotel; we might benefit from tradition."

"Why didn't I think of that?" Being in America, all the hotels I'd stayed in recently had plastic swipe cards designed to open doors. Fancy that, real keys.

We walked up the carpeted steps to the second floor.

"We're breaking and entering, you know," Lennox said.

"So what?" I hadn't seen any cops in Edinburgh, or armed officers at all since the airport. "I don't think we have to worry about that."

"You're not a Black man," he said. He was suggesting that there was a lot left over from the modern world, not much of it good.

"That's true." I wanted to show him that I understood his point.

"You know, one time I was drinking with my brother, Ethan. He was visiting from Texas. Marguerites at an outdoor place in New York. I think we split a pitcher. He went off with some school friends. I was feeling no pain, and I get in my car afterwards. Pissed. Not a good idea. I drive down a side street and race up the entrance ramp to the highway, but I must have been doing fifty or more, because the cops pull me over. They make me get out by the side of the road, do a few silly road tests, like standing on one leg and touching my nose. The one thing I remember: being petrified and intimidated, and how that focused me. I was loaded, but locked in. I performed every one of those tests perfectly, and they let me go without even a warning.

"The point being, what if I was a Black man? And not a white red head, and on the shy innocent side?"

"It wouldn't have ended well," Lennox said.

"No, most certainly not. So we find a double, share a room, and if anything goes wrong, like if the police come, I'll do the talking."

I think it sucks that we had to make this kind of

contingency.

At a small bar near reception, I began harvesting what I needed: two liters of San Pellegrino (I would return for more), and a fifth of Belvedere vodka and Laphroig 15-year-old. I find a copy of ***The Scotsman*** from one week ago, and on one of those shelfs of random books displayed for guests, ***Lord Byron, Selected Poems.***

I knew I was going to have long, lonely evenings ahead, if I was still uncertain exactly what they were going to be like.

We fetched two keys from behind the desk, as I had a change of heart about sharing a room with Lennox. He'd be alright next door to me. Mine was 25D, his 25F.

As soon as I entered the room, I shut the door, locked it, opened a window. A nice breeze blew across the bed sheets. The wind was cool, as the sun settled into the countryside outside of Edinburgh. A sea-scented air passed through the trees on the side of Calton Hill.

I lay down on my side, with a bit of sheet pulled up to my ear, and passed out.

My stomach growled when I woke up. I had no idea what time it was, but I'd slept through the darkness. Outside, the light was fuzzy, with the birds making morning cries. The room seemed safe, for now. I pushed the sheets aside and sat on the edge of the mattress.

I thought of my father, Roy Blair. My mother Evelyn had already passed. My father lived north of here in Inverness. Ethan was still in Austin, Texas.

I last talked to my father a week ago. He seemed okay. He said he was safe, "for now.' I sat and pictured his face; friendly eyes, a shock of white hair, a scruffy beard. Big arms, like those of an old iron worker. I needed coffee badly. Then I decided I'd head for my father's place in Inverness.

The room had running water; for this brief time I felt like a normal visitor on a trip, but I told myself, *you're dreaming. You're deluding yourself.* I drank gulps of water and splashed some on my face. Ethan sent me text messages when Will was getting sick, saying that the virus was in Austin but that he was okay and not to worry.

He was a software engineer, texting from his cubicle. It was hot in Austin then, about 100.

I thought it would be a miracle if I saw my brother again. Pre-virus, the last thing he told me was that he wanted to move back to Scotland, maybe Glasgow. He missed the U.K. Austin was too big for him, and hot. You should see New York, I'd said.

I believed the virus was moving more slowly in the U.K., northward, as if carried on the wind. Inverness might not be affected. But this notion was no more than a belief, pure speculation.

I looked at myself in the mirror above the sink. I seemed pale, eyes a bit rheumy. I wanted to wash my hair, bathe. I needed a big meal; I couldn't start losing weight and weakening.

I opened my hotel door and walked down the hallway, padding quietly in sneakers, my only footwear. I descended the carpeted stairs to the reception area, through there to the dining room, where I saw a person sitting at a table like a statue.

CHAPTER 9

An old man sat in a square of sunlight. He'd left the door to the street open. I heard only birds chirping, a pleasant sound. He had thinning white hair and a beige sport coat. I said "mornin' to you," and he mumbled in response. My voice sounded too loud.

I quickly scanned the room, for more people, but mostly for food scraps that I missed before. I already felt that I had no other status than that of scavenger. I was a little shocked at how swiftly I'd made the transition, away from civilized, productive behavior as the default. Was I different, as in, of inferior character next to the scientists at the hospital?

The man stared straight ahead, zoned out, as if he was trying to remember something. I walked past him to look outside. Instantly, I suspected he was infected. I thought of the breakfast and coffee at the hospital; but I'd check the kitchen first. I kept my distance.

I thought of that man in Walgreens in New York, when I went to get Tylenol for Will. The man who didn't know what the packages were in his hands, then collapsed in the aisle. It seemed like the start of all this. This was only weeks ago.

"Do you work here?" the man at the table said.

"No. The hotel is empty."

"Oh. I thought I could get some breakfast. My wife usually makes the meals." He had a thick Scottish accent. He sounded normal, not that I was an expert at detection.

"Where's your wife?"

"She was at the hospital. Elizabeth. She didn't make it." The last part was only mumbled.

"I'm sorry to hear that. What's your name? I'm Emma."

"Malcolm Abernathy. From Aberdeen."

"Listen Malcolm, they have food at the hospital, I reckon."

"I don't want to go back there."

"I understand."

"A rat. They had a rat at the hospital. Elizabeth shouldn't 'a been in a hospital that had a rat."

"No. Oh my."

I turned and headed outside, to breathe the fresh morning air. I didn't see a soul. It was still early, but I didn't have the impression that people were hiding, locking themselves down.

Only the birds were about: Starlings and Larks and Robins, racing around in the early, clean air. A Raven squawked by, as I gazed up. I wanted a view of the ocean again.

Edinburgh was an old, worldly, worn-out historic place, but I didn't sense the sudden decay and collapse that I did in New York. Just chatting with Malcolm gave me a sad sense of normalcy.

I came back inside and went to the kitchen in back, and the first thing I did is switch on a gas burner. It didn't flame up, but I could smell the stinky propane and hear the hiss. After a search, I found a box of wooden matches, voila! They were almost spent, but I used two and got a tremulous blue flame going.

I found a silo-shaped box of oatmeal, poured it into a pan of water, boiled it up. I located used coffee grounds at the bottom of a stainless steel pot. I added one envelope of instant chocolate to the grounds, mixed it altogether for me and Malcolm. And Lennox, if he was still here.

I added a little salt to the oatmeal. Salt was needed, and potassium, to keep my systems going.

I found more dry goods, lining up the cardboard containers triumphantly. None of it would be left or abandoned. The hotel felt not quite like a home, but a suitable refuge, for a morning. I took nothing for granted, not after New York.

Northumberland Street, I thought. I reminded myself, that's where Ned lives. I stepped out of the kitchen, wiping my hands. I told Malcolm wryly that breakfast was ready. I was already thinking, one step ahead, of finding Ned and driving out of that city, before the virus took over.

CHAPTER 10: Emma Winslow, London, 2051

We watch the boat drift out of control in the choppy Thames, beneath Blackfriars Bridge.

"How come the people don't do anything? Hey you!" I scream at them, waving an arm vigorously. "The river's dangerous! That's not a game!" No one turns their heads or responds to me.

"What's up with them? Are they daft?"

"Beats me," Jason says, straddling his bicycle. "You know how some people are. Senseless, mindless." He shakes his head judgmentally.

"Is that all?" I say. "Senseless? I think they're barmy. I better get back to the hospital." I swing a leg over my bike.

"I'll see you later," Jason answers, looking away from the foundering boat on the Thames. "I have to meet Randolph Braden. Talk about plans."

"Do you think we should help the people on the boat? What if there are children?" I'm a bit incredulous. There are no other pedestrians watching on the bridge.

"From here?" Jason says, skeptically. "I don't see any kids. Only nitwits. We couldn't do anything, realistically, from shore. They have to throw an anchor or tie up to a dock. No one's navigating; he or she must be three sheets to the wind. People do that on boats, you know, get pissed."

"I'll say." I ponder the foundering vessel with its statuesque figures, rather than a crew, poised lethargically on the deck, then I turn away and pedal hard onto Queen Victoria Street. A side street gets me to the hospital. Jason continues going straight on New Bridge Street.

# #

My medical ward in St. Paul's Cathedral is chaos. I'm used to it. The large room smells like pot, given that cannabis is one of the primary painkillers. All the windows are open. We do this even in winter.

We've got a place on the roof for fresh air and sun. People with the flu or TB or other germs go up there in bathrobes on lounge chairs. They often recuperate quicker than they would in a stuffy ward.

I've got a few long-term patients, older men and women with chronic ailments, staying in beds lined up along the walls. We typically encourage everyone to have as short a stay as possible, because we don't have the manpower or resources to look after them. In most circumstances, they'd be better off getting well wherever they call home. We give them what remedies we have, herbal ointments and disinfectants and CBD oils and alcohol rubs.

We patch them up, send them on their way. It's understood. We don't have people begging to stay and see doctors, because real doctors, those who've been trained in medical schools, are all old, and few and far between.

Other than the elderly, the people we help at St. Paul's are accident victims, or the occasional sick child. Right away, I begin to tend to the bruised, banged-up, and gouged.

"Slips, trips, and falls," bloody heads, punctured hands, lacerated legs. Most of it caused by bike accidents, and people getting hurt while building or fixing something; rarely fight injuries come in here.

There's always been a rule: if you're going to do something as idiotic and senseless as clobber and stab at each other, don't come here. We serve innocent and accidental victims.

I take wads of gauze and tape up the wounds. Sometimes someone needs stitches.

First in line is a young man with a nasty gash on his wrist. Looking sheepish, he holds a white, blood-soaked cloth to it, obviously his T-shirt, because he's bare-chested. He's scrawny and his skin is white as a lily. At first glance, he doesn't look to have the constitution to bear a lot of blood loss. I tell him to take a seat.

"Are you okay? Are you light-headed?"

"Nah. I'm alright." I've seen him around. He's one of the older teens on the street.

"What's your name?"

"Calvin." The position of the gash on his wrist raises

some red flags.

"We've got to stitch that up, Calvin. Hold your wrist out." A pause. "Let me ask you, did you have a go at cutting your own wrist?"

He hesitates. I can't tell whether he wants to lie, or is offended by the question.

"If you did, would you tell me? Or would you try to hide it? Because the best way to deal with this stuff is to get it out in the open..."

He interrupts, "Wouldn't do a thing like that. Nope, not me. It wouldn't cross my mind. I was cutting some hose, and when I follow through, see, the blade of my knife slashes my wrist. Just a bloody...pardon the slip, mistake on my part. I know it looks bad, due to where the cut is. But I swear..."

"I believe you. This is going to hurt." I have a needle sterilized by a small flame, and a roll of black thread. I sew up skin more than I darn socks these days. Calvin looks away toward a window, his jaw set.

"How old are you?" I ask. I gently tug the needle through the first two holes. Honestly, I've never had stitches myself, so I can only imagine what it feels like.

"17."

"Do you need some whisky, or weed? For the pain?"

"Nah. Not right now."

"Where do you live?"

"Chelsea."

"Got a Ma and Pa?"

"No. Roomies."

"Any mates with you now?"

"No. I came alone."

He's still looking out the window at a calm, pale blue sky. I'm on the sixth stitch. Not a peep out of him. His cheek twinges now and then.

"You're brave. Better than most."

"It don't hurt. Just a little sting." Then he looks from the window to me. "Many thanks, by the way. The blood wouldn't stop. So Grunge, one of me mates, he says, take your shirt off and wrap it up tight. Go to St. Paul's. So I did. I'm glad it was you." He swallows, almost sadly.

"Well it was my pleasure, Calvin." The eighth stitch goes in, and it's time for clean-up and the bandaging. "No worries at all."

"The bleeding is the only thing I'm scared of. Not the pain. But losing all my blood, that's scary."

"I don't blame you. I'm almost done."

The wound didn't stink yet, but I thought he needed a disinfectant.

"This will sting a bit lad." I seize the nearby bottle of alcohol that the local distilleries produced. I pause for a moment.

"What happened to your Ma and Pa?"

"Don't know. Never met 'em."

"So you're like me then. I never met my father and mother."

"Does it bother you?"

"No. You?"

"Never. Can't miss someone I never knew."

"I've been told a lot of stories about them, by my Uncle Harry."

I hate the word "orphan," with its negative connotation, as if the label was a kind of incurable malaise or a scar. Most of us are orphans, anyway. The suicide rate among young people is low, on the other hand. I cannot speculate much why–I think it's because of the uniformity of our station. We're all pretty much in the same boat, merely eking out our livelihoods and spending lots of time in the London wilderness.

CHAPTER 11

"I play for a football club," Calvin offers. He digs a tattered card out of his pocket. The card looks like it's been through the wash.

"That's a real antique."

"Lionel Messi. Barcelona, 2022. I carry it with me for good luck. Messi is my nickname." He grins from ear to ear. Just the thought makes him buoyant.

"A real hero on the pitch, huh?"

Deftly, I uncap the alcohol and pour some directly on the wound.

"Ow, that hurts like a bastard!"

"I told you that's the hard part." I lift his forearm and wrap the wrist in gauze, then adhesive tape.

"Now you get a move on, Calvin. And keep an eye on that wound. It won't get in the way of your football. No hand balls, remember."

"I'm playing tomorrow, Stamford Bridge. Spurs."

"What's your position?"

"Striker. Messi, remember?" He gives me another gap-toothed smile, standing up. He reaches into his pocket and removes a rather impressive looking, folded-up red Swiss Army knife.

"I want you to have it," he says. "As a gift of appreciation for fixing me up."

"Oh no, I can't. You keep it."

"Come on, you can do everything with it. Open cans and bottle caps, saw sticks, even protect yerself. It makes a good weapon."

"No, thanks. I have kitchen tools. I appreciate the thought. But I could never pull a knife on another human being. Ever."

He shrugs, returns the knife to his pocket. Then he's gone out the exit.

An older fellow, one of the old-timers, hails me from across the room. I need a coffee or tea break. I walk across the creaky wooden floor.

"Good day to you, Mr. Taylor." Jack, as he's commonly known around the hospital, is the old duffer who still wears his private-school tie and blazer and insists on dressing well for the ward. He's about 80 y.o., one of the older Londoners.

"Florence Nightingale. I say."

"Yes."

"I think it's the white lace scarf and your selfless dedication."

"You're so kind. Can I get you some CBD oil." We use it for pain and inducing calm among the elders.

"I could use some scotch, instead." We keep whisky and vodka around the ward. For medicinal purposes, of course.

"I'm going to join you." I fetch two short glasses and fill them halfway with the amber-colored liquor.

It's a different era, I think. If a patient smells scotch on your breath, they're not going to freak out and report you to the authorities. It's like the Battle of Britain, from historical accounts I've read. Fight, eat, skip sleep often (although I love my sleep), have a dram, a coffee, back into the plane. Do what has to be done.

It would be unheard of to fly off the handle when one's had a dram in the ward near the end of the day. People cut me some slack.

Jack takes a sip, savoring the scotch. "Just delightful."

"Now, let me tell you a story," he says. "Had an older girlfriend once. I was in my early 20s in the Royal Marines. She was 30, married. Took a fancy to me. Her name was Emma, too. Wilson, Wilcox, Waddington, don't remember. Had some wonderful afternoons in the Hotel Belmont in Surrey, had a pub on the first floor. Can't remember its name, but I vividly recall her legs and bust. What afternoons! Just gorgeous! Outstanding!"

"***Mister Taylor,*** you better not tell me more." The booze had gone straight to my head. His, too.

"Did you hear the one about the Chinese man called Olly Olafson?"

"No."

"So this Swedish fellow gets off the boat on Ellis Island, stands in line in immigration. Finally makes it to one of the immigration inspectors. 'What's your name?'

the official asks him. 'Olly Olafson.'"

I interrupt. "What's Ellis Island?"

"An island near Manhattan where the Americans processed immigrants who'd arrived in ships. Over 10 million emigres went through Ellis Island, beginning in 1892. Went on for 63 years."

"Wow, okay."

"At any rate," he chuckles, "Olly Olafson, the Swede, moves on. Behind him was this chap who'd sailed from China."

"'What's *your* name?' the inspector asks. 'Sam Ting,' he says."

There's an awkward silence. "Get it? Chinaman named Olly Olafson? Sam Ting?"

"Okay, very funny. Ha ha. What's up with..." I nod to a man sitting quietly nearby, staring off into space.

"That's Simmons. He's a bit off his game, you know. You see, Simmons was in the war." He could have been talking about World War II, given the clipped tone. Simmons was well-dressed in a Navy blue sport coat. A yellowed *London Times* from years ago lay in his lap.

"Which war?"

"Afghanistan, with the Americans. You could have been a combat nurse there, and a damn fine one at that. The Florence Nightingale of Kabul."

"I wasn't born, you know, until 2029. What year are we talking about now?"

"Quite. That would have been 2005, 2006. We were both in the British Marines, at the end of our service careers. Simmons had a bad time of it. Don't ask him for that story."

"I wasn't intending to. What happened?" I whisper.

"He was in a helicopter crash in Helmand Province. Hurt his back, crawled into some rocks, for concealment. Hid from the Taliban. Wasn't rescued for 48 hours. It ended for us the following year. He's never been quite the same. His brain was injured. You know how it is." Then he brightened visibly.

"We don't have wars anymore."

"Just pandemics. Sometimes."

"True. Pandemics. They come, and go." Simmons stands up stiffly, the paper fluttering to the floor. He shuffles over to the open window. We don't have screens in the windows. That makes me nervous.

"How come I didn't know this before?" I say to anyone who cared to listen. "About his anxiety?"

At the window, Simmons erupts. "Jill! Jill!" he yells, staring out toward the Thames and the bridges and shoreline.

"That's not Jill, you fool!" Jack says. "He thinks he sees his wife."

"What happened to Jill?"

"Died of the fever, you know. Long time ago."

"Right about when I was born."

"Mr. Simmons," I said. "Can I get you some tea?"

The confusion melts away from his face. An eager focus returns.

"Whisky," he said. "*Scotch* whiskey, not Irish."

"Coming right up, one dram." I give a dram to anyone who wants one. Sign of the times, or simply habit.

There's a bustle at the door, another injured family

member. I go over to wash my hands. Now *I* need tea. Jack Taylor and Henry Simmons gaze out the window, standing in a square of sunlight. I go over to pour Simmons a Scotch, before I tend to another visitor's injury. A small line forms by the table where I had repaired Calvin.

"I'll be damned," Taylor says, staring out at the city below. "Four lads, stripped to nowt. Running down the street toward the river. Nobody's chasing them. It's *them* chasing something, or someone. I'll be damned. Buck naked sods!"

CHAPTER 12

I leave the hospital a few hours later and walk to my second-floor flat only a block and a half away. The facade of the building is covered in vines, with pretty purple blossoms. For the life of me, I can't name them, which takes nothing away from their beauty and sweet fragrances. It's a nice time of the year. By November the vines will look like coarse gray snakes.

Now I can smell them through my bedroom window. When I get to my flat, I fall onto my bed, stomach first, and crush a pillow to my face. I've seen too much blood today, too many stitches and festering wounds. I've wiped away too many tears. Not to mention imbibing the scotch. I'm knackered, and sleep will be delicious relief.

I wake up in the dark, having slept through a thunderstorm. The air feels cooler, with a scorched scent.

My sheets are wet from rain the wind has blown through the open window. I wake up lonely.

For some reason, I acutely miss confiding in my Mum Emma, who I've never actually known. She's like a statue built in my mind, almost a myth, but for her diary and Jack's and Harry's stories.

I sit on the edge of the bed with an empty, deprived feeling. It's a void I've been trying to fill with other people for my young lifetime.

Pre-epidemic, before 2025. How my mother lived! It's a fairytale to me. She took jet planes and traipsed between New York, Edinburgh, London, and Geneva. She fell in love with different men. Many men, I'm sure, got crushed on her.

The sun has gone down over the darkened skyscrapers. All I hear out the window are crickets, and the creaking gears of a bike riding beneath my window.

I put on sneakers and head outside, where the air is charged and cleansed. In the next block, I find Harry sitting on a stoop, using a flashlight to read a frayed hardcover book. He's sipping from a pint mug. A cricket bat sits next to him.

Given the richness of the foam on top of the beer, I can tell the beer was brewed locally and is esteemed, not "reindeer piss," as they call the cheap stuff.

"Cheers," he says, looking up.

"Whatcha reading?" His presence buoys me. Harry is a de facto big brother.

"Science," he says. "Human physiology and immunity."

"Wow, heavy. How does the beer do for

concentration, and absorption of the material?" Then I feel bad about saying that. I should encourage his in-depth reading, not poke fun of it.

"Did you know..." he says, ignoring my wise-ass remark. "...that a virus can mutate in different ways. It can change, but not enough, so that if you were sick with it before, you still have the antibodies to defeat it. They call that antigenic drift. The proteins change on the virus, but the body still recognizes it, moves in to kill it. That's a good thing."

"No, I didn't know that."

Harry is tall and sturdy, wears collared shirts when he can find them, and slicks his brown hair back with water. He has a poet's classic profile, perhaps like Byron's, a big, aquiline nose. He lately grew a scrappy beard, which he trims and attempts to make stylish.

The women love him, but he's still unmarried at 31. Playing the field; he has a posh blond named Gwen who fancies him now. She's smart and has apparently motivated his reading.

Most of the other men here take the opposite approach. The pickings are so slim in London that they tend to settle on someone early, if that lady will have them.

The ladies hold out until they feel they have to get pregnant. This is, of course, *very* important for the city, increasing its population.

Harry continues: "The other path a virus can take is antigenic *shift*. That's a mutation that avoids past antibodies. That's *not* a good thing. Meaning we could get a plague going again here."

"That's a cheery thought."

He marks and shuts the book, then says: "I was looking for you before."

"Why?"

"I have something for you." He stands up, fetches another object from the top of the steps, then walks down and hands them both to me. "Congratulations. You've earned them. Your mom Emma's cricket bat, and her little axe."

I fist the bat by the handle, setting the axe down on the steps. The bat has an unusual heft. It seems to embody her persona, like if someone gave you Muhammed Ali's boxing glove.

I got quiet for a minute, then,

"What was she like? I just had a dream about her. We were standing on the roof, looking at London. We were going to sail to New York together the next day. Somehow, in my dreams, she appears like an older version of me."

"She was a redhead," Harry says. "Really smashing. I was only a small lad at the time, living in the church. We liked her. She was pregnant with you when we met her. She was maybe a bit bossy, like a drill sergeant, but we were only orphans in the ruins and weren't used to supervision.

"I thought the bat was the coolest thing. See those notches, right there?" He points along the handle of the bat.

"Yeah, I see them."

"Every time she took out one of them sick freaks, she added a notch."

"They were real people who got a disease, not freaks. They were someone's loved ones."

"They were freaks, zombies, believe me. I was alive then. There was nothing real human about them, except you could hack 'em down with that axe, like your mom did."

"I'm aware of that. And she didn't do it that much."

Harry scoffs.

"She did it a lot. She was a badass, Miss Blair, that one. She could do everything. She was a genius, could take care of babies, and when I first saw that axe, it had blood dried on it. She told me the viral zombies grabbed her and she took the axe and..." He makes a big chopping motion.

"I know I know. She called them ***reivers*** by the way."

"I knew that. People still call 'em that."

"My mom Emma was an inquisitive scientist, too." I feel my temper rising. "Brilliant. A free-thinking woman."

"That she was. A sweetheart, yeah. She was kind, like a mom, to me and the lads. And you know what? I was more sad when she died than when my own mum died. Fancy that?"

"Tch tch. That doesn't sound quite right. Didn't you get along with your mum?"

"Sure. I was more sad though, when Miss Blair passed. That's just the way it was." Then he stands up, gets that far-off look, and brushes his pants off. "You should keep those things. They're yours. Use 'em if you have to."

I run my finger over the notches on the bat; they feel primitive and like an embodiment of history, like a petroglyph. The bat itself feels like it should be in a museum.

Still, I was reluctant to picture her gritting her teeth and dispatching infected people. Finishing them off, as it were, with cold precision.

"Listen," Harry says. "Let me give you some advice. I've got a couple of years on you." He looks out across the shadowy trees, over the dark tops of countless roofs. The blackness above hides the stars and the clouds.

"I spent my childhood with that barmy fever, raging through the city. My home. I saw what it did to blokes and girls. You're like a sister to me. We're all here for each other." He paces back and forth a bit, agitated, then picks up his book.

"But if you're alone and in trouble, for whatever reason, you're going to have to protect yourself. Pacifism is all fine and dandy. A nice idea. It makes me all fuzzy and warm inside. But if you have a pistol, an axe, a cricket bat...use it on one of those things...to protect yerself. Better them than you."

"One of those *things*? Who?"

"Your dad called them the daft bastards. The infected, whatever you fancy for a name. Reivers, mad dogs, I call 'em."

"The virus disappeared," he continued, somewhat paternally, which irritates me. "But it could mutate, you know, and reappear in a different form. Once infected, a person isn't human anymore. It's like slapping a wasp before it stings your arm. You gotta just do it."

That was a lousy comparison, I thought. A poor metaphor. "You slap at a wasp, it's more likely to sting you. I just let them fly around, and they go away. I never get stung."

"Lucky you."

I cross my arms tightly.

"Nothing ever happens to me in London."

"There's a first time for everything."

"Aren't you a beacon of hope," I say sardonically.

Of course, he has a point, even though his delivery lacks tact. I hang onto both the axe and the cricket bat, because holding onto them makes me feel like I'm closer to the first Emma.

All daughters feel this way. But I assume it's different if you never knew your mother.

I put the two cherished objects back in my flat, then Harry decides to accompany me down to the Thames for my evening walk. Like Jason, he doesn't like me walking alone at night, and my insouciance and bravado only drives them crazy.

CHAPTER 13: Emma Blair, Edinburgh, 2026

I needed a bigger, better backpack than the wimpy one I escaped New York with. From the Marriott, I aimed for an Edinburgh neighborhood off Princes Street and Frederick, where they had outdoor retail stores. Although I'm nominally shopping for gear, let's call it what it is–stealing or looting. Even "harvesting" seems like a euphemism.

The city still functioned, but if the shops weren't open, and more or less permanently closed by this epic emergency, I still needed gear and supplies. I knew what I needed to survive.

I hadn't talked to Lennox that morning. I thought he was still conked out in our "private hotel," the abandoned Marriott. I made my way to the empty pedestrian alley, where I found an outdoorsy store with a Norwegian name.

The plate-glass front window was smashed, the cobblestones littered with glass shards. No one was around, including the looters. This let me off the hook. I was supposed to be ashamed, appalled, by the damage and the crimes. Under other circumstances, I would have been. I don't advocate anarchy, I thought, as I stepped through the glass and entered the store.

"Anyone home? Hello!" It was silent. Stuff strewn about; there were lots of empty shelves and racks, but still copious gear. It was a bonanza for a "harvester" like me. Backpacks lined the walls up on hooks. I chose a roomy, dark-blue one with lots of webbing and pockets. I stuffed it with hats, gloves, socks, and buffs; two water bottles, and camping snacks like freeze-dried packets of soup and bags of gorp.

I'm an anarchist, a looter, I thought, as I left the store. In fact, I'd seen no Scottish policemen around, a dubious excuse for what I'd done. I was still not sure what state Edinburgh was in, other than of emergency and fright.

One more time I yelled out, carrying an armful of bounty, "Anyone around?" I still had a wallet; VISA card, U.S. cash. All of it was presumably useless as currency, I assumed. They wouldn't take dollars and the New York bank that issued my credit card had been rubbed out by a catastrophic pathogen.

The alley was still empty, an otherwise pleasant pale-blue sky above it. Fluffy white clouds drifted in from the sea.

I hitched the backpack to a shoulder and began walking. I already missed my bike dearly, the one from

New York. I tended to invest beloved inanimate objects with human qualities, like people festoon their cars with stickers and flags, give them cute names, then mourn them when they're finally towed to the boneyard.

I thought of my poor bike lying on its side on a bleak access road at JFK Airport, and it seemed like a sad symbol for everything that was lost in New York City.

I hadn't showed up at the hospital yet. The W.H.O. had probably fired me by now. I'll find Lennox, I thought, and we'll stop in at the labs to see what's going on.

Biochemical research is complex, endlessly time-consuming, exceedingly detailed; could it even be done with all this crap going on around it? I was highly doubtful. Still, I felt obligated to lend a hand, but not to stupidly leave myself and others without essential survival gear. I saw what happened in New York, and how quickly it struck.

Before I reached Princes Street, I spotted a teenager on a bicycle about three blocks away. Fancy that, I thought, a pretty normal scene for Edinburgh. He glided along, lacking a frightful urgency, and turned down another street. Walking along with the backpack around my shoulders, I felt more prepared, and this view of the kid on a bike lifted my spirits.

I stopped to sit down on the grass next to a tall tree in a park off Princes. Again, no other pedestrians around, even in the park. The grass was soft, lush, and deep green; it smelled like dark loam. I lay my head back for a moment, let the sun bathe my face. Then I pulled out the bag of sunflower seeds I'd copped from the store. I poured some out in my palm and chewed them down. For a brief moment, I breathed easier and Edinburgh appeared livable, safe.

I shared some of the seeds with a chipmunk that darted by. He stuffed his pouchy cheeks with them, then disappeared. Later, I'll think of this as a unique moment in time, a brief respite that occurred as if Before Carnage. I poured out another little pile of seeds in the grass, then returned the bag to the backpack.

I stood up to leave, and when I got back to the hotel, the old man, Abernathy, dressed in his beige coat, was gone, the oatmeal mush I'd served him half finished. I filled the backpack with all the food I'd harvested from the kitchen. The pack was actually feeling bulky; with water it will be heavy, I thought. I'd left the door to the room locked, but the key worked fine. I entered the room, half expecting a maid to have appeared and made my bed; yet, the sheet and blankets I'd slept under were still bunched up, the pillows dented with the impression of my head. I won't make the bed, I thought; I'm not that impulsive to preserve old habits. For a female, I was rather sloppy about the flat anyways.

I added the medical kit to the large backpack, and went to find Lennox.

His door was locked and he didn't answer. That was odd; he would have waited for me. It was time to locate Lennox, and Ned.

CHAPTER 14

Out in the hallway, I knocked on Lennox's door, loudly and urgently, but he still wasn't around or awake. I'd scrawled a note to him before, on hotel stationery, and I slipped it under the door, before I went downstairs and through the empty dining area to the street.

I had everything with me I needed. First, I headed in the direction of the makeshift lab center, but I didn't want to be roped into some last-ditch, doomed-from-the-start attempt to cure the pandemic on the fly. That wasn't how it was done, with a novel pathogen exhibiting this virulence. The research had little future; it was like scrutinizing the blueprints of a ship as the Titanic sinks.

Edinburgh was still silent and windy. The city's vibrancy was gone, evaporated; one couldn't know for how long. I saw a few passersby rush past with masks, including a gang of four teens, all boys. They were laughing; the pandemic was an excuse to be unruly and riotous. Their masks were designed with ghastly, toothy grins.

I figured I'd find Lennox, out on the street or over in the hospital. I wondered how Marie was doing. I felt bad for her; she didn't appear equipped for what was coming down.

I crossed the park where I'd rested before, then veered away toward the small river called Water of Leith. It winds through the city and its outskirts, ending up at the Firth of Forth, then the North Sea. That's when I saw Lennox stride urgently toward me from across a boulevard. He stopped about ten yards from me and put up a "halt" signal with both hands.

"Don't come any closer, Emma!"

"What's wrong? I was looking for you."

"I think I'm infected! I'm sweating my ass off and my heart's racing!" Lennox's face reminded me of Will's, a mask of bewilderment and fear, in Manhattan only weeks ago.

"That could be a seasonal flu," I insisted. "A common, hard-hitting cold virus. That's the thing with pandemics. You think you always ***have*** the virus, when the probability is that it's something else."

"No, this is something different. This shit's got me in its grip. My mind's racing."

I put the backpack down and fished out the medical kit. "Look, you remembered my name. You knew the way back to the hotel. That's where you were going, right?"

"A chicken with its head cut off still finds the coop!"

"Nonsense. Catch." I tossed him a small bottle of pilfered ibuprofen. I'd added key vitamins and minerals to it before: vitamins D, C, magnesium, zinc.

"Take a couple of those pills, the ibuprofen and the vitamins, with lots of water. Believe me, you wouldn't have known my name if you had H7N11. When did the headache start?"

"An hour ago."

"You have a common influenza A from the plane, or whatnot. Get some sleep." And call me in the morning, I almost said.

He stared at me unblinking, and I couldn't help but notice the anguish in his eyes.

"Emma," he said with a tender, desperate tone. "The lab got an outbreak. Don't go there. It's chaos. One of the guys dove out the window. He just looked at everyone, said he didn't know where or who he was, and dove out. About half the people lost their minds, wandered away."

"To where? What about Marie!"

"I don't know. I don't..."

He removed an envelope from his back pocket.

"Why didn't you knock on my door, before you left?" I asked.

"I wanted to let you sleep."

"That was kind of you, Lennox."

He handed me the envelope, then declared like a man heading to the gallows, "Send it, if you can, or give this to my sister."

I took the letter, knelt down, and put it in one of the pockets of the backpack. I stood up, and he looked at me across the empty road, his eyes conveying a moist uncertainty. He had sad eyes, like an Irishman.

"Look," I said, perhaps a bit too sure of myself. "In times like this, even if it's just a hangover, you think you've caught the germ. It could be any of a couple of dozen germs, or even sleep deprivation. Jet lag. Do you have the key to your room? Here, just in case, take mine." I dug mine out of a pocket and tossed it to him. "I'm going to find Ned. I might see you in the lobby in a little while."

"Alright," he said weakly. I think he realized, without me telling him, that I wouldn't be going back to the hotel. I was plagued by guilt. ***Does he need me? Am I abandoning him?*** I tried to reason my way out of it: If he has the virus, there's nothing I can do for him but give him a lethal, compassionate dose of a potion I don't presently possess.

If it was just the flu–I clung to that notion because it released me from commitment–then he had everything he needed at the hotel. He was a big, strong lad. He could sleep it off.

"You want me to walk you back?"

"No. I want you to keep your distance."

"Lennox, if I was susceptible, I'd have the virus by now. I was in New York. I was in crowds at the airport."

"Go do what you have to do," he said, turning away, quieter and calmer than before. "Thanks for the pills, and the key. I hope my sister can get the letter. Is that too much, putting that burden on you?"

"No, not at all."

"Now, you take care of yourself Emma, okay?"

"You too my friend."

"You'll do okay," he said, over his shoulder. "I know you. You're a fighter." The world has good people and bad people, I thought, or, broken people where the damage manifests as badness. For sure, Lennox is one of the truly good people.

We were both walking away and I called out, "Lennox, take care buddy!"

He wiped the sweat off his face with a shirtsleeve. He said, "These rough times, one can't know when they'll end." He shoved his hands in his pockets and strode off down the hill towards the hotel.

Now I was sure I wouldn't go to the lab. Ned had said that he lived near the river, I thought, so I'll go there and look for Northumberland Street. I was itching to go, to leave Edinburgh. Northern Scotland, my home, pulled me away from the city like a magnet.

I reached the Water of Leith. The river was sluggish, mossy, shallow, moving over reeds and rocks. Thick green shrubs grew from the banks down to the water. There was a railing and a footpath beside the river. I stood at the railing and watched. Leaves floated along down the middle of the current, with branches washed in from the last rainstorm.

Something heavier lay in the water. I leaned the backpack against the railing and sidestepped down through the shrubs. It was a water-logged overcoat, of no use to me. I climbed back up the steep bank and stepped through the railing.

As I watched, a larger object drifted into view. It was a man in a dark sweater, shaved head with the face submerged, legs underwater, floating heavily like a lump of debris.

Behind him, another body drifted in, and another, until the river was full of corpses, some snagging on roots and forming little eddies around them, knocking against each other. I broke out into a sweat and pulled the pack onto my back and walked hurriedly toward Northumberland, fleeing the little river clogged with the dead, vowing never to look back at it. Never look back.

CHAPTER 15

I'm better on my own than I thought I would be. I think it's because I've been straight out since fleeing the coast and Edinburgh in Ned's Rover. So far, no time for wallowing in loneliness or self-pity.

The battered Rover got me as far as the Kyle of Lochalsh, in the far northwest of Scotland, then I left it, started walking with the backpack crammed with every last remaining morsel of food and water bottle I could carry.

The little town located at the Kyle itself proved too dangerous, or I would have camped out there. I would have slept in the Rover, which ran out of gas, for at least a night. I saw too many of the wandering, muttering sick as I cruised through town. One small gang of crazy thugs chased the car, looking utterly bonkers, aiming at me some rabid retribution, cooked up by fatally warped minds.

For what purpose? I thought, as I watched them through the rearview mirror. What did *I* do to *them*? What do they want from *me*? I thought of the crowds of infected on Manhattan's avenues, and that dream I had of being borne along by those crowds while Will screamed at me from a window.

They had this way of grouping up and becoming lethal. If they're not tearing their clothes off or hurling themselves into rivers and bays, they're tearing after poor me.

I left them behind and drove across the isthmus on a bridge, when the Rover gave out. Good timing by the empty tank, lucky for me.

# #

I was stealthy now, avoiding people. I walked down a rural road; fields, isolated homes, solitary trees, bare brown hills. The homes appeared empty. I slept outside last night in the long grass of a meadow at the foot of a bluff.

The bluff had sheep tracks on it and I could smell the manure. The stars were out, and the silence was so pure I could hear my heart beat. I slept fitfully, but some.

It was October and chilly at night. I had my thick coat, and I used another as a pillow. I woke up with my nose in some grass, to sunlight mingled with clouds, my stomach growling. I could smell rain in the air, and the brine of the sea, which smashes its waves and pushes its tide against the ever-present rocky coasts of this remote island.

I was still taking little eyedroppers of CBD oil. It

calmed me, slowed my heart rate. One time I counted beats-per-minute with an index finger on the inside of my wrist; 54 beats. I've always had a slow-beating heart, which explains why I always could run well, a slim lass who was good at cross-country but didn't care for competition.

I went off the silent road and approached a faded white house. It was mid-morning: I needed shelter, and always, more provisions. My wariness had increased 110 percent, after what happened in the small town near the bridge, what happened to Will, what happened to Ned at the coast. That will haunt me forever. It was partly my fault because I convinced Ned to escape Edinburgh.

Best not to think about it. If I ruminated on my short-comings and faults the effect would be paralysis. I couldn't prevent what happened, and I can't change history.

It was a modest, bland white house, no lights on, no car in the driveway, no dog barking. I need smashing things, I thought, tools and weapons. Lennox told me to take care of myself, and he meant hit back, no hesitation, if them evil things have a go at me. It's a cruel new world, it is.

I stood and stared at the house, for minutes on end. Unless there was an invalid imprisoned in a room or an injured person lying on the floor, I concluded this home was unoccupied, which freed me to break into it. I found a heavy stick in the yard. Sturdy enough, it broke through a first-floor window with a couple of swings, then I reached in and unlatched the window from the inside.

I pushed the backpack through first. That was

unwieldy but I refused to leave my stuff, even for a moment, by itself on the grass. Never leave any space between myself and my provisions: the medical kit, food, water, and the warm clothes I pilfered from the outdoor store in Edinburgh.

I found myself in a sort of decent living room. A carpet, a sofa, cushy chair, fireplace and hearth. What caught my eye first were the photos arranged on a mantel: a man fishing in a Scottish loch, five folks at what looked like a birthday dinner, a school picture of a smiling lass. She looked about 12 y.o., blond hair, and the spitting image of my younger sister Jenny.

I was 26 y.o. then; that meant Jenny would have been 21, if she was still alive. For a reason that completely escaped me, and was obviously propelled by the photo and the likeness, Jenny filled the living room with her spirit. I could hear her voice, calling out my name, *Emma! Look! Look what I did!* She'd hold up a drawing of something like a horse or a turtle, a reasonable facsimile.

We used to splash in the ocean together, play silly games with Star Wars dolls, watch cartoons on cable, then ride bikes. Always smiling, always laughing, such pretty, clean hair, green eyes.

One day she rode her bike into an intersection and was hit by an SUV car and killed instantly. Happened in 2017. She was 12, I was 17. That blew me away: the laughter, those eyes, silenced forever. Little Sis dead, violently, trying to get a grip on that, failing. Miserable. I never could get over that, and that's when cell science and disease research, being so complex and meaningful, helped distract me from this inconsolable grief. On top of guilt, since I'd taught her how to ride a bike.

So here I was, standing on the rug, looking at a picture of a stranger's child, in a stranger's house, where I'd broken in, on the Isle Of Skye, marooned by an apocalypse, and crying my bloody eyes out. Crying so hard that I have to bend over at the waist, and put both hands on my knees. Little salty drops hitting the rug.

CHAPTER 16

I spent a little while sitting cross-legged on that rug, letting the interior storm pass. And when that finally seemed aimless, I began addressing Jenny, as if she were here, and that becomes consoling, soothing, motivating.

I was all on my own, in this dull white house with its dull furniture and not much else, and I decided to head straight for the kitchen. I felt this sudden surge of boldness, and I yelled straight up the stairwell, for someone, and heard nothing in response, so I made a beeline for the fridge. Fridge was packed; I'd say it hadn't been 48 hours since those folks left. Where? Who knows. Nowhere else to go on the Isle Of Skye except to remoter areas or onto some boat; some ship to nowhere, because the pandemic seemed to follow people wherever they go. So the fridge was stocked...

Milk, I opened the bottle and guzzled half of it down.

Cheese…I unwrapped the plastic and frantically searched through drawers for a knife, then I had at it and shoved slices of gouda in my mouth. I found a cooked breakfast sausage; down it went, in four chewy pieces. Remember those waffles and pancakes you loved, the ones you put in the toaster? I found two boxes of those, now soggy because they're defrosted, yet still delicious, still worth saving, and one box was consumed, another went into the backpack.

Unfortunately, no fresh fruit or veggies (you used to hate those–I remember how hard it was to get you to eat your peas), but beggars can't be choosers. I wouldn't have minded finding a meatloaf with a salad and walnuts, and that reminded me that I would make my way to the town of Portree (the largest nearby one, meaning, about 15 miles from here) and loot all the abandoned restaurants and shops I could find.

I took your picture off the mantel, I decided it was you, and stuffed it in the backpack, which had room for hardly anything more.

Before ditching the house, I decided to creep upstairs for one look. Very creaky stairs, unnerving, but you never know what useful stuff you can find. More portraits in the bedroom, which seemed to glare at and admonish me for going through their stuff like any common grifter, but I found a Swiss Army knife in a desk drawer before I left, which made it all worth it.

It was nearly mid-afternoon by the time I hit the road; I decided not to sleep in the house. I know that doesn't make sense, but my gut told me to move. That the owners would return any minute, find the broken window, catch my hand in the cookie jar, and then react in whatever is in character for them, which might be furious and violent.

I always go by my gut, letting the chips fall where they may. Of course, within a mile of leaving the house and walking north along the coast of the Isle Of Skye, it rained. Heavy sheets, blown in curtains from the nearby loch. I trudged across a field and stood under a tree. I still got wet; the rain came down hard, as if purposely defying the decisions I'd made so far.

For survival is making decisions, isn't it?

Always have a plan, even if it seems far-fetched and hasty.

If the plan sucks and fails, formulate a new one. Keep going, plow forward. What's the plan?

Failing to plan leads to panic, paralysis, and often, in survival terms, death.

So there you have it, Jen. The state of my mind, right now.

The rain ceased; it was followed by pleasant and penetrating sunlight. The same field where I found my shelter tree, had a lone apple tree. It had a nice, round shape, and from a distance, I made out its hanging fruit. I picked up the backpack and walked through long grasses, then I got to it and picked perfectly round, medium-sized, pale green and red apples. We used to pick apples at that orchard near home, Jen. Remember? They used to charge a quid per large canvas bag and I always thought so many of the apples went wasted, lying around on the ground. We took them home and made apple crisp.

I devoured the ones I picked, dropping the cores and

the stems, which had a couple of green leaves popping out of them, in a kind of path as I walked around. Some of the apples, whatever I had room for, went into the backpack.

This reminds me of a story Will told me. He spent some summers as a kid in bear-populated Vermont. He said the bears would eat the apples off the ground; the apples were often rotted and fermented. The bears would get drunk on these fermented apples, and sway around on their hind legs, seeming buffoonish rather than threatening. No bears, or wolves, that I know of, on Skye.

Standing there eating, I thought I needed some Scotch, speaking of drunk, and some vodka (as a disinfectant).

In the afternoon, I made my way down the road toward Portree. Strange I hadn't seen any people. I also felt like the kiss of death for other humans, having lost Will, Lennox, Marie, and Ned. It's not my fault, Jen! Not! It's important for my morale, not to suffer this survivor's guilt, a luxurious, self-indulgent emotion given that I might be next on the Reaper's list.

The land was sheep's country, bare and sparsely forested and rocky. At this pace, I would certainly be spending the night outside again, I thought, with coats and apples and leftover cheese, until I heard a familiar rattle in the distance.

I turned the corner, with a fast stride. It was an old pickup truck, pulled over by the side of the road. Motor running. I walked closer. A man sat in the passenger seat, staring straight ahead. My instincts told me to, rather than run and hide, check him out. Gauge if he's friend or foe. Instincts. Go by my gut. Never stop planning.

CHAPTER 17

The pickup, an old Ford F-150 model, containing only loam dust and an old rusty gas can, leaned to the right, toward a drainage gully. Pulling over seemed to have been a rash decision. I hiked over to the driver's side. The window was down.

The guy looked at me as if I was a ghost, then he was startled by the nerve of a stranger who dared to sneak up on his left shoulder.

The truck smelled like smokes, and this older, unshaven, red-eyed bloke just gawked at me. Finally, I broke the ice.

"By any chance, are you going to Portree?"

He scrutinized me for an awkward moment, then said, "I don't know where I'm bloody going."

"I thought I might grab a ride with you. I'm Emma."

"You don't want to ride with a guy who doesn't know

where the hell he is, do you?"

"You're on the Isle Of Skye," I said, looking around, trying to stay calm. "Aren't too many of us here, apparently."

So then he shut off the motor. By now, Jen, I'm thinking he's got the disease, the forgetting fever. H7N11. One side of me says, 'just keep going...put some distance between yourself and this guy.' Then there was the truck. I needed transportation. I didn't even have a bicycle.

"I'm Emma Wallace, from northern Scotland. Do you know what your name is?"

He scoffed and looked at me with scorn.

"Why the bloody hell wouldn't I?" He opened the door, stepped unsteadily onto the gravel road, dug a wallet out of his back pocket. Opened it. Hand shaking, handed me the driver's license. Wouldn't even read it himself, for Chrissakes.

"'Damn it all, read it!' he said. 'I don't have my glasses.'" I took the license. We're standing there alone out in the middle of nowhere, like the last two people on Skye.

"Robert J. Hardy. Birth date, March 1, 1972." He was 54. I felt bad for him; it was just a matter of time.

"Aberdeen..." he mumbled, filling in the essentials of his lost identity.

"That's right!" I said brightly.

"My wife's Beatrice. Irritable and needy, she says I've become, in my middle age. That's all I remember. Couldn't say why I'm driving on Skye."

He looked back to the vehicle. "Hey, where's Bundy?" Then he gazed around the surrounding landscape frantically. I was instantly afraid he'd lost a child.

"Who's Bundy?"

"My dog! She was sitting right there in the passenger seat. Hey Bundy!" he called out, answered only by the wind that scoured these sheep-trod fields and bluffs.

"When's the last time you pulled over?"

"Back at that town, before the bridge. I've got to go back, look for Bundy!"

He got back into the truck, started up the motor, I backed off to the side of the road. He accelerated away, squealing into a U-turn, leaving a cloud of diesel smoke and dust. He didn't go 200 yards when he stopped all of a sudden, jerked the truck to the side. Braked. Emergency lights went on. Red, off and on, off and on.

The truck idled; wind, red lights blinking, I'm just standing there, watching what he'll do next.

The driver's door opened, Robert J. Hardy stepped out gruffly, gripping a crowbar. He raised it over his head, get this, and smashed it down on the cab! Then he moved over to the back of the truck and gave the fender a couple of angry whacks. Apropos of nothing. Robert dropped the crowbar onto the road. He clutched at his hair, manically, then he trooped off across the adjacent field, towards some woods.

I knew what that meant. I knew what was happening to Robert J. Hardy.

I hiked back toward the truck, and when I got there, threw the backpack in the bed. I bent down and picked up the crowbar. I went over to the driver's door, opened it, got in. I vowed to keep an eye out for a stray dog, Bundy. Then I put the truck into gear and pulled out, aiming for the short drive to Portree.

When I looked over toward the woods, through the passenger window, Robert was gone. It was just me and this quiet, windswept coastal wilderness.

CHAPTER 18: Emma Winslow, London, June, 2051

I really sleep in the next morning. I'm not due at the hospital at St. Paul's Cathedral, London, until 3 p.m. Then I'm awoken by someone pounding on the front door. This doesn't happen much; the people who know me know I like my sleep. I'm never late for work or oversleep. I throw the quilt aside, thinking it's probably Jason. I need coffee desperately.

I go down barefoot to the front hallway and peek behind a sliding curtain on the front door. It's Harry, again, shuffling his feet on the stoop.

All I have on is an oversized T-shirt that goes past my knees. It's only Harry. I open the door; he appears a bit hang-dog.

"Do you have a coffee or tea for me?" I ask.

"I wish. Then I could have some for myself. Listen, I was walking by, and I thought I should tell you..."

"Come in, and I'll make a pot. Have you had breakfast?"

"Nah."

"Did you sleep?"

He shrugs, "Enough. I was with Gwen."

"That explains it." My eyebrows raised, we stroll into the kitchen.

"The coffee is only going to be Nescafe mixed with old espresso grounds."

"That's okay." We learned to make do long ago.

He sits down at a kitchen table while I make the coffee.

"Why did you come over, and wake me up?"

"We had some problems in the neighborhood last night. I think some nutty blokes have gotten their hands on bootleg opioids. Got themselves strung out. Now they're running around with their clothes off, like a troupe of naked lunatics. Bloody buck naked sods. It's not safe for women or old people, at least, at night."

"They're *attacking* people?"

"Not that I know of, but acting like they will."

I thought of the boys me and Jason saw near the park; the alley, and the dog barking.

"So what makes you think it's drugs?"

"Just a guess. It's been happening a lot, people getting hooked on opioids."

"Did anyone get hurt or sick?"

"Yuh, the older brother of my friend Benji, Kyle, got it."

"Got what?"

"The shakes. The Joneses. Whatever. He lay in bed with the sweats for a day. Had a fever. Then he says he's okay, seems normal, but before you know it, he rips his bed sheets off, runs down the middle of Savoy Street buck naked, and throws himself off the Waterloo Bridge. Drowns."

"Sheesh, that's awful! Benji Jameson's brother, you say?"

"Right, Kyle was a drug addict. Crying shame. But it's spreading, spreading through the city, like a bloody...epidemic. People getting hopped up on bad opiates. So you should stick close to the neighborhood, for now."

"But I thought you said Kyle had a fever, felt sick first?"

"Yeah I know, it's curious. It could have been withdrawal symptoms. At any rate, thought you should know first, with your hospital work and what not."

"You always did look out for me, Harry." I place the mug of coffee in front of him. He fists it, then chugs from the mug, placing it back down on the counter and rotating it thoughtfully.

"Thanks for the coffee. Tastes like it's from an espresso bar."

"You're just saying that."

Ever since a long-lost cache of Oxycontin, boxes of it, was found in a warehouse, we'd been having trouble with opioid addiction. But nothing to the extent that couldn't be managed.

I scrape a chair across the wooden floor and sit down.

"What were Kyle's other symptoms?"

"Well, a fever, and a craving for opiates."

"What about forgetfulness? Don't know your name, why you're in a room. You kind of blank out."

"No, I haven't heard that. It's more like, just going completely bonkers, he couldn't be contained in a room, at least that was Kyle. I know where your questions are leading to and yeah, it could be a disease, rather than the drugs. Anything's possible. I'm not the expert. But I know a lot of people are dabbling in opiates."

"Any women involved?"

"What do you mean?"

"You keep mentioning blokes only. Has anyone seen, that you know of, a woman get sick, then exhibit some of the same behaviors?"

"No, *that* I would have remembered. It's all been men."

"Strange," I say, gazing out the window, through a white, gauzy curtain. Pale sunlight struggles through a morning murk draped over the city. ***With the barmy fever, women were primarily affected, or were infected easier. There are some differences; this mania was not present with H7N11. Although herd aggression and violence was.***

"I haven't seen it in the hospital," I say. "No sign of it. You'd think I'd see it there first."

"You can't take these lunatics to a hospital, unless they're restrained and sedated. Anyways, that's what I came to tell you. You have to watch out for it."

Harry finishes his coffee and stands up, appearing disheveled and like *he* can't be contained in this small room. He runs a busy food-delivery business throughout London.

"I'll be off." I follow him out.

"Listen, knowing some of the lads around here," I say. "Don't you think some of them are doing it on purpose? They see an opportunity to have fun and act like arseholes. They used to call it streaking."

"Fake a fever? Then your own death? That's a stretch. Anyway, I saw Jason, too, last night. He told me he was leaving for mainland Europe."

"When?"

"In one day." I'm standing at the door in silent shock.

"Didn't he tell you?"

"Not exactly."

"I thought you two were tight?" he says, opening the door and stepping outside. He turns back to me and adds, paternalistically, "Get some clothes on."

"Of course..." I'm still spacey from the Jason news. I call after, "Thanks for telling me, Harry. About the dangers."

"No worries. Be careful Emma."

When I close the door behind him, I see the cricket bat and the axe leaning against the wall, as one would place an umbrella.

CHAPTER 19

For some people, life is little more than a series of heightened sensations. Nothing is pre-thought or plotted out. Thrill, fear, joy, lust, satiety, intoxication, all these things are desired minute-by-minute, with no self reflection. For this very reason, they are magnetic to other people, who want to experience life as vitally and intensely as they do.

Jason is like that, a good-looking, zesty man. A guy who has a new plan every hour, making it a bit slippery to be his girlfriend. I think now he may have split London to mount an adventure on the mainland, just to test me, to see if I would follow him.

Whatever he did worked, because I desperately want to find him. I think I discovered I loved him, but about an hour too late.

My search of London for Jason is going to be on foot;

no way to call or text. Yes, we know about those defunct technologies. The jury is out, in my mind, which way is superior: word of mouth, in-person, or instantaneous texting, which certainly has its benefits, and the big downside of constant harassment and addiction.

All I know is my mum texted and emailed, then she had to learn a new way of communicating when TSHTF.

Uncertainties swirl around in my mind; maybe the hesitancy to fall overtly head over heels with Jason has scared him off. Maybe he's decided he's done with me.

He wasn't at his flat, so I go look for him at the distillery, which is located on the other side of the Thames. I take Fleet Street to Queen Victoria, then walk over to the long steps going up to the Millennium Footbridge. From that vantage point, I see ribbons of smoke rising from several different places across the river.

Small groups of people flee along the riverside sidewalk, across the river from where I'm standing. Buildings burn, a few random fires licking and spewing black smoke. I can't put my finger on it, but some decentralized riot is taking place. That side of the river looks like a no-go, for me, so I pause on the empty bridge. I stare at the fires and the sudden emergence of violent agitation.

We don't protest, because government bodies that antagonize people by their policies do not exist. Any existing protests are person-to-person ("You nicked this or that bicycle or cache of food!") or internalized.

I watch people bolting out of fright; they are clearly being pursued, or getting out of the way of a riot.

A teenaged kid appears on a bicycle and starts to cross

the bridge opposite from me. The bike wobbles, as though he's just a beginner, then it teeters and falls. He lies there unmoving in a heap, a lone crumpled body on an empty bridge.

So now I move into first responder mode. I *am* a nurse. I stride quickly, half the bridge, listening to my own foot strikes, not quite thinking about Jason, as the sudden urban chaos has taken my mind off the issue, if only temporarily.

The young lad's only wearing a loose pair of black-knit Nike shorts. Barefoot, lying on his side, tangled up with the bike; lips blue, eyes closed, red face, not palpably breathing. Heart attack or seizure I think. He looks like he woke up on a couch, didn't know where he was, and jumped on a bicycle to randomly pedal, in a panic.

I pick up his wrist and check his racing pulse rate; he's clearly alive. His forehead is afire.

The eyes snap open, frightening me. He makes eye contact and moves his mouth soundlessly.

"What's your name? Where do you live? Do you know where you are? Where are the rest of your clothes?" All the answers are "I don't knows" or blank stares.

I hear footsteps on the bridge nearby. I stand up. Four young people bolt past, coming from the opposite side of the river. South London, a place that I like; my parks and gardens.

"What's happening?" I yell out. They seem to be on the normal, reliable side of the humanity scale.

The first guy says, "Get to safety, Mum. The crazy gangs are about. The city's gone mad!"

"Yeah, but why? Who is it?"

"Beats me. They're throwing burning trash cans through windows. Attacking people...ripping their own bloody clothes off. I think it's drug addictions run amok! Or some kind of sickness!"

"Jonathan, let's go! Let's get a long ways out," a woman yells back.

"You better leave. They're crossing the river!" Jonathan says over his shoulder, then runs after his companions.

Who's crossing the river? Random sick people? I wonder if this is the beginning of a city-wide epidemic, fast- and hard-hitting, like my mum described so long ago. Manhattan avenues densely packed with the ill. H7N11, it was.

The fallen man has gone limp at my feet. Realistically, for the moment, I can do nothing for him. I'm empty-handed and ill-equipped; I don't have my medical kit, and the hospital's several blocks away. I disentangle him from the bike, drag him across a patch of concrete, and lean him against the bridge railing above the river. His head slumps over on a shoulder.

Off goes the sweatshirt I'm wearing and I drape it over his saggy, bare shoulders and upper body. Then I back off.

I want to wash my hands and face in the worst way. I wish I had a mask, medical grade or not. I stand up; I'd have to get help from a couple of guys with a stretcher. I only see a few vehicles driving in the distance, on adjacent bridges or in the streets.

I lean against the railing, suddenly wan and exhausted. I watch the steady, green-blue Thames surge past, its swollen, muddy surface swirling with eddies. It takes me away from the chaos, like feeling the heartbeat of the city by watching its bloodstream.

"Just like Jason to leave at the last minute without telling me his plans," I tell the river. The guy lies silently slumped on the railing. Urgent, random shouts carry across the water. I walk quickly back over to the City of London, heading for St. Paul's Cathedral and the hospital.

Obsessive speculation swarms my mind. *There are loads of available opiates–even for people who have a lot of pain and cannabis isn't enough for it–but something else is at play here. That guy felt viral, feverish and ill.* I think about the book Harry was reading, *antigenic shift*. A virus mutates and the population has no built-in immunity mechanism. Defenseless, small-population place; potential wipe-out.

Jesus, I need to wash up!

London would be utterly defenseless against a pandemic. We have no advanced medical technology.

I walk back across the Millennium Footbridge to Cannon Street, the thoughts spinning and awry. Over my shoulder, I hear the distant shouts and the pops, echoing off concrete bridges, of exploding fires. I see ribbons of dark smoke snaking amidst empty glass towers.

This street is vacant. Silence like shutting a door on the noise, stifled by the banks of trees. A dog barks, a cyclist pedals past on a side street, yellow blossoms shake in a sunny breeze.

I breathe easier.

The buildings here are still covered with those vines

and purple blossoms. Another small tree that adorns the lawn of an ancient church has huge, carnation-shaped white blossoms, which turn violet during the early fall. I feel like there's still a large part of London we can protect. I wonder if we can block the bridges, preserve parts of the city, and quarantine this outbreak?

If that's what it is.

A few blocks from the Cathedral, I see a nurse that I work with coming towards me on the sidewalk. She breaks into a run when she sees me.

Her name is Grace, and she's my age. She never does anything slowly. Her engine runs in a higher gear than other women. Her black hair, with a luster in the sunlight, bouncing along. Somehow, from the expression on her face, I know she has important news for me.

CHAPTER 20

"We've been looking for you," Grace says breathlessly.

"What for? I'm not due for a shift till 2 p.m. I was just checking that everything's okay here."

"Isn't it terrible? What's happening in the city?"

"What about in our ward? Are our men and women doing well?"

"Yes, it's alright. But no one knows what's happening. Jason was looking for you. He said he went to your place first, then he came here."

"Shoot. He must have just missed me!"

"He gave me this to give you." She hands me a folded up piece of paper, a note he's written me. I instantly feel edgy, raw around the corners, like pieces of my world are calving off an edifice and shattering on the ground. I'm also starved, which is one of the ways my body responds to stress.

I open the note and read, standing there on the breezy road, the sun popping in and out like someone passing flash cards over it:

Dear Emma,

I should have told you this a long time ago, so here goes. I have a son, William Fairfield.

My hand drops to the side. Then I lift the note up and keep reading.

He's four years old. He took his Mom's last name. Her name is Amelia Fairfield. I split with her years ago, and we never had much of a relationship in the first place. I only found out about William a year ago.

Amelia left London with a caravan four years ago, and now Amelia is sick. I heard she might die. They live on the mainland near Lake Geneva. Alright, the purpose of all this writing, and I feel rotten not telling you in person, is that I feel responsible for poor William.

I have this opportunity to be reunited with him by going on the trip with Dr. Braden, so I took the job. I lied to you, or didn't tell the whole truth. I feel bad that I made you think it was all about the job, my prospects, when in truth it was about my estranged son.

Braden is an arrogant sod and has to leave tomorrow. He'll be financing the trip and wages when I go get William. Braden's got this idea that London has an outbreak of a germ or poisoned opiates that will take hold of and strangle the city. He thinks these gangs of *infected thugs will terrorize the city for quite some time.*

Emma, I will come back for you as soon as I get a chance. Just sit tight. Stay safe. Stick with Harry and the lot. They'll know what to do. It may only be a few weeks. You can still come with me if you pack up and meet me at the Southwark Underground by 2:00 p.m. We're taking the vehicles through the Chunnel tonight.

I want you to come, I really do! Dammit, I screwed up things between us. Sorry.

Love and all my heart, Jason

This note is *so* Jason. Especially the last part, *love and all my heart.* What the fuck does that mean, coming from Jason who doesn't express his emotions like that? There's something essentially inarticulate about him that makes the emotions raw and unrefined, and therefore genuine. See, I can't stay angry with Jason.

I'll betch you I'd even like this Amelia. I'm not jealous or bitter at all, at least right now, only disappointed that he couldn't tell me before. He couldn't be the honest, stand-up guy that I want him to be.

Now I'm making calculations about whether I could intercept him. My changing world...it's faster than I can react. We hurry back to the hospital, and I think of all the stuff I could fetch at my flat and take through the Chunnel.

"What are you going to do?" Grace asks, again, breathlessly awaiting my answer.

"Did you read the note?" She looks at me, stricken and guilty.

"Of course I did."

"That's alright. I'd have done the same thing."

"So what are you gonna do?"

"I don't have a bloody clue."

CHAPTER 21: Emma Blair, Isle of Skye, October 2026

It's ages since I've driven a pickup. Did it on a farm when I was young in the north of Scotland, before I became a city girl. An academic with only crude survival skills that I already sense being pushed to the limits.

I've stolen, or "commandeered," a truck, for Chrissakes. Robert J. Hardy's. He's run off. Is stealing a skill or a deviance? An instinctual desire to promote one's survival, at all costs.

The flaky old dented Ford had a wobbly stick and was hard to get into gear. I didn't see anything but yellow dust in the rearview mirror. I threw it into third, with a loud grunt from the transmission, then I yanked it into fourth and rattled along on the road to Portree. It was only a few miles to town. I feared being the loudest thing on the landscape. No secret to anyone in Portree, infected or not, that Emma was coming into town.

After a few miles, I met a single flashing yellow light. The first modest homes appear amongst these sheep-grazing fields. I went at a wary cruising speed, trundling onto the main drag. It was no surprise that the streets were empty and barren. I didn't see one crowded block in Edinburgh, and here I was in a tiny town on the Isle Of Skye. Robert J. Hardy dashed any notion that the island was spared H7N11.

Main Street took me past vacant homes (I could never be sure...), a service station, a restaurant called the Sea Net. I slowed down at an intersection; nothing in the rearview mirror but a skewed view of pavement and ineptly parked cars. Drivers having abandoned them in a panic, I gathered.

The town appeared neutron bombed.

That reference came from the old days when merchants of war designed a mass-destruction weapon that kills all people but leaves the buildings and bridges intact. Little did they know, those unimaginative doom merchants, that a microscopic pathogen would produce their desired outcome far better: silent, lightning quick, thorough.

I planned to gather supplies and squat at one of these homes, *if* I deemed the small town safe. I rolled the window down; the air was cool and salty, mingled with a faint fishy odor. A low-lying fog fought with the sun. In the fishing-town manner, the buildings sloped down to a cozy harbor and had little space between them.

I pulled a U-ee, then drove up to a gas pump at the

petrol station. I was going to fill up the truck and the gas can that sat in its bed. I was already treating this truck like it was mine, which gave me a sharp twinge of guilt. I thought of keeping an eye out for Robert J., and Bundy.

I got out of the truck to inspect the gas pumps. They were modern, and by silly habit–the same one that impelled me to "do errands since I'm in town"–I fished around for my credit card.

A loose metal sign banged against its steel pipe and I whipped around, then laughed at myself. ***I'm alone, I've nicked a truck, I'm stuck in a ghost town in the middle of the baddest pandemic. You have to laugh, right?*** Sure. Otherwise, I'd scream and bawl my eyes out, not necessarily in that order.

I pondered the petrol display, figuring out how to get the "gazzoleen," as Ned would say, to flow, which reminded me of Ned, and I got all choked up. In the old days, that was one month ago, I'd fish around for my VISA. I took the fuel nozzle from its cradle, the numbers on the pump display scrolled like a slot machine's and reset to zeros. Voila!

Then I heard a gravelly female voice, "That's Bob Hardy's truck."

I turned, still clutching the fuel nozzle. Gray-haired lady in a white knit sweater and jeans, holding a clipboard by her side, not a handgun. A voice inside said, "This is rural Scotland not the U.S.A. She isn't automatically going to be holding a handgun or a rifle."

I stood there awkwardly gripping the pump nozzle, hand in the cookie jar. "This *is* Robert J. Hardy's truck. Yes."

The lady looked at me quizzically, then burst out laughing, apparently at my formal usage. When she got her breath back: "Mind my asking, what are you doing with it?"

"I asked him for a ride. His memory was, sadly, all but gone. He showed me his license, then he ran off into the woods, for no reason." I understand that this was the abbreviated version of what happened.

"And you took his truck?"

"I said I'd gas up and go look for his dog for him."

"What happened to his dog?"

"Bundy? I don't know. I think he just ran off. Robert was upset."

"She."

I looked at her blankly.

"Bundy is a she, a border collie."

She sighed, which dissipated the tension, at least for me. I was essentially stealing gas for a stolen truck. In the absence of anything else to do, I jammed the nozzle back into its cradle.

"What happened to Bob is no different than what happened to everyone else in this town," the lady said sagely.

"Did they get sick, forget everything?"

"Worse. They grouped up and started killing, like."

"That's awful."

"It was. Is. You can pump the gas, I don't care."

"You sure?" I fetched the fuel dispenser again. Gotta finish my errand. "I'm Emma, by the way."

"Gladys."

I squeezed the nozzle handle like I was milking a cow,

and the flow started. I smelled the "gazzoleen" fumes.

"Do you live around here?"

"Right next door."

I looked around, a bit perplexed, but I felt I already knew what happened to the rest of the Portree citizenry.

"Is anyone else around?"

"I'm the last. They took my Bill. I hid out. I have plenty of food. There's lots around."

"I'm really sorry to hear that. Do you mind if I fill the gas receptacle in back? I have some cash."

"Don't bother paying, and no I don't mind. I wouldn't have anything to buy. Everything is...well you could say that everything is free. Like that truck you're driving."

"I'm going to look for him." And Bundy, I thought, sticking the nozzle back in its cradle and getting the can from the back. I sensed the streets around me with their loud silence, the echoes of all the young children that were gone. The boozers from the pubs and the teenagers and the chit-chatting moms. I wondered if Gladys had kids too, or even grandkids. I wouldn't even ask.

"I'm going to give Robert J. Hardy his truck back, too."

"Oh, don't mind me. I was just ribbing. Why don't you come for some tea, when you're finished." Gladys laughed, more of a cackle bred from loneliness. She turned and walked toward the house next door, with its sooty brick chimney and flaking white clapboards.

The wind gusted over the empty loch down by the harbor. The sound of the clanking broken sign and a shutter that banged against Gladys's house was like an unsettling language I didn't understand.

CHAPTER 22

I parked the dented Ford, now all gassed up, with reserves in the can in back. I noted the petrol station itself had a convenience mart, which I would mine for necessities, after a short spell with Gladys. I fully expected her to ask me to stay. I will decline, I thought, hoping somehow to make my refusal diplomatic.

My gut told me I needed to do things my way for at least the first few weeks, and I'd had too many companion fatalities as it was.

I followed Gladys across the broken pavement with its tufts of coastal grass sprouting through the cracks. It was awkward entering her house, accepting her hospitality. A moment ago, she didn't know what had happened to Robert J. Hardy, and what my role had been.

As I creaked open the screen door to her kitchen, over my shoulder the fog seeped into the streets, Styrofoam food containers and cups caterwauling into vacant lots that appeared never inhabited.

Gladys must be going crazy in this town, I thought.

"Tea?" she asked, standing over an old stove.

"Love some, thanks."

"Got any kids, honey?"

"No."

"Did you ever want some?"

Odd question, given that our universe had changed, procreation had screeched to a halt, as far as I knew. Possibly, the green shoots of some post-apocalyptic romances were sprouting. Any planning was out the window.

"I do, as a matter of fact. I'm not sure I'd want to bring a daughter into this world right now, though. Lately, I haven't thought about it much. A lot has gone on my back burner."

"I imagine so. You're still young. You have plenty of time."

The tea kettle emitted a wheezy whine.

"When was the last time someone bought gas here?"

"Bob Hardy, just last week. Before then, a month."

She stood on the wooden floor dipping a tea bag in the hot water, dipping it in up and down and up and down.

"My Bill ran the petrol station, I kept the books, and the house. We have a daughter, Gretchen, a single mom in Glasgow. Grandchild's name is Amy." She started to choke up, eyes welled with tears; one streaked down her cheek.

"I don't know what's happened to them, my

daughter...my granddaughter."

"I'm sorry I got us talking on this subject."

"No, it's alright." She was revved up and the tight ball of twine must unwind. "One day I see this group of young men coming down the hill. Hear them first, muttering, a humming, like a chant. I go to the door; they're like a whole football team that's been at the pub, rowdy, wild-eyed, all packed together. Scary. Bill, I says, come in! He's standing on the pavement out there, wiping his hands with a cloth. Don't pay 'em no mind, he says."

"You don't have to go on..." My own tears well up...Lennox, Ned. Gazzoleen. The sand, the shadows, on Balmedie Beach. Me and Gladys needed to talk about food, cooking, the gardens, something else.

"Bill goes back to the garage, comes out with a crowbar, like. He didn't have a chance." She clapped the cup down on the wooden table, stood holding her head.

"They swarmed onto him like hornets, beat him. Carried him away. I watched it from the window; that awful chanting, muttering! I'm glad we didn't have a rifle–I doubt it would have saved him from that mob. And I would have turned it on myself!"

"I'm sorry." I gulped my tea down, set it on the table, twirled it in a circle.

"I've almost taken the sleeping pills with the Scotch as it is. Look now, I've ruined our tea."

"You've got it off your chest. It's good to talk it out." Everyone's got something like this, I thought, and it's only been about a month.

"If it wasn't for the few visitors who've come, like

yourself."

"And Robert J. Harding," I added.

I finished the Chamomile. It was, as advertised, mild and calming.

Gladys flashes a perfunctory glance. "He might be gone now. That's how it starts. For him, there'll be no going back. It's a crying shame."

I sat silently in this depressing kitchen, sipping the end of my tea, feeling sorry my presence dredged up the misery, realizing it can never be far from the surface for her.

Gladys took a deep breath and stared out the window.

"Don't you worry, Dearie." She patted me on the shoulder. "This will blow over, someday. You'll fancy a young man, have a daughter. This too shall pass," she said emphatically, shaking an index finger like a pastor to her rapt congregation.

"I have to go. Thanks so much for the tea, and the gas." I stood up.

"You won't stay for a meal?"

"I don't want to impose." That sounded, well, stupid, given the situation. Gladys wiped her hands off with a towel wrapped on the handle of the stove. She still kept an organized household, given all, I thought.

"I'll check in on you tomorrow," I said. She looked at me with warm understanding.

"There's an empty farmhouse, just outside of town. I'll give you directions. Fancy it's safe, for now. You can drive your truck there." I looked outside the window, distracted by the sign that kept banging against the metal pipe.

Right then, outside of town sounded good to me.

CHAPTER 23

The farmhouse was located at the end of a rutted road bordered by tall, stately trees. I bounced the truck along the road, driving unconsciously, forming an attachment to the vehicle after only a few minutes. I thought of Jen again, the photo in my backpack. Just me and the truck, alone.

The surrounding meadow was quite big; a stone wall meandered through it. The fog lifted, showing tall wet grass gleaming in the sun. Birds scattered from the meadow as I pulled up.

I idled the truck at the end of the dirt driveway. The brick farmhouse had a slate roof and a slightly crooked stone chimney. The structure was choked by shrubs; it had a falling-down, detached barn.

I felt grounded, for once. This homestead would have some supplies and tools, and provided at the very least a solid roof over my head.

The isolation gave me the creeps, however. I was alone in a strange land. Without companions in a friendless wilderness, other than Gladys, is not where I expected to be at age 26.

If you were alive, Jen, would you be with me, right now?

I decided to beep the horn; if someone was in there, they'd come out. The sound was jarring. A heavy, rural silence permeated everything. I was the loudest thing on the farm; afraid that the horn would bring the evil fairies onto me.

Then I regarded my new home, yes, my house and barn, if the Owen Fergusons would permit me. Gladys told me they were the owners and they had flown the coop. No cars or trucks or tractors were in the yard; no chickens pecking at the lush grass. I shut off the engine and stepped out of the old Ford F-150. Windows at the farm were all dark and I had this creepy, defensive feeling, Jen, but it was time to explore.

"Hello!" I yelled out, stepping through long grass and weeds to the front door. Seemed a good two weeks since other humans had trod this lawn. A flock of ravens alighted from the trees. No one seemed to be about to disturb. All the windows in the house were dark, with some curtains drawn. Only the wind and the leaning, creaking of a dead tree looming above me.

It was October. The flowers have withered, the leaves in the trees were changing colors and flaking into piles on the ground.

I trusted Gladys's recommendation for this farmhouse.

No reason she'd lead me astray. I didn't ask her what happened to the Owen Fergusons. I simply accepted her generous and sensible recommendation to re-occupy it. I repeated these things to myself, building my morale.

Reached the front door, tried a brass front-door knob, which turned cleanly. The thick door stuck, but opened when I gave it a concentrated shove.

Why didn't you knock first fool, I thought, until I realized that "abandoned" is the operative term here. I wasn't going to find anyone alive in this town, Robert J. Hardy notwithstanding.

The front hall air was musty like a closet. The floor boards bowed and creaked under my tentative steps. It was an old house Jen, virtually reeking of generations of Owen Fergusons. A shadowy hallway; portraits on the wall, a coat rack, a stuffy chair, a flight of frayed, carpeted steps leading to the second floor. Several doors to other first-floor rooms.

You know I was not going upstairs alone. You know I was not going into the attic. Too scary! Remember how going upstairs in empty quiet houses used to scare the crap out of me? Attics are like nightmares come true!

Get a grip on yourself, I said. See Jen, I felt your presence. Not like a ghostly spirit or anything weird or mystical like that. Merely something that would boost my courage. Strength in numbers. Why did you have to die then? Why does life throw us those wicked curves, when we least expect it? You were part of the mental game, Jen. You're a morale booster, a lifeline.

First priority: kitchen.

"Anyone home?" I yelled out, twice, just to make sure.

Old plaster walls with dusky landscapes and portraits gobbled up the words. The first door gave way to what was probably a dining room; thick wooden table with a cloth and a single candle in the middle. No food scraps. Four wooden chairs (fire material? Potentialities if I run out, I thought). A clouded, paned window with a gnarled shrub brushing against it, more long grass leading downhill to a small copse of dark woods.

I went back into the front hall and tried another door; bingo! The kitchen. I sensed a lift as if I was finally re-centered, in my element. The rest of the home had clung to me with a doleful, claustrophobic loneliness.

A real kitchen!

An oven hearth made of stone, wooden shelves with pots and pans stacked on them, cardboard boxes of supplies, including salt, dried potatoes, oatmeal. Old? Yes. Appreciated and needed? Unquestionably.

A fridge, tucked into a corner. Electricity off; might have still had a few food items that hadn't spoiled. A real drawer of forks and knives. And that's what I found in the first 15 minutes. I knew there was more. My own kitchen Jen, a real place where I could hang my hat and feel human again.

I hurriedly dumped my backpack on the floor, eager to sift through everything and make myself at home. Make it mine.

I spent the next hour arranging things precisely to my liking, putting my stamp on them. Then I cooked a glorious four-course meal of canned sardines, mashed potatoes, black beans from a can, and Cheerios with powdered milk (sorry, that's dessert).

I found a bottle of Laphroig 15-year-old on an upper shelf, two-thirds full. Scotch whisky precedes and accompanies dinner. Yes! It goes without saying Jen, I got a bit pissed, in my new home. It helped me forget my predicament, and at the same time, made me loopy and celebrant in the "new" farmhouse.

The Scotch and the carb-rich meal knocked me out. My eyes drooped. Knackered City. I scraped the wooden chair across the flagstone floor, stumbling as I stood up. Two jiggers of Scotch, four ounces, a chick who doesn't weigh nine stone. I like wine too, and a lager, and a Scotch on a proper occasion, but I get drunk on just one. I staggered beyond the kitchen to the bedroom.

"Jesus Emma," I bawled out as if to a separate self, then laughed. Another voice in the back of my mind, the avenging, admonishing one, told me I'm toast if any intruders find me now. But I wasn't exactly thinking about that at this moment, gratefully.

I reached the hallway, noticed through a window, the night was black, autumnal winds swaying trees in the darkness. A branch scraped against a window somewhere, which indisputably scared the shit out of me. I investigated it, deciphered the noise because otherwise I wouldn't sleep; I couldn't let go of a cloying paranoia.

A young woman, alone in an isolated farmhouse at night amidst pandemic carnage.

What I needed to do is turn off this internal churning and sleep. Off to bed I went. I made sure all doors were locked from the inside, all windows. I settled down palpably. When I ducked under the covers finally, it felt like my bed.

Remember when we used to sleep together, in the big cushy mattress with heavy covers? Well, it wasn't like that, but the memory was soothing. First night.

The farmhouse. I slept.

CHAPTER 24: Isle of Skye, October 2026,

First Day At The Farmhouse

The metal bed frame had a head stand in the shape of a suspension bridge. There were two pillows and a nice blanket with a velour texture. The blanket tented over my head, I curled up on my side, left cheek denting the pillows. The Scotch did it. I don't remember laying awake pondering my plight, or ruminating too much, until I tugged the blanket aside and found light flooding the room. Sun through the window. Morning.

# #

I couldn't only hide out in the farmhouse. That was just not gonna work, nor was it in my nature. I'd go stir crazy. I woke up purposefully, and did a complete inventory of the residence. The kitchen was well-equipped, if not wondrously stocked. I eventually had to go outside, find more food.

I made cowboy coffee, old grounds soaked in hot water, which took me half an hour, but by darn I had a cuppa Joe. Then I went outside and searched the barn. The Owen Fergusons undoubtedly left with the finest of the tools, but other useful implements were scattered about, hanging from hooks, leaning in corners. I came away with a pick and a hoe; a shovel, a small axe, a long apple picker with a claw-like basket at the end.

Gut feelings, which I take seriously, flowed in like the morning tide: I would never use this dingy barn as a shelter, except in the most desperate circumstances. It was musty, structurally rotten in spots, and littered with mouse droppings. I made a pile of the tools outside the front of the barn, and walked back inside the house gripping the axe like a tomahawk.

I wanted to use it to chop up kindling for the kitchen hearth. I was thinking I'd keep a fire going most of the waking hours, to heat up my food ingredients, and heat up me.

It already felt that way, *my* farmhouse. I needed that sense of ownership and possession, the Owen Fergusons be damned.

I will certainly cultivate a garden, I thought, but that's not for six or seven months from now. Will I be alone for that long? I'll have to stop in on Gladys again. I'd promised to today. No, it's not going to be today. Too busy.

Gladys had mentioned a schoolhouse, down the dirt road that passes my driveway. Off I went to check it out. The school was three miles down the road, but I took a shortcut across the meadow behind the farm.

Down the hill, through the long grasses and wildflowers, past the woods, I found a small footpath through the fields. The day was fair, about 12 C. (54 F.), cloudy, yet I didn't sense rain. I actually planned to collect water; set up some kind of cistern made up of empty buckets and pots and a bird-bath on a wooden pedestal that I found in the barn.

I crossed a narrow and mossy stream that looked too boggy for drinking, yet we did have a small river beyond the woods. I saw it winding along into this valley when I drove in the truck.

Perhaps the school has a well, I thought. You have children there every day, you have to water them. I'd drive the truck over there, by the way, but it gets crap mileage. How long will gas be available in Portree? Probably not very; I have to take every opportunity to conserve. I'm going to need the truck when the weather gets cold and I need supplies. I'm going to need the truck to flee threats to my life.

After I crossed the stream, I came upon ancient graves spread throughout the grasses. Sturdy, stone memorials for powerful clan members that lived in these parts hundreds of years ago. Carved, engraved figures lying prone with their arms and hands crossing their chests. I walked quickly among them, wondering on what solemn rites I have trod.

I sensed heavy medieval religious symbolism, emblematic for brief, violent, pious, and orthodox lives. I reached the top of a hill, and at the bottom was the road leading to the schoolhouse.

I crossed another meadow to reach the school. The sun flared from behind clouds that drifted in from the ocean. White and yellow wildflowers clung to life, bending over in the breath of a wind, buzzing with bees. I put the axe and small backpack down, sat cross-legged in the grass. I stared at the flowers, mesmerized and meditative, passively following the industrious progress of one or two of the bees.

For once, I wasn't on the run or hiding. My heart rate slowed; the scars began to heal, psychic and otherwise; the weight of recent experiences fell away. I lost track of time, perhaps half an hour, before I stood up and made my way to the building.

This was a one-room schoolhouse, with flaking white clapboards and black shingles. A cracked pavement lot with a lonesome looking basketball hoop, minus a net. I've heard there are entire school districts in these parts with less than 20 kids. Met a guy from a Scottish village who boasted of being both at the top *and* bottom of his class, since he was actually its only member.

A ramshackle shed sat nearby, where they probably kept sports and building upkeep equipment. I tried the front door of the school; it was locked, duh. This place was evacuated weeks ago. I wouldn't let that stop me. I was driven by a relentless, compulsive instinct to harvest and prep.

I looked around the surrounding road, meadows, glen; as usual, nobody and nothing around. I began trying windows. They'd done a fine job of securing the building; and I wasn't in the proper mood for a violent, glass-breaking entry. I was grateful and hesitant when the cellar door creaked open after a stiff pull, in the back of the building. I'd come all the way here and this was my only way in. After a deep breath, I stepped down into the dark and dank room and made my way quickly through the equivalent of a squalid, dark root cellar, praying that the door at the top of the rickety wooden stairs would open.

It was blocked by a desk; a couple of tough shoves and I was officially a schoolhouse break-in. Entering that room was like stepping into another century. Rows of small wooden desks, almost crude in their simplicity. Cubbies lined the wall, some still draped with a hat or coat. I saw a Frigidaire at the far end of the room in the back. Snacks, I figured, teachers' lunches. I found a shelf of single-serving, spoiled milk containers, but also a few plastic water bottles, unopened.

The bottles went into the backpack. Above the fridge was a basket, how quaint and domestic, containing several packets of animal crackers. ***Class going nuts, time for the animal crackers, I thought. Bring on the docility. Sugar is the brute force method to win discipline.***

I placed my pack down on the wood floor and stood there in the middle of this space, as quiet as a museum, chewing down crackers, surrounded by the invisible presence of chattering children. ***A bell rings, school's out, screaming and laughing kids stream outside, the door shuts. Oh, if only it was true. A thick silence trails in their wake.*** It was composed of their absence.

In the front of the room was a chalkboard and lessons that covered almost an entire wall. A math lesson: long division, then multiplication involving decimal numbers.

Automatically, I completed the calculations in my head.

In fifth grade, Miss Cornish had me stand up in class and rattle off the answers to numbers other students shouted out, two-digit numbers multiplied together. I'm a math jock, a numbers geek. I didn't forget that I was an infectious disease researcher. I did all the problems in about 15 seconds, then I picked up a piece of chalk the size of a cigarette butt. I wrote out, "H7N11."

Below that: "Transmission: Airborne, possibly saliva and blood-borne." Below that,

"Symptoms: immediate, no delay, presentation acute and neurological." I hear the chalk: scrape, squeak, scrape, squeak. Below that,

"Resistance: Significant and exceedingly rare (myself). Source: Unknown, possibly DNA-based."

Below that: "Fatality rate:," squeak, scrape, squeak, scrape..." 100%. Proviso, victims otherwise group together and roam..." Wait, I erase that roam and write, "maraud, like reivers."

I like that, reivers.

"Survival rate of packed reivers: Unknown, as long as food supply (live flesh, water, blood?) remains. Death soon, 1-24 hours, when separated..."

All very curious. All very mysterious and unprecedented for a virus. That couldn't have evolved from nature. You don't see bats catching viruses then flying around in packs of...whatever number. Similar to rabies though. I colored in a period (.), the chalk was yellow, then said to myself, "There, enough. Enough of the pathogen shit for now."

It would be good soon to have someone else to talk to.

The rest of the board lists global capitals. This must have also been a social studies lesson, before the kids and their teacher skedaddled: Edinburgh, London, Madrid, Paris, Berlin, Zurich, Stockholm, Budapest, Rome.

Only weeks ago those metropolises stood astride the western world and hummed with vibrant humanity. Millions of people. The *teaming masses,* one is wont to say. All of the leaders of these cities and city states had an urbane, smug complacency. The cities bristled and hummed with something else now, this infection apocalypse, which reminded me to go to the window and scan the surrounding meadows, roads, and dales.

Gotta watch my back. Always. No one to do it for me. Like Ned. Or Will or Lennox.

I saw the dust rise in the breeze off the dirt road, Meadow Larks and black birds, but nothing much else.

I thought about how I could never have lived in a place quite so remote and de-populated, except for hikers and tourists, in pre-pandemic times. The boonies. Now, dominated by the oppressive silence of the countryside, minus people. I was aware that some people find that untouched-ness sublime.

I cranked open the window, letting in cool, fresh, briny air. There was still no movement or human presence out there.

I moved to the teacher's thick wooden desk up front. I rifled the drawer's contents, without hesitation. Pen, pencils, stapler, thick pad of unused paper, a stack of ancient postcards from who knows where, two nip bottles of Dewar's (bagged, immediately), and shoved way back in the rear of the drawer, a threesome of wrapped condoms. Surprise!

Now *that's* funny, I thought. The boys in the front row, "Teacher, teacher, caught with rubbers." I laughed out loud, just let it rip because of how good it felt, and the noise echoed and jarred, like an outburst in church.

No one ever said teaching was easy. One needs an escape valve. I took the Dewar's, everything. Into the pack they went. I felt like I was done looting the schoolhouse.

Before I left, I spotted a cricket bat leaning in a corner of the room, a classic model. A Bradbury. I picked it up, took a few practice swings, which felt playful and good. I wanted it; so the axe filled the rest of the backpack and I carried the cricket bat by its handle to the front door. I unlocked it, stepped outside to the top of the steps that lead into the school.

Something got my attention at the corner of my eye, on the road below. I had company.

CHAPTER 25

Striding through the long grass, feeling the weight of the axe in the backpack, breathing hard, thumping along, clutching the cricket bat by the upper handle.

I headed into the sun-dappled meadows with the centuries-old graves, thinking I could lose my pursuers. I knew nothing of what awaited me, except what I'd watched happen to Ned. That was enough.

I remembered him waving me on, a true mate. A mensch, a hero. "Just go!" he shouted. "I'll be alright." He didn't know, because he hadn't been in New York.

Now I pumped my arms, tears misting my eyes, wind in my hair, the adrenaline coursing through my limbs like a manic drug. I listened to my own footfalls smack the grass and the weeds and the wildflowers brushing past my thighs. I heard nothing else, but my tortured breaths. Maybe, just maybe, they were gone, I thought. I could have outrun them.

I finally ventured a look behind, and there was a pack of them about 40 yards away. Closing. They were smiling at me. Insane, strenuous, grimacing smiles.

Fuck that.

I dropped the backpack in the grass. Discarded the weight. *Get it later. Move Emma! Move! Move honey, get going!* There was a whole ravenous squad of them; eight. The way they ran, deviant and sick like that, obsessed and tireless and warped and driven.

I ran past a small thicket of trees that led down to the river, then ducked into them. Stopped, listened. Maybe they needed open spaces, I thought, but no! I heard them thrashing through the underbrush, charging into these trees, so I ran out of the thicket, through the long grass, toward the river. Downhill.

Carrying the bat like a javelin. *How do they go so fast? What's their fuel? What's the mechanism?* Mother nature is cruel in her inventiveness.

They were 25 yards behind me.

Fifteen yards. I counted them. Eight. *How so fast? There's middle-aged people in there too; I saw glimpses of faces, ghastly faces with rotten teeth and dreadful grimaces.*

A lone tree sat in the meadow. I ripped past it, like a hunter-gatherer with her spear.

I felt like I was going fast, but not fast enough. I wished I had a machine gun.

They forked at the tree, two separate rivulets of maniacs, and suddenly three of them were isolated, cut off. They stopped in their tracks, started puttering, meandering, aimless and doltish. Now the main assault was composed of five. I guess I'd run hard for a mile; almost out of gas. Thirsty as hell, scared as shit all.

I slowed to a jog, mouth pasty, heart racing, sweat trickling down my ribcage.

The five came on strong. They plodded along the same meadow path that contained the graves of long-fallen warriors. Pious, orthodox, deeply meaningful graves. Thick with history. Haunted with combat, blood, and death.

I took this as a sign; these graves. I halted. *I take a stand, I have to. Here, now.* I gripped the cricket bat with both hands, gritted my teeth, felt my forearms tremble, shoulder-width stance, facing the on-coming reivers.

I had nowhere else to go. No one to help me.

"C'mon!" I yelled. Then,

"Ahhhhhhhhhhhhhhhhhhhh!!"

The best battle cry I'd ever heard from me.

The feeling was, *this is my ground now.*

Five of them.

First was a burly, portly teen boy with an unwashed Black Sabbath T-shirt. Patchy, pathetic excuse for a beard. Darting eyes, a twisted leader. Four in a line behind him.

I saw a skinny brunette in a black track suit. Barefoot. The third, a lanky looking flat-top, older half-starved looking sod. Beady eyes and a tattoo on his neck.

Bringing up the rear was another chick in bluejeans and a hoodie sweatshirt. The sweatshirt said, "St. Andrews U."

Black Sabbath was 30 seconds from the target. Me.

Shoulder-to-shoulder with Track Suit, of all people, was Robert J. Hardy, the buttons of his shirt ripped open to the belly and his beet-red face wet with, I don't know, *slobber*? I was nauseated, I was frightened, I was gripping my cricket bat and taking aim.

Inexplicably, I yelled out, "Bob Hardy! I have your truck!"

He stopped and fell to his knees.

The other four were right on top of me. Black Sabbath came first. He lowered his head like a piggish rugby player, as if he would run full-tilt into a stone wall if nothing else was stopping him, except I was the immovable object not the wall, and I swung the bat with an American batter's stance and connected with all the might my eight stone, 112 pounds, could put behind the stroke. I smashed him solidly on the forehead, feeling the mushy crack vibrate in my forearms, as if I'd struck a rock on a stonewall.

He plunged face-first into the grass.

Track Suit, going full tilt, flew with a squeal over his prone body, pitching and rolling onto the hummocky ground.

Brandishing the bat, I flailed wildly at the two other assailants, greasy, bony hands now tearing at my hair, my face, my arms, the loose pieces of my clothing. The appalling smell, the dreadful muttering and humming and teeth gnashing.

A nauseating odor, the loud grunting an assault on my ears.

There I was with the bat, smashing and slashing and clubbing, and I had this image in my mind of the savage beating administered to Ned at the ocean's edge at Balmedie Beach, me crying and beseeching from a distance on the sand dunes, them hauling a bloody Ned like a side of beef for disposal in the ocean waves, and I turned and ran, on the sand at Balmedie, bawling my eyes out with fear, sadness, nausea...

...and there in the meadow with its bloody history of killing and survival, I swung at the lout rearing up behind Black Sabbath, the one with the crew-cut and an ugly neck tattoo, striking him with the edge of the bat on the Adam's apple and hearing the bones snapping like a chicken's.

I kicked out at St. Andrews–she actually had her teeth on my trousers at about the shin–then I golf-swung a bat stroke that crushed her straight in the face, smashing her nose back up into her eyes.

Robert J. Hardy, crawling pitiably in the grass, tugged at the baggy bottoms of my trousers as I backpedaled dizzily, still clubbing away at St. Andrews, when I saw Track Suit back on her feet, that baleful look in her red-streaked eyes like a corpse's returning from the dead.

I knocked Robert J. out cold with a wicked downward swing of the bat onto the crown of his head, feeling no remorse, thinking only of my mate Ned, who'd sacrificed his own life for mine.

I heard my own bitter sobs, desperate grunts of exertion.

Only Track Suit was left. She gave me a skewed glare, not a watt in it of warmth or humanity. She came on with her relentless savagery, fueled by the germ infecting her crippled mind. I swung the heavy bat in a loop over my head, like the bulky swords wielded by the ghosts of the fallen Scotsmen buried in this sun-spangled field, clubbing her once on the head, once more as she fell past, then finally administering the fatal *coup de grace*, with another sideways to downstroke.

"Ahhhhhhhhhhh!"

The bat dropped to the ground. I gasped for breath, bathed in sweat, hands on my knees.

Five bodies all around, as if dropped from a plane in the sky. Lying still as can be.

I had scratches and gouges on my hands, arms, neck, cheek, forehead; they pulsated like hell, everywhere.

I'd never even, up till then, struck a girl or a boy with a closed fist in my life. I was a gentle, sensitive, smart lass, remember that, Jen? Remember how I was? The bullies left me alone. I tended to have protectors at school. I was one of the lucky ones.

Black Sabbath muttered, moved an arm, shifted a leg. I walked over, picked up the bat, lifted it high over my head, then brought it down with my now familiar savage, bitter victory lament. More like an exhausted scream or a shriek.

It all hadn't taken more than two minutes; a brief firefight. Which *I* won. Victory, short-lived. Survival. For Ned. For humanity, the rest of us, if there still was an "us."

An us that used to be them.

I knew they were wicked, relentless, tireless in numbers, but also shambling and tactless and one-dimensional. No working cerebral cortex, only poisoned, implacable wills. They were the very definition of overkill.

Dragging the cricket bat, I wandered in a sweaty daze back over the meadow for my backpack. Found it. Walked slowly to the farmhouse, thinking of it as my refuge, my *home*. My ground.

I'd paid a dear price, but it was mine now.

CHAPTER 26

A bank of gray clouds, under which I'd fought, gave way to full sunlight. I was exhausted and starved. First, I had to tend to my wounds. Prevent infection, and not just with H7N11.

I pushed open the heavy door, rushed past the kitchen, headed straight for the vodka bottle.

The Smirnoff had a twist cap. I opened it up and propped my left leg on a chair, rolled up my pant leg, and dribbled vodka on a long scrape that traveled from my inner thigh to my ankle. Those were the bite marks, the ones that Track Suit's so-called older sister gave me. As if'd run through a thick thorn bush with track shorts on.

The vodka stung, but I poured it liberally on the bites and scratches, gritting my teeth. I ripped my T-shirt off; scratches were everywhere on my arms. I poured vodka on both elbows, forearms, and hands; nothing was deeply gouged or still bleeding.

I experienced a wave of nausea; plopped down on a chair with my head in my hands. I still felt that adrenaline, that valiant rage, coursing everywhere through my body. I seized the Smirnoff, then put it down. I stood up and took down the 15-year-old Laphroig, and poured a couple of fingers. Chugged it. Calmness, for a brief shining moment.

I scraped that glass across the wooden table, then poured more dribbles of Smirnoff on both arms and then all over my neck, and even my face. I smelled like a bloody besotted vodka drunk, but the smell wasn't like whisky. It was antiseptic and made me think–*clean.* Because when I got back to the farmhouse, I'd felt like I'd been raped and pillaged.

Gotta get some propylene glycol, I thought; gotta gather some real disinfectants and medicine. More vitamins and minerals...I splashed the vodka on my skin again, stinging all over.

Then I patted my face with a cloth, placed palms over both eyes, elbows on the table, and bawled my head off. Real convulsive, visceral, cathartic crying. Two minutes. Another sip of Scotch, and it felt all over, for a brief moment.

I guzzled down two bottles of the water I'd found at the school, tipping the bottles up and watching the bubbles at the bottom of the bottles and the declining volume, as if I was a snotty-nosed kid again. I went out into the yard, sat cross-legged in a patch of sunlight, ate leftovers: apples, animal crackers, pasty, salted mashed potatoes. I was in a daze; the food was nevertheless brilliant. I went back inside, locked the doors, went out like a light under the covers.

# #

Next morning. Over hot scavenged school tea, I took out the pad and paper and the pen, wrote:

October 16, 2026, Emma Wallace Blair, Isle Of Skye, Scotland. Fair to cloudy, about 58 degrees F. Good sleep, decent breakfast. Took my vitamins and supplements. Drank lots of river water (used it to thoroughly wash off the foreign saliva–yuck!–last night). Explored the nearby school yesterday. Skirmished, a really bad one, with reivers. Killed five.

What happened to those other three? The ones that ran off? What's the outcome? I suppose I could guess.

What is the metabolic source, seemingly bottomless, of their attacking energy? Does the virus mobilize fat stores? Steroid hormones? Both? The symptoms have some kind of strong social component; an instinct to make violent, vicious groups.

Nazis, KKK, Pol Pot, Rwanda circa 1990s–was that viral and related?

This disease is like rabies, may be related to it, but also quite different.

Why don't I get it? (Thank God.)

Then I scrawled:

H7N11 infected do not respond to kindness or reason or gentleness or empathy.

It won't work. I saw Ned, I saw it myself. In their ravaged faces, not a watt of human warmth.

I was otherwise a kind, reasonable, gentle, empathic person.

I imagined those masses of people in crowds at Hitler's speeches, in black and white footage. Adoring faces, but something was *off* in those expressions. *Something dazed and manic.*

Then I wrote,

The disease presents with traits that never would have evolved naturally, because they kill off the host. Must be with at least four others. I saw the three calve off in the meadow and immediately crumble, fall apart.

A multi-celled organism needs its other cells.

The reivers were a many-headed beast.

I sat for a while and enjoyed nature. It was a beautiful farm and view. I gathered empty pots and a plastic gallon bottle I'd found in the barn, and walked down to the river.

The sun sparkled on the water, which gurgled over polished round stones that dully absorbed the sunlight. The banks were grassy, showing no signs of being trod upon. It was soothing. I felt normal again. I should fish for food, I thought. Yet, I had only the axe with me. Left the cricket bat leaning against the back door of the farmhouse.

I filled the pots and the plastic gallon bottle with the water. (I really could have used some disinfectant pills...that would come with scavenging later...). In the back of my mind I planned to drive to Portree, loot a pharmacy. Visit Gladys. Get propylene glycol and more vodka and disinfectant pills and Scotch and food. Necessarily in that order.

My cuts and gouges, one day later, were doing pretty well. They were black and blue and yellow around the edges. Watch out for a stinky smell and pus and a green color, I told myself.

After everything was filled with water, I sat down on the banks of the river, drank some, and took out the pipette. I began to make sounds with it, not music. You have to start somewhere.

I really loved it down there by the river. There was a clean cool scent where it ran briskly. It was soothing, that's right.

I made more flute sounds, listening to them carry over the water. They blended in with the bird cries. The birds seemed to answer them.

I had a sense, my gut instinct, that there were no reivers around, anywhere near. I made some more music, drank water from one of the pots and filled it back up again, then wandered back through the wildflowers to the farmhouse.

I took the cricket bat, sat down at the wooden table, and carved five notches into it.

A tufty white and black bird sat on a tree branch outside the window. "These are victory marks, birdie," I said. It turned its head in my direction, then flew off.

CHAPTER 27: Emma Winslow, French Countryside, June, 2051

Harry agreed to come with me south, to my surprise, enthusiastically. He wanted to get his arse out of London, for at least a short time. For him, it was an adventure. It was an impulsive move for myself, motivated by fondness, love, fear of being left behind, and fear of one-dimensionality and my life only going in one direction.

It was not motivated by fear of the new outbreak, which hadn't been diagnosed yet. We didn't have that kind of technology or expertise.

I'm 22 now. The city is being overrun by a new strain or outbreak of a pathogen, or pollutant, or opiates abuse; simple, widespread hysteria, or a combination of all four. I've gone numb by contemplating it, and I don't want this outbreak to dominate the fast-moving years of my youth.

The ward at St. Paul's Cathedral, and the nave and ornate murals and warren of rooms, is all I've known these years, along with London's many parks. I was literally born in St. Paul's. Who lives nearby, and works in the hospital where they were born, all their life? This is not for me.

Instinct tells me to move on to another stage in my life. Find out what's truly going on with Jason and his estranged son Willie. Be in another place for once; Lake Geneva in what used to be Switzerland, an alpine haven that may still be intact. We don't know for sure, but one can always hope. When you're 22, you have plenty of capacity for dreams.

Harry jumps at the opportunity. He refuses to let me go alone; I doubt I could have anyways. I know of no caravans going in that direction. Harry, however, has Gwen's feelings to consider, and his own feelings for Gwen.

The hospital is okay without me, I tell myself, although I leave it with considerable guilt. Grace understands; she read the letter from Jason. She thinks it's cool that I've launched an impetuous journey. I sense she wants to come.

The puzzling and disturbing London contagion, as it's come to be known, has no known cure or treatment (beyond stopping the abuse of opiates altogether). One doesn't know how long it will last. A lot of unknowns.

The thought that dealing with its victims will be my life for the next five years or more is impossible to bear.

Journey logistics: no more Chunnel trains or regional lines, that's for sure. Travel is by cobbled-together vehicles and home-brewed gasoline, boat, horse-and-wagons, bicycle–you get the picture. We've been all but thrust back to the 19th century.

It was said, a Saudi Arabian described the end of oil this way: my grandparents rode camels, my parents drove cars, I fly in jet planes, my grandchildren will ride camels.

For our trip, however, we're lucky. Harry is well-connected; always has been. He has an ingenious friend who's built an electric van with a battery installed in back. The battery is rechargeable, if you have the gizmo for doing that.

He's bartered a deal for the van, battery, and crank-operated recharging device–by offering much of the cool stuff we have in our apartments. He spared our bikes, however. They'll hang from the back of the van. You have to have a Plan B. This is a risky, long trip, during an era when virtually any trip outside of London risks life and limb.

This is the world I know.

The distance between London and Montreux on Lake Geneva, which is the closest settlement to where Jason left to, traversing old Belgian and French routes that have undoubtedly fallen into disrepair, is at least 900 kilometers, or 560 miles.

In France they used to be called *routes principales*, and in Swiss-German, *hauptstrassen*, but now they're merely broken down roads of dirt and crumbled concrete. Not much better than the trails forged by pioneers in the U.S. West.

Logistics: We have good tires, Michelins from the old days. The van gets no more than 400 kilometers on a charge. We won't even have a chance to test it, so we keep our fingers crossed that we can recharge the battery up to two times. Or, we'll never make it out of Belgium.

From there, the route passes within about 160 kilometers east of Paris, and then we continue south toward Lyon.

We always have the bikes, hanging from the back of the van. That's part of Plan B.

There's no *one* accepted name for where we are going, driving off south into the shadowy wilderness. Only sentimentalists, like me, refer to it as the European mainland or ***Europe***. To many, it's frontier, backcountry, or terra incognita. Null Land, in German, or Zero Country. There are many risks, not the least of which are bandits along this abandoned, lengthy, un-policed road.

# #

On the first day we make it all the way through Belgium. By the time it's dark, we're somewhere northeast of Paris. Harry did all the driving at first, with Gwen in the front and me in the back, gazing out the window and dozing.

We see very few other vehicles, but plenty of other settlements and what we assume are isolated homes. After the sun goes down we see the bonfires in the darkness. Our own headlights stab obliquely into the thick stands of evergreen forests, which appear to march forever into the fields and hills on both sides. The trees are tall and straight and they have wide spaces between them that look like dark hallways.

Gwen and I switch places. We're looking for a place to pull over and recharge the battery, get something to eat. We're all on edge about whether the recharger will work, and if not, whether we'll be stuck on the side of the road, only halfway through our journey.

No one says that could happen out loud. We don't want to jinx it.

Once in a while we'll see someone set-up along the side of the road with open carts, selling stuff. We stop once and buy some apples and pears. We don't know what currency to use. The people appear to be a family of farmers or orchard caretakers, but they take a few of our old faded and crumpled Euros, which are seldom used in London. Apparently they're still traded in France. We don't have much to trade them in return for the fruit; we have to hang on to all of our own supplies.

It's reassuring to be involved in such a commonplace transaction; it makes the route we are taking seem orderly and civilized.

We ask the man and woman about the road ahead, going into southern France towards the former border with Switzerland. The Alps. They know nothing about beyond a five-mile radius of where they sell their fruit. They seem wary and guarded when we ask them questions, so I change the subject to how wonderful the apples and pears look.

I try to speak a little French, and that lightens things up. One doesn't know, in 2051, exactly which languages have died or morphed into obscure or local dialects. I can only guess, but it seems that plain-vanilla French is understood well enough.

A cracked smile breaks across the woman's face. She wears her hair tied up with a scarf, and a flannel shirt and jeans. They seem like gypsies. We get into our car and pull away, waving goodbye.

When the sun goes down it's crushingly dark, without the city lights in the distance. Without Paris.

This mate that traded us the van said to not let the battery run completely down, so we pull over about ten miles beyond the fruit stand.

It's an empty lot that looks like it used to be a weigh station for trucks. Harry glances at me devilishly, as if recharging the van is part of the pleasure of adventuring, which for him is true and yet it fills me with an unsettling uncertainty.

I don't like the feeling of being surrounded by a dark wilderness and fractured, strange human communities. The fruit sellers were nice enough, but stopping the van, shutting it off, and being swallowed by the dark mysteries of lightless France gives me the creeps.

CHAPTER 28

We get out of the van, because Harry wants to make a fire. We have some soup broth and stew meat to heat. We need to try to crank up the battery.

I'm not sure how the dynamics are working with the three of us. I'm the third wheel, which I find awkward. Harry keeps his cool and doesn't do a lot of cuddling and snuggling with Gwen. He's 31 y.o. and holds himself a cut above public displays of affection. I sense he understands that all that stuff is uncalled for at the moment.

I've always found Gwen standoffish and somewhat posh and high-and-mighty in her attitude. She comes from money, from back when it still mattered. But of course, the barmy fever and the pandemic had a way of leveling the playing field.

Nor have I ever remembered Harry making any kind of commitment to a girlfriend before. He is by nature fey with women; here today gone tomorrow. He seldom has problems attracting new ones. I sense that this Gwen soiree is different. He has an altered vibe about him, more sober and attached, which is shocking given that the concept of "attachment" would have previously evoked terror in Harry.

I guess I'll find out sooner or later. I'll also find out about what's going on with me and Jason. This journey, among its many other unknowns, is going to be an acid test for the boys and the girls.

Gwen stays behind for several minutes in the van "changing." Harry and I sit cross-legged next to a fire, lit only by its wavering circle of light, as if we were the only people within 50 miles. A cloud of embers swirls into the inky black sky, two pots sizzle with meaty fragrances, and all I can hear is its crackle. It's been a long time since this *routes principales* was jammed with evening traffic, streaming back and forth to Paris.

Right now the road is empty, dark, and unsettling. You could have seen a vehicle coming from 25 miles away, but no other cars or vans pass our little camp site.

"You had grandparents," Harry says, the light from the flames flickering on his impassive face. He lightly nudges burning tree branches with a stick. "Do you know anything about them?"

"No. Unfortunately, my mother, Emma Blair, didn't write much in her diary about her childhood. She wrote in the here and now."

"What about your Da, Winslow. I remember him and his Harley. He was a good chap. What do you know about him?"

"Probably not much more than you, since you actually met him and interacted with him. Terry Winslow."

I stare into the fire and conjure what I think his face looked like. "He was a big man. Super clever and inventive, with trains and mechanics and such. He had a wife and kids, before us. That must have been so sad for him. Of course, Emma and Terry, my parents, weren't married. Making me 'born out of wedlock'," I say with mock outrage.

"What do you know of ***your*** parents, Harry?"

He swallows, looks away into the darkness. I've nudged a psychic bruise and am sorry for it. I don't regret our topic though. Life is so day-by-day and provisional, one has to remind oneself and others about your lineage and background. You have to give your life back its fiber and bone.

"We had a nice big flat in East London. My mum was a homemaker, I guess you'd call her. Everyone liked her; she was kind to everyone on the block. We nicked about and caused trouble, hit cricket balls through windows, bloodied noses, made up gangs based on the shows on telly, the usual rough-and-tumble London childhood."

"Was she pretty?"

"Who?"

"Your Mum?"

"Are you kidding? Like I'm checking out my own mother?"

"You know what I mean."

"Sure. The other lads thought my mum was pretty. Not sure about my dad though. He was always at work, some kind of accountant deal, and then off to the pub. Kind of a gruff bloke after a few pints. Sound familiar? I was only a kid; didn't get to know 'im much." He's silent for a few minutes as the fire crackles.

We put a pan of rice and lentils and tomatoes on it. The stew meat came from a lamb someone had slaughtered back in London, poor thing.

Gwen joins the fray, sitting down next to Harry. The flames spray embers as we toss sticks onto them, glowing clouds of dots that rise and fade out. The woods sway in the wind around us, which carries a sappy pine scent. Everything on this continent has sunk back into the primitive and the rustic. Of course, I've never seen it before, only in my mind's eye from pictures and stories.

Europe and its myths and dramatic history, seemingly snuffed out, like an inhabited planet struck by an asteroid.

Where we were going, Lake Geneva, may only have a population of 2,000. Or, it could be 500, or 5,000. Who knew? The remaining people would be drawn to its shores and resources, like us.

Harry keeps talking about his parents; usually we didn't, because we were young, it was old news, water under the bridge, and we only looked toward and yearned for the future.

"When the barmy fever came, they didn't last long. Everybody's parents were going bonkers and wandering off. It was a weird sort of nightmare for kids. One family down the block committed suicide together. I remember thinking that was a crazy, bogus move, worse than the daft bastards themselves.

"It was also exciting, in a warped way. You're seven or eight, and it's just you and the lads in East London, with no grown-ups, no coppers, no supervision. No one to tell you, don't do this, don't do that. I hardly knew my parents, so I didn't mourn them that much. We took to the streets, me, Max, Jack and the rest. Started squatting in other people's homes, playing in the ruins. It was one, big, twisted, fantasy game."

A smile creeps across his face, with the memory. "Let's spit all at once..."

"What?"

"The blocks near our house had weekend festivals, Indian and Pakistani food, music on the streets. There was this chimney above the street, and someone had spray-painted on it, 'Let's spit all at once and drown the bastards.' It's funny what sticks in your mind. That was wise swagger for me back then."

"What about you, Gwen?" I say. She hugs a sweater around herself with her hair pulled back. "Remember your folks?"

"Sure I do."

"They lived over in Westminster," Harry quips. He puts his arm around her, to reassure Gwen that he's mostly kidding. "To the manor born."

"Sure. They were a lawyer and a fashion designer. ***Philip and Margaret Court***," she says, gently mocking the upper-class status. "We *did* live in Westminster, third-floor flat overlooking the Thames."

"*Big* third-floor flat," Harry says.

She looks over and smiles. "How would you know?"

"You told me once it had 12 rooms."

"Ten. Maybe three designed for children. There were the bedrooms for me and my sister, and a playroom. The rest were for the grownups. All the dinner parties and social connections, you know."

"What's your sister's name?" I ask. Getting to know the details of Gwen pulls us closer, takes a bit of the vinegar out of my biases toward her. Isn't that the way it always is.

"Philomena."

I'm afraid she's dead, Philomena, so I don't say anything. But Gwen reads my mind.

"Philomena is married to Roy. They live in South London."

"I might recognize her. Does she go by Philomena Court?"

"No. She changed her name to Virginia Woolf. Our generation can do whatever it likes, you know. I still call her Philomena. She hates me for that. All in good jest."

"Philomena, or Virginia, is nice," Harry says. "She's a hippy. A hippy feminist."

Gwen looks at him disparagingly. "You have *her* figured out. And what, that doesn't make *me* a feminist?"

"You're a feminist too," Harry says. I find that to be a shocking admission. He usually didn't care a jot for social movements, protests, and the like; this remark seems like a concession. Or an evolution. I also never knew that crusading side of Gwen. She was looking up, in my eyes.

"Does Virginia know you left London to go south through France?" I ask.

"Yeah. She wants me to go claim our boat in Nice."

"Nice?"

"Her parents kept a yacht in Nice," Harry points out proudly.

"A yacht? No, it is hardly a yacht. I've seen yachts and this vessel is much smaller and cozier. But I loved it. I went out on it about six times. Before the curtain came down on everything. I think I miss the boat and the south of France at least as much as I miss my parents. Is that horrible?"

"The attitudes of children always surprise," I say. Gwen frowns at me.

"Are you calling me a child?"

"I meant, in our memories, the way we see our childhood and parents now."

"Okay," Harry says, slapping his knees and standing up. "I have to crank up the battery. Hope the bloody thing works." Both Gwen and I look at each other with a hint of consternation.

"...It will," he says, noticing that.

"Hey Gwen," Harry adds. "Maybe we can check out that boat since we'll be in the neighborhood."

"That would be smashing! Could we? Truly, please?"

"Why not? The possibilities are endless. We have no real plan."

I wanted to say, 'Hardly. I've left London specifically to find Jason and his son. It's not like we're going to traipse another 300 miles to Nice.'

"You two keep enjoying your dinner. Just sit tight," Harry says over his shoulder. "We'll be ready to get back on the road soon."

He strides away from the comfort of the fire and its

warm circle of crackling light.

We have hundreds of miles to travel, along a road fraught with uncertainties, before completing our last leg to the big lake. I pensively chew and watch the fire die down. Harry works the crank on the machine, around and around and around, until I find myself holding my breath...then the van starts up, its weak interior light flickering on.

He leaves the motor running. We wolf the rest of the meal, stamp out the fire and throw dirt on it, then pile into the van. We bounce over divots and bumps back onto the route, seeing only about 20 feet of road ahead of us.

"Do you want me to drive now?" At this point I want to, if only for the distraction.

"I'm good for now. Maybe in an hour or so." Gwen has lain down on the back seat and pulled a coat over her head. The van's engine rattles; I smell burnt oil, even though the motor is battery, not fuel powered. I desperately need a tea or coffee, but we feel in a hurry to leave, now that we have a working battery. For now.

We drive along in a southeast direction, the weak headlights providing shadowy glimpses of broken down cars and the worn-out shrubs that border vast acres of untilled fields and dark, abandoned suburbs. Sheets of sparkling mist drift past the headlights.

It has begun to rain. We are somewhere outside of Reims, France.

CHAPTER 29

Middle of the night. I can't sleep; I'm too excited. An impenetrable darkness blankets the fields and the forests. We could be the last vehicle left on the continent; the only inhabitants on this crumbling *routes principals* still moving on four tires.

We see stragglers, on occasion. One, two people or more, suddenly appear for a moment in the headlights; bereft, toting meagre possessions, wary eyes glinting in the darkness. Sometimes with hopefulness, other times with anger or fear, as if we had roughly intruded on their solitary musings. We don't stop; there were no children.

Sometimes a biker, pushing determinedly on the pedals, hauling small trailers and not looking up. I felt sorry for them, all of them, the refugees stuck in the witching hour on this lost road to Old Europe.

They don't seem lost, they seem desperate to get

wherever they are going, something we all have in common.

A vehicle appears going in the opposite direction. The first one we've seen. Instead of dimming their headlights, they blast us with high beams.

"Fuck!" Harry says at the wheel. "Shut off those fucking lights!" He pulls half on to the gravelly roadside, because they're hogging the road. He gestures at them angrily when they go by; a medium-sized truck full of young punks, rowdies with their shirts off and dark-painted bellies and stubbly, patchy beards. I hear loud music, shrill electric guitars and pounding drums. They curse us out as they go by; a glass bottle shatters down by our tires.

"Fuck them!"

"Just let 'em go, Harry," I say suspiciously, looking at the rearview mirror, looking at the truck slowing and turning around.

"Yeah," he grumbles. He's looking in the rearview, too.

"They're turning around," I say.

"They are?"

"Step on it. Go faster."

"Bloody idiots." I see them making up ground behind us.

"Faster."

"The van doesn't go faster, Emma."

Gwen is still asleep in the back seat. The bright lights hover behind, until they're like a searchlight aimed into the back window of the van.

Suddenly all the lights in our vehicle go out, including

the headlights. We're covered in darkness, but still moving.

"Harry, what happened!"

"I shut the lights off. Hold on to your hats, I'm going to pull off to the side, on the next right turn. Let them go past. They can't see us."

"How do you know?"

"Because it's dark as shit out." He's stepping on it; I see nothing out the windshield but blackness disappearing under the wheels.

I call out, alarmed: "We're going to hit something, a tree, a person! Harry!"

"No worries," he murmurs. The lights dim behind us. There's a right turn, and Harry jerks the wheel onto another anonymous, unlit roadway, unpaved and covered in leaves. We bounce down it a ways, then pull over to the side. He switches off the motor.

"Let's wait a minute." He suddenly jerks around and looks behind the van. We see a dot of moving light, it floats past our right-hand turn, then it goes out.

Harry opens the door, gets out, leaves the door open, stands in the darkness with his hands on his hips.

Everything's changed, the curiosity I had for our journey, its novelty, now everything and everyone is a vague threat. We're vulnerable. In a girlish way, I crave London again.

"Sh-sh," Harry says. I get out on my side; the night air is cool, bracing. Harry tells me not to shut my door and make any noise. Everything is velvety black, silent, like a desert, but without the starlight. Wind blows through distant, shadowy trees. I leave my door open and walk over to his side.

A light flicks on nearby, another. A wavy light, two torches. They're coming towards us. Harry swiftly re-enters the van, rummages about in back, and emerges with a vintage pistol. From the Middle-Eastern wars that the boys at St. Paul's told me about. I take his cue. I reach into the front seat for my cricket bat. It doesn't seem like much; it doesn't shoot or stab. But I do it for Harry's morale, and my own. The bat embodies a mysterious power.

"Ah, bon soir!" a man, clutching his torch, declares. He's with a small group of men and boys, the punks from the truck. The flames of two torches flicker in their pinched, sweaty faces.

Harry brandishes his pistol, I don't even know if it's loaded.

"What do you want?" he asks.

The guy in the front is short, with a black stubble on his head, a mean little face.

"So, English?" he says. Harry makes sure he sees the gun.

"We were just leaving," Harry says.

"We thought you were lost, need help," the man said. "*Soyons amis, ok?*"

His French seems unfriendly, as though he knows we don't understand it. He deploys it as a kind of weapon, to gain leverage over us. Gwen, apparently, is still passed out.

The shirtless, painted, and ragged louts standing with him break the silence with mindless giggling. One of them spits off to the side. All of them have dirty, long matted hair, torsos smeared with paint, like hooligans at a rugby match. Drunk as lords, probably wasted on other substances, I think. Opiates. Not again.

"We're not lost. We're leaving," Harry says, raising the gun so it's obvious, the gate between us and them.

J'aime ce van, says one of the guys. He steps forward and runs his hand along the roof admiringly.

"Hands off the car, mate," Harry snaps. The guy appears to notice Gwen, who's slept through it all.

"Ah, *la femme.*"

"What's your names?" the mean little shit says. He doesn't seem to have a gun.

"Queen Victoria," Harry says. "And I'm King George."

The little shit laughs.

"What's your real name, Sweetie?" he says to me.

"You'll never know."

"Jamais, jamais, merde!" he spits.

The snotty lout who's got his grubby hands on our van knocks on the back window, and I notice Gwen stirring. Harry raises the pistol and fires it into the dark sky. I jump; I'm shocked how loud it is, how the noise carries and lingers in the dark valleys, the vacant roads. It leaves a gritty, cordite scent in its wake.

"I'll shoot the bloke with his bloody hands on the van, then the rest of yah!"

"Okay, okay, calm down," the leader of the rowdies says. He looks back to the rest of his grubby crew, then at us, smiling, more of an acid little grimace.

"Lac Leman is near. You're not lost. You're just unfriendly, cuckoo. Maybe you'll be arrested there, or worse. You won't be welcome, no?"

"*Allons-y*!" he calls out. "*Au revoir*." He turns to go. One the yahoos sneers at us and says, "Fuck you! We'll see you later!" They walk off into the darkness, laughing and muttering. I hear the beginning of a drunken fight song, in French.

Harry gets into the van. He lingers, with one leg and foot still outside the vehicle, his head half turned in the direction they went. I stare out of the back of the van, watching the torchlights get smaller. Soon, the nearby road is illuminated by their truck lights, and the vehicle moves away east down the *routes principals*.

Faintly, I hear heavy metal music switch back on.

Me: "I'm glad you had the handgun. It came in handy." Harry scoffs, looks at the gun, gets back in all the way and starts the van's motor. The lights come on reassuringly.

"It's a Browning, 40 caliber. Now you know we have it."

"My God. What was all that!" Gwen says groggily from the back seat.

"Just some bloody sods on the road. They're gone. Now we're leaving. You two can get some sleep again."

I no longer want to drive. "Thank you, Harry."

CHAPTER 30: Lake Geneva, 2051

In a few hours, we watch a glorious sun-up. We've been alone, once again, on the road.

I'm a biker, not accustomed to the mentality of car dependence. When we near the Swiss border, with only a drop of a charge left in our battery, the praying for the van to keep going, the helplessness, is foreign and irritating.

I was ready to get to Lake Geneva, whatever and whoever we were going to find there.

As the van rattled along, I distracted myself by thinking about Jason. Where exactly was he? He had told me he was headed to where his son was kept, near the former Lausanne.

I don't know much about that city, or nearby Montreux, except they were exceptional and coveted cities in their time and were settled well before they were part of Roman settlements centuries ago. They grew wine, and were famous for their splendid, mountainous location on the lake. For now, that was enough for me, even with the unknowns, the frightening uncertainties of exploring new terrain in 2051.

Had bandits and hostile tribes settled this region, like the sods and rowdies? It's impossible to know, since London has an effective news blackout about distant regions. Everything is rumor or hearsay. Our own drive over France's broken and neglected ***routes principales*** has been eventful, nonetheless.

This area of the Alps has a temperate climate, a scenic, resource-rich lake, and majestic mountains. I won't let the mean little shit, and his ***Lac Leman*** references, ruin it for me.

Jason doesn't know I'm coming. I haven't heard from him since that final letter Grace showed me.

We climb steep grades now, the steering column quivering with the laboring motor. Harry grips the wheel tightly, eyes weary, fastened on the road. The green slopes on each side glint with dew; moss-covered cliffs jut out from them. High snowy mountains grace the horizon. The van crawls over one more grade, then Harry's shoulders visibly relax. He sighs.

"I'd say it's all downhill from here."

I'd taken on some of the driving late last night. The pale beams of our lights jumped around on the gray, rutted road. I'd watched grainy light gather, then the blooming of an intense, titian sunrise over the French Alps.

"Did you sleep before? While I was driving?" I ask.

"I got a little sleep," Harry says, staring at the road. "Could use some more."

"And some tea or coffee."

"Some tea or coffee," he repeats robotically. He'd looked at the old map we had for mainland Europe. No automatic Global Positioning System for *this* van. Yeah, we read about that technology, and those satellites, the ones the GPS depends on, are no longer operable. They spin uselessly around the earth, apparently.

This route has brought us into a rolling, forested wilderness called Parc Jura Vaudois. It has fast-running brooks and rich green slopes and fir forests, with old, almost hidden stone dwellings tucked away in its hollows. It's located north and above Lake Geneva, which we can't see yet, but we are tantalizingly close and I eagerly await the first view, as if it's our salvation. This is a new feeling of discovery; it has me joyously on edge.

Everything is so new; I can't contain myself. We've almost made it–most of 900 kilometers through a dark, strange, Middle-Ages–like stage of the continent. The van has gotten us here, despite my fears about the crank tool. It seems a miracle.

We need one more charge, however. I'm relieved when Harry utters, "Let's stop and crank 'er up for the final haul." We've gone more than 800 kilometers from London, or just about 500 miles.

Gwen wakes up and leans between the two of us, groggy, muttering, "Where are we?"

"Near what used to be the Swiss border. Well, maybe it still is."

Harry pulls the van off the road over to a dirt, gravel,

and grass overlook. We don't spend 15 minutes there. The hand-held charger has a red metallic grip and a black one, which clip onto the respective terminals of the van battery. Then you crank the handle around and around and around, for minutes, more or less praying for the thing to work.

The engine turns over with a guttural cough; it lives, for another hour. We're back on the Parc road, topping one final grade. "This is *so* not like London," I whisper, gazing around eagerly with wide, youngster's eyes. "It's breathtaking here."

"Feel like a pioneer? I do," Harry says.

"More like an emigre, a kind of gypsy. Pinch me so I know I'm not dreaming."

Harry laughs hoarsely. He seems fatigued, but triumphant. Like me, I get the sense he feels the worst unknowns are behind us, however naive that is. Hopeful, in a forced way, in a manner that comes naturally to us nomads.

"You feel like a Swiss yet? An alpine farmer?"

"To be honest, I feel a bit guilty. About the hospital. About everything. We left London in bad shape. What if it's another pathogen? What if they're having a epidemic? We just booked out of there. Like cowards would, people just looking after themselves and with no responsibilities."

"If it *was* another epidemic, then we would have caught it," Harry quips. He doesn't want any part of my guilt, any negative-Nelly talk, after his nearly sleepless slog across France. Shooting off the Browning and all, to ward off the thugs. At least that's my impression. I don't really blame him.

We're silent for a minute. The van makes it's lonely way through the beautiful, empty Parc, with its ordered rows of trees and the gauzy sunlight shining as if through the roof of a cathedral.

"No worries, right?" Harry says, palpably more chipper. "We find your Jason, then in a couple of weeks, we figure out what to do." That sounds upbeat but vague, as if he's hiding something from me.

I look back at Gwen. "What about Virginia Woolf? Your sister? We just left her back there."

"She can join us when we find the boat in Nice," Gwen says blithely.

We reach the top of the rise; we see the lake, blue, shimmering, through a lattice of trees. Its waters are spacious, vast, like an inland sea, soft yet rich, enameled blue water, with layers of hazy sunshine hovering above it. It's "a lake that changes color every day," someone once said.

It was a lake that people for centuries desired to paint, had to capture for an eternity. Harry pulls over and stops the van. We get out.

We stand silently and admire the view, the rugged terrain of mountains bordering the water. It was a promised land, just having emerged for us over the horizon. Tiny boats make their way over the sunny water, leaving wakes like white pencil lines.

The opposite shore shoots up to high mountains that have no cities or towns, barren and inspiring.

London, all I'd known till now, suddenly appears frenetic, blase, and cramped.

Beneath us are small villages, surrounded by endless acres of terraced, green vineyards. Wine grapes are still being grown on an unbelievably large scale. I rub the fatigue out of my eyes and the image refuses to go away, after the regions of red and yellow float by the insides of my eyelids. Precisely spaced, green vineyards baking in the sun, almost as far as you can see.

We have serviceable greenhouses at home, and hardscrabble vegetable gardens. Yet at first glance, this new place seems like The Garden Of Eden.

Cicadas noisily fill the hot, hazy air; larks, robins, and jays dart about. A road winds down below, heading toward the shore. Cities, or the remnants thereof, lay farther up the lake, planted on the edge of the water. We leave the van and begin walking down the road, this section mostly composed of well-worn dirt, carrying a few provisions.

Gwen appears reluctant and lethargic. "Where are we going?" she blurts out, stepping out of the side of the van and dragging a coat. "We're leaving the van?"

Harry and I are of the same mind. "We've been stuck in the van for two days," he says. "Let's walk down to the town, see what we can find."

"I have to move my legs," I say. "We'll bring our backpacks. Can you lock the van? It'll be okay."

The road, still paved in spots, but with cracks and divots, curves down through quiet neighborhoods and a quaint village. On both sides are the vineyards, which cover the hillsides in immaculate rows.

A old man with a cane walks toward us, ambling up the hill. He wears a black suit and a cloth surgical mask that covers his long white beard. I wave at him; he slowly gestures to me with the hand not leaning on the cane.

"Maybe he's sick," Gwen says.

"Maybe they have a epidemic," I say, feeling alarm, vague disappointment, and familiarity all at once.

Gwen's voices rises: "An epidemic? Of what?"

"Not the Barmy Fever." Harry seems exasperated, clearly sick of the idea of yet one more disease to have to deal with. "No mask protects against that."

Seeming determined to complete his walk, the elderly man ignores us as he shuffles past. I'm not sure of the language here. Before, it was French, with some German. "*Au revoir*," I call out after him. He turns toward me, but only smiles and continues on his way.

I feel it's necessary to comply with his mask, since we're newcomers and don't know what's going on.

"When in Rome...we should wear our masks, until we find out down below what's cookin' around here." We'd carried them from London in our rucksacks.

Harry pushes back. Somehow I expected that. "Not unless I have to."

"We're in someone else's city now. Don't be an arsehole." That makes him sulk as we walk along the road. I feel hot for the first time; the heated air, rising from the lake, seems sub-tropical.

I get the impression something's eating at him, but Harry has mood swings that become more apparent the more time you spend with him.

There is simply nothing like a long road trip for burrowing under the surface of someone else's emotions.

The road enters a walled passage through vineyards,

orchards, and the outskirts of a small, antique village. There's a gate that permits an entrance to the fields. The orchards include apple and peach trees. It's too much to resist. There's no one around to order us off their property; the old man was the only person we'd seen.

We approach an arched entrance in the ancient stone wall. We walk through the arch and out into the fields, and like children abruptly released from confinement, we pick as many apples and peaches as we can carry, ravenously eating them, soaking our cheeks with the tart juices, as we tuck uneaten ones in our packs.

Behind us is a large stone house, presumably meant for the caretaker of these acres of fruit trees and grapevines, but no one is about. The beauty of this realm, its peace and silence, feels saintly and almost otherworldly, as if we'd stumbled upon Utopia. But another, practical side of me fears someone will literally set the dogs on us at any moment, for raiding their property.

The voice repeats itself inside me: *There are no utopias. Am I irreparably jaded?* I think.

We're startled by the aggressive pealing of church bells, from the village below, like a warning of invaders.

CHAPTER 31

The noise shatters a divine silence. The bells continue their cacophony, as if warning of invading, barbarian tribes. Honestly, I don't know whether it's Sunday or not, and I've never taken part in old-fashioned religious ceremonies, but it makes me feel guilty for trespassing these lovely grounds, and devouring the fruit.

When the bells stop, I take it as a signal to collapse down into the soft grass of the sun-baked orchard, with its trees heavy with peaches and apples. I sit next to Gwen in the sunlight, eating one of the peaches, feeling the juice run down my wrist, wiping it off on my pants, and then leaning back into the grass, the bright sun hitting my face.

"You can't get a peach like this in London. Do you feel better, Gwen?"

"A little." With a blank, wan expression, she lays back in the long grass and shields her eyes from the sun. "It's been a long trip, but I'm glad I came. I'd be miserable in London."

"What's the matter? What's ailing you?" I plan to spend as much time in the sun as I possibly can, while I'm here. I glance at the skin of my arm; it's so white it's almost translucent.

Gwen merely shakes her head, noncommittally.

Harry sits down next to us, chewing thoughtfully on an apple and gazing off to the lake, the tiny boats like precise models someone has etched. It's as if Harry's sorting out some conflicting thoughts.

"We haven't really come clean with you," he says to me. "On all the reasons we came on the trip."

"And so?"

"This guy Jason works for, Braden, he says this place is a spa region. It's a place where people come to get well from their ills. So that's why we came, to help you in your travels, and get Gwen well again."

Gwen's eyes open wide, glistening with a desire to explain more to me.

"So what's the big secret? Why didn't you tell me days ago?"

Harry shrugs, then fiddles with the grass at his feet. "Because we're not going back, probably ever. I thought you'd be mad, like we were going to come here and abandon you. We weren't ready to tell the whole story, I guess that's the honest truth. Gwen doesn't like to talk about it."

"No worries, you two," I say, not quite understanding the earnestness, the angst. "What's specifically wrong, Gwen? You can talk to me about it."

"I haven't been able to get out of bed–too exhausted. And I've got these pains..." She caresses her abdomen. "My mom died young of ovarian cancer. I had to get rid of the pain, so I started to take the Oxy."

Now I start to see the problem...

"I got addicted. I need a place like this to get well."

"Where'd you get the drugs?"

"The black market. Out on the street," Harry says.

"What? Are you kidding?" Harry will shock me with his impulsive, thoughtless actions sometimes, because he isn't a stupid bloke. He just makes rash decisions.

"You should have told me before. I could have gotten you alternative pain meds, like cannabis and CBD. I don't see why you didn't just tell me back in London."

"The stuff worked," Harry says, typically dismissive. He doesn't like accepting blame for things that go wrong. "So we just went with it. Now we see it was a mistake. So we're telling you now."

"Do you have a destination here in mind, already?"

"There's a medical clinic and spa recommended, in Montreux. I have to work for them, cleanup and maintenance duties, and they'll take Gwen. That's the deal."

"Who's deal?"

"Braden. This guy Jason's with."

"Ah. He seems Mr. Connected in this place."

I stare at Lake Geneva, the sun glinting off its robin-egg blue surface. A slow wave of loneliness washes through me. They have all these plans that don't involve me.

Harry points down the shoreline. "That direction's

Montreux. Down here, the direction we're walking in, is Vevey." (He pronounces it like "wavy.") Famous wine town. They're doing well. Braden knows this area. It's a good place to settle."

"Hopefully so." What I've seen so far is impressive, but what are the settlers like?

"We'll help you find Jason," Harry says, with rising earnestness. "That's a promise. You're my sister in spirit, and I wouldn't just come here and piss off so I can get a job, and Gwen can get well."

"I didn't think you were going to do that." I glance wearily around at the vineyards. It crosses my mind: maybe I can find a spot of work with a vintner. Nursing is gratifying, but hard work. The divine simplicity of these vineyards, the way they're preserved in time as if encased in glass, would do my soul some good.

We stand up with the fruit stored securely in our packs. We get going. The old paved road winds down steeply through the vineyard terraces. I feel fine walking along, without much concern about Harry's revelations, beyond hoping Gwen could get over her addiction and illness.

I thought about the sick men I'd seen in London, with their opiate rages, ripping their clothes off and assaulting people. I'd been lucky to have lived trouble-free in London up till then.

The road passes through a sparsely populated village. It has old plaster or wooden residences, with their shutters open and colorful flowers displayed in boxes. The center of the village has a fountain. Two young girls on bikes ride by, laughing and talking. Up ahead is an outdoor cafe; they're serving food to a table full of casual diners.

As a waitress comes in and out, I notice she's wearing a cloth mask, too.

"Can we?" I say to the others.

"We'd love to," Gwen says.

We angle past the fountain, with its rainbow-colored spray, to an empty table. It seems a simple, long-lost luxury, scraping a wire-mesh chair across the flagstones and sitting in the sun. Someone waiting on you, serving fresh, tasty food. Un-London, at least my London. The smiling young waitress, with long black hair, hands a menu to each of us. We put our masks on.

These simple masks, which matrons sew in London, were packed before we left. There are no widespread meds for the treatment of outbreaks in 2051. We had to be prepared.

"Will you take Euros for the food?" I always keep a few Euros with me.

"Yes, of course."

"One more thing. We're new arrivals," I tell her through the mask. I notice that her eyes are friendly and receptive, above her own face covering. With a lot of mask wearing, one gets better at eye reading. It's as if we've relearned the sweeping expressiveness of eyes.

"This might seem like a naive question. Is there an epidemic here? Why the masks?"

Her eyes glaze over. They lose some of their warmth.

"Did you talk to the district authorities when you came into the lake region?"

"What authorities? We came through the Parc

Vaudois," Harry says, looking up from the menu, taking an interest.

"Oh, so you took a more remote route. Most people coming over the trade routes are stopped, searched, interviewed. They find out about our health-maintenance requirements. The mask policy."

"Health maintenance...?"

The waitress steals a shifty glance over to the other table of diners. "Everyone must adopt preventive health steps, wear the mask, keep their distance, take the prescribed vitamin pills. We always have an epidemic going, in their eyes. Now I have to take your order."

Their eyes.

Harry looks at Gwen, fretfully. Quickly, he changes the subject. I get it that he doesn't want this lady, or the "officials," to know we're from London. Or about Gwen's condition.

"What's this lovely village called?" I ask.

"Chardonne."

I order a salade nicoise. I hand her back the menu. I hardly know how to act in a cafe. We don't have too many working ones; mostly pubs.

It must be fake tuna in the salad, I think to myself. Who catches a tuna in 2051? What do I know; this is a major trade route. Maybe they're still pulling tuna out of the water in Japan, Norway, and Vietnam, if those places actually exist.

Gwen orders the same as me; Harry has schnitzel and pommes frites. We order a small carafe of the local white wine. The waitress nods and smiles agreeably. You can't wander through a vineyard, then turn down the chance to drink the local wine.

One must savor every moment in life, for tomorrow may be nigh.

CHAPTER 32

We walk from Chardonne, with full stomachs and light heads, to the Vevey lakeside. Jason left no forwarding address, I think fretfully. I don't have a clue where he is, or how to contact him. I just *expect* to find him, eventually. The lake's shores, compared with a generation ago, are lightly populated. It's not like either of us can be lost in a crowd for too long.

Unless this farm he talks about is high in the hills, and he never descends to the lake. This bloke, I think, Randolph Braden, is *too* connected for my liking. Too many rackets going on. His name keeps coming up. I'm not sure whether Jason has taken up with a grifter, but I do know he's sincere about seeking out his son.

All these thoughts and assumptions swirl through my mind; I'm torn between hedonism, thoroughly enjoying my first foray into a strange, opulent land, and doing something purposeful, like seeking out Jason.

Having a good time is winning.

The surrounding hills are knit with vines for hundreds of acres, the land drowned in placid sunlight.

The path down from Chardonne spills out into empty city streets, a square that was once busy with traffic: Fiats, Volkswagens, Renaults, Audis, and sidewalks flowing with pedestrians. Now, a few cyclists, a few people in cafes, leaves blowing about the empty boulevard. Vevey, circa 2051.

I see a few tractors in the vineyards and orchards, probably running on biofuel. A car approaches in Vevey, we watch it from several blocks away. It seems like a rarity, an oddity.

The lake shore is visible, beyond an old hotel named Europa. The waitress said, if we had to, we could inquire there about rooms for the night. I thought we'd be staying in the van.

I've been looking forward to reaching and at least dipping my toes into the lake. We walk past Europa on a path that leads to a promenade along the water. The shoreline is composed of amazing palm trees and floral bushes, with jumbled rocks collected and piled up along the water's edge. More people, the citizens of Vevey, lie and sit on grassy areas near the shore.

Lots of parks here. My eyes are wide open. I expect these people to look different than Londoners, but they don't.

It's multi-racial and -ethnic, and they have the cosmopolitan diversity of my city. Well, we only drove 900 kilometers. It's not as if we or they are aliens from distant shores.

To my surprise, only because I'd rarely see it near the Thames, many of the men and women lie completely nude with towels draped on the grass. Delighted, I say out loud: "I could use some of that. I really could." The sun on my skin, I mean. I feel not a bit of embarrassment as I survey the park, the disrobed bathers, indulging their "health maintenance practices."

"I wish I had a towel. Maybe we can borrow some, or get a room in the hotel and use the towels. I want to swim. What do you think, Gwen?" She seems wan and tired. "The sun would do *you* good, too."

"Oh, I don't know about swimming. I will sit." We reach the edge of the water. The shrubs have a big space in them, allowing an entry to the jumbled rocks and the lake shore, where the blue water calmly laps against the stones.

I pull my shirt over my head, down to my bra. I reach around to undo it. I'm going in!

"Don't think that's Gwen's thing," Harry quips, looking away out of his own shyness. This amuses me. He likes to think of himself as thick-skinned and modern and fearless. I detect in his tone a little jealousy and possessiveness. ***No one else is permitted to see Gwen's body, not even Emma.***

Now *that's* silly and sophomoric.

"Well, let's check out the lake." I saunter down to the water's edge, now topless, with my arms draped across my breasts. Small waves and froth strike the edge of the rocks. I sit down and take off my shoes, carefully arranging the rest of my stuff in a pile on a flat rock. I stick my feet in, move my toes around. It's warmer than I thought it would be.

A smile cracks across my face–the shimmering lake water is irresistible. No bathing suit, no bother. I strip down to my panties, then on second thought, take everything off. Grinning ear-to-ear, laughing, because I can't force myself at first to dive into water, which is always colder when you're nude.

In I go, with a squeal, a splash. I'm underwater, the sounds muffled, bubbles gathering around my face. The water delivers a bracing jolt.. Beneath the surface, the view is murky green; sunlight pulsates, and more rocks cover the bottom.

I swim underwater for a few body lengths, then breach the surface, grinning with the water pouring down my hair and cheeks, treading water with the warm sun in my eyes.

I see Harry wearing a rakish smile. He's doffing his shirt. I've inspired him, but Gwen seems dispassionate. She sits cross-legged on grass and watches us, mopey, with sunglasses. I feel bad for her, not feeling well. It's been a long trip.

I swim around a bit, not self-conscious because I'm surrounded by about 100 nude people. For the first time in a long time, I feel fully connected, as if I've arrived some place where I truly belong.

I swim farther out into the lake, stroking hard and fast until I can see the coastline, the jumbled rocks and the palm trees and the old hotels that entertained the devotees of jazz and wine festivals. Villas and sailboats; they're all still there, as if projected from a postcard.

I go over on my side and stroke and scope out everything; the well-appointed residences climbing steep, tree-lined streets into the hills, into the mountains. A grand hotel farther up, still lording over everything. Sure, I can make this my home, if they'll have me. If Jason will have me.

Who am I kidding? Where's Jason?

I expect him to be overjoyed to see me. I see a splash as Harry dives in off a rock, sporting only his boxer shorts. I glance at the rocks, at the neat little pile of clothing I left there. I can't afford to have someone nick them. I take one grand look again, all around at the mountains, never having experienced this glorious sensation, the tall peaks rising from the shoreline of a vast, emerald blue lake, and me swimming like a nude nymph. Then I stroke back to the rocks, several yards because I really had swum way out, to catch the distant view of the shore.

A woman and two men approach Gwen, where she's sitting on the grass. All three wear surgical masks. Gwen stands up, brushes herself off. She digs into her pocket, removes a mask, puts it on her face.

The people wear starched white uniforms, like orderlies in a hospital. I'm breast-stroking to shore now, feeling the sun on my back, watching the people on the shoreline. I'm still nude; unable to forget that inconvenient detail, as three strangers gesture and chat with Gwen.

Harry, still dressed only in boxer shorts, pulls himself out of the lake onto a rock. He stands dripping; we have no towels.

Now this was going to be embarrassing. "The district

authorities." I guess we should have expected it, after chatting with the waitress back in Chardonne.

I see the woman in white leave, walking briskly in the direction of somewhere else on the promenade. The two men still talk with Harry. He puts a mask on; he dries himself off with a T-shirt.

I see these black things, like night sticks, hanging off the strangers' belts.

Dammit Emma! I'm angry about leaving myself in a compromising spot, but why should one ever be punished for wanting to swim *au naturel*?

I'm half tempted to swim away, until these two blokes with their stiff uniforms and nightsticks finish whatever business they have with Harry.

I swim up to the rocks and yell at Harry: "Can you ask them to turn away, so I can come out and get dressed?"

My teeth chatter, as much as from nerves as cold. I'm also aware that my feminine shape is not hard on the eyes. I don't want these two stiffs on the shoreline, whatever their business is, leering at me over their masks. I'm not going to give these guys a free show, despite the apparent local permissiveness, with everyone lying around in their birthday suits.

Oh wait, right, *health*, that's what it is.

Harry yells back: "He says the lady is coming back with towels for us." He tears off his boxers down to his fanny, then pulls dry trousers on, in about 10 seconds flat.

"What do they want?" I yell back, treading water, still considering a brisk, escapist crawl down the shoreline.

He shrugs. "Tell you later."

It seems to take forever, but the lady, with a brisk officious manner and her gray-streaked hair tied up in a bun, shows up with not only towels but white terrycloth robes.

She wanders over to the rock where my possessions are neatly piled. Suddenly, I feel at her mercy, a complete stranger on a nebulous mission. I'm thinking: ***this would be a really good time for Jason to show up! He could explain, then we could leave with him. Oh, Jason!***

She holds this white robe out, suggesting, with the gesture, that I'm to climb out of the water and slip my virginal body into the kindly-held folds of the robe, before prying eyes rob me of thereof, my symbolic virginity (if it could be taken by someone's look alone). Despite her somewhat cold-eyed expression, I do it. The alternatives, at this point, are down to nil.

This land and lake, which had welcomed me into its dreamy embrace, now seems spoiled by its human squatters.

I wrap the robe tightly around my waist, staring longingly at the lake. The swim will stick in my mind a long time. It's the small-scale revelations that last for a lifetime, even if they take only minutes, merely seconds.

"Where are you from?" I ask the woman, who stands next to me impatiently, as if ready to bark out another order. I have a right to know. Her uniform, it can't be anything else, has no logos or insignias. "I mean, what's your *agency*?"

This is all foreign to me. You see, in London, we've developed very little bureaucracy. We don't have government bureaus. Authority and bureaucracy are primarily about power, and power is an obsession held mostly by adults. In London, we were largely kids.

"I'm from the district council." Her voice is distant and self-contained, especially behind the mask, as if this council has got everything figured out.

"We don't recognize you or your companions as residents. You must come to answer a few questions."

"Where?"

"Our offices are not far from here. You can change back into your clothes." She hands me a towel and I use it to dry off my hair.

"I can change right here."

"No, I don't think that's recommended." I glance around at the sunbathers and am suddenly taken by their self-isolation, glistening bodies on the grass, lined up in neat rows like shiny mannequins.

"District council, you said?" Still drying my hair vigorously.

"Yes."

"What's your name? Mine is Emma."

"Simone," she says, standoffish and official. She has a French accent.

Gwen sobs quietly, unsteadily leaning against Harry, who's dressed and flanked by the two men. I'm out of earshot, but Harry keeps talking, keeps trying to iron out this new wrinkle in our star-crossed journey.

"Come," Simone says. I want to give her a good shove and dash away from this. I want to get out of her cloying clutches. I don't believe her intentions are good. My red alerts, the ones honed since childhood, are triggered and blaring all at once. But I can't just run, and abandon my companions.

A block farther down the lakeside promenade, I see a young man sprinting and pursued by two more of the men in the white uniforms, clutching their nightsticks.

CHAPTER 33

This guy sprints all out, trying to get away. We all watch him intently. He trips, falls, scrambles to his feet. Has a scared-out-of-his-wits look. The two guys catch up to him and each seize him by an arm, but he breaks free.

He's fighting back. One of the uniformed guards swings hard with a nightstick, but the pursued man ducks, grabs his assailant by the loose parts of the uniform around the neck, and tries to hurl him to the ground.

I sense my hands at my side, fists clenching, unclenching.

The guard's partner pulls out a weapon that looks like a pistol, with a black handle and yellow barrel. He aims, and with a loud, hideous bright spark like a blown electrical circuit, zaps and incapacitates the escapee. The guy screams in pain, freezes, and collapses in a heap onto the ground. The two men drag him away, his limp shoes scraping along the pavement.

I snap a glance at Simone. "What was that?"

"That was a taser. The CRS officer had to use it. The man was assaulting them."

"He looked like he was running away and defending himself. What was he running from? Would you know?" ***The tranquility of Lake Geneva is beginning to seem like a misleading facade, I think.***

"The man was an offender, doubtlessly, a resistor. He may have been openly exposing citizens to disease, or flaunting an infection."

The large group of nearby sunbathers appear perfectly blase, as though they couldn't be bothered.

"Infection?"

Simone turns away from me. "Follow me."

What if I don't? Will I be tased? This is the first time I've ever seen one of those bloody things.

We walk a couple of blocks to what I assume is an official "district" headquarters. I'm still dressed only in the terrycloth robe and carrying my clothes. Wearing a mask, I turn to Simone, voice muffled, feeling stifled.

"Where can I get dressed?"

She points to an outdoor loo, which is marked with the symbol of a woman on it. "The rest room is there. Don't take long." I come out five minutes later and hand her the robe. She never budged from just outside the door of the lady's room.

I feel like a delinquent who's been swept off the street and sent into detention.

If it was just me and Harry, well, I'd think we'd make

a run for it. The whole demeanor of these people is a toxic mixture of piggish authority and veiled threats.

The promenade is much busier compared with the quiet charm of those boulevards in Vevey. I sense a different atmosphere. Small crowds of masked people, keeping their distance and not making eye contact with me.

I turn to Simone: "Is there a particular disease about?" I'm trying to shed light on the general weirdness of it all. "Is there an epidemic?"

"There are always transmissible diseases, no? Viruses are always in the environment, and brought in by outsiders. We catch them before they take hold and wreak havoc. Where did you come from, by the way?"

"London."

"And do you have epidemics there?"

"No. I mean, I'm 22, and I've lived there my whole life. I was born into the barmy fever, but it subsided years ago. All the sick died off."

"The barmy..."

"Another name for H7N11."

"Of course, I know what you're talking about. That almost wiped out the human race. It could come back, though."

Jeez, I'm thinking, she's quite the germaphobe.

Changing the subject: "Is the Castle Of Chillon still around here?"

"Around? Of course. It's called Chateau de Chillon. We haven't torn it down. Why would we? It's that way." She points down along the water toward the rest of the ornate neighborhoods of Montreux. "How do you know about it?"

"Byron's poem, *The Prisoner Of Chillon*. I looked it up and found that it was on Lake Geneva. I actually didn't think of it when we planned this trip."

She regards me curiously, as if impressed by my erudition.

I ask her, "What's it used for now?"

She hesitates, implying the answer is secret. "It's a clinic."

"A medical clinic?"

"Yes, it's used to heal people..." Another suspicious hesitation. "And for research."

"What kind of research?"

"You ask a lot of questions."

# #

We walk along the water, caressed by the warm winds off the lake, delicately shaking the palm trees. Gwen leans languidly on Harry's shoulder. Roses and big-blossomed carnations decorate the lakeside. I suppose a little discipline is necessary to protect what beauty you have, I think. They have it in abundance here, but this pushy group, with their bellicose tactics, has everyone on edge.

The "district council" building is a converted hotel, right on the lake. It has four stories and a large Royal Plaza sign. What used to be a cafe seems to be set aside for council cadres on a break. People, their masks hanging from an ear or set to one side, sit under trees and sip coffee, chew on croissants.

We enter through the back, by the lake. The interior is a sort of conference or banquet room. As we walk in, we have our temperature checked, with a battery-operated device aimed at our foreheads. The thing looks like a taser and freaks me out when, immediately a man standing by the entrance, waves it at my forehead.

I'd never seen this device before, since batteries are almost impossible to come by in London.

The device reads my own temp as 35.2 C., about 95-6 F., then add one, so I'm only 97 Fahrenheit. But Gwen is 100.5. Simone raises her eyebrows, acts smug and pompous and authoritarian, as though she has expected the high reading.

"Where did you get this device?" I ask. "I work in a hospital. We don't have them."

I'm hoping if Simone concludes I'm professional and rational-minded, she'll let us go with a brief interview.

Hope is cheap.

"Which hospital?"

"A clinic in London. St. Paul's."

"How long ago did you leave London?"

"Just two days."

"You will have to quarantine."

"What's this all about?" She asks us all to take chairs at a long table. I sit down tentatively, still wet from the swim, feeling awkward and annoyed.

"Laws and regulations," Simone says dryly. "We don't want sick people coming here from other places." She can't help but aim a contemptuous glance at Gwen. I swallow; the situation seems to spiral.

One of the men, standing nearby with his arms crossed, speaks up. "Your companion is running a temperature. She will have to be isolated." Gwen's hand darts to her chin fretfully. Harry stands up, his rage simmering, on the verge of being uncorked.

"We can go stay in the van," he snaps. "We'll just stay up there for a few days, until she's better."

"What van?" Simone says, in a demanding tone.

Harry doesn't say anything. We're beginning to feel like prisoners; refugees who are taken for criminals.

"The protocols require isolation," the man says smugly, virtually looking at the ceiling, not Harry.

"Listen mate," Harry spits.

"Harry..." I don't think I can calm him down. This is Harry; he's combative.

"You'll both be living not far away. For your quarantine," Simone says, implying there's no alternative.

Nobody tells us where to live. We're Londoners, of the 2051 generation.

I stand up and move over next to Harry, put my hand on his shoulder. Defuse him, or at least attempt to. He's already had enough of this "house arrest."

"I'm a nurse. I truly don't think Gwen has a contagious infection. I've examined her..." (Exaggeration, there...) "She has abdominal pains and sporadic fever. I think it's appendicitis. We could get to the bottom of it, at one of your advanced clinics."

"Advanced clinics?" Simone says, skeptically.

"We've heard you have good clinics and spas." I try to explain the trip as planned and thought out. I talk faster, nervously.

I look outside a window and my gaze settles on the pastel blue lake. I keep watching, willfully blocking out what Simone is saying. She's like the wicked private-school headmistress, antagonizing her imprisoned students.

Mankind, warts and all, I think, gazing at the blue water, immersing myself in it all over again. *We'll disappear someday, that I'm sure of, leaving the lake in its lofty, windy silence.*

"...Here in District 10," I hear her prattle on.

"What exactly is this region called, other than 'District 10'?" I ask. I think of Chardonne, the quaint, quiet, narrow street winding through vineyards and peach groves. Sitting in the long grass, eating fruit, basking in sunlight. That mindset has been vanquished; it seems to exist only in memory, banished to another dimension.

"We came through Vevey," I explain. "After driving through the Parc Jura Vaudois."

"This is Lac Leman, District 10." She takes all of our full names, ages, origins; she demands to know where we left the van. I wish I was resting in it now. Harry, standing off to the side, is red-faced, seconds away from blowing a fuse. I know it.

The two men pull on plastic gloves and eye goggles, adding to the antiseptic look of the masks. I want to point out, *if you're afraid of catching an infection from Gwen, then it's too late for the gloves and the goggles.*

They want to take *her* one place, us another. Harry suddenly has one of the guys by the collar, handfuls of the man's shirt in each tightened fist. I've seen this look on his face before, like the time he slugged two guys because they were cat-calling me outside the pub on St. Thomas Street. Had a donnybrook because they wouldn't apologize.

"I won that! I won that!" I remember he said, as I

patched up his scuffed and bloodied fists and face at my own clinic. All because these pub guys said I had an "awesome round arse." I didn't give a pauper's copper about the comments, but I was still proud of him.

Harry's an inherent protector. Which is to say, he's going to fight for Gwen now, for *her* freedom. It's in his nature, his blood.

The other guy removes a black night stick and the first one backs off and reaches for his own club, and I fear the unknown punishments meted out to miscreants from afar.

A scuffle breaks out, chairs topple over, Gwen cries hysterically, Harry throws one of the guys to the floor and is seconds away from being tased, and I scream,

"Harry! Chill out!"

Everybody stops what they were doing; everybody in the room is watching us.

Harry tears himself away from the two men, straightens his shoulders, glares at everyone, still spoiling for a brawl. Gwen sobs quietly. The two guys are joined by a third, and I wonder if they're going to tase Harry.

"Let him go!" I yell. "He's just lost his temper! We're okay now." I shoot a glance at Simone, appealing for intervention. Her expression is cold, imperious, still plotting, still conniving.

"Okay men, that's enough!" Simone finally barks, just as a white-uniformed orderly with a hypodermic needle hits Harry's shoulder. Harry roughly back hands the guy and breaks free.

"What was in that?" I yell at Simone.

"A harmless sedative."

"He didn't get me!" Harry declares, loud and triumphant.

"Okay, everyone calm down," I say, playing the peacemaker. I stand between the three men and Harry. Two of them have pulled out their tasers, thrusting them forward, threatening to trigger that awful, hot spark. I flinch, anticipating its burning odor, the excruciating electric jolt.

Simone says: "We'll go now. We'll take you to your rooms for quarantine."

That's just not going to happen, I think. This isn't why I left London. I have to find Jason.

The whole disheveled group of us stumbles just beyond the entrance door, where a small group of spectators have gathered. Harry and Gwen are arm in arm. He's enraged, she's distraught and weepy. Simone takes me by the arm.

"I want to show you something, Miss." Temporarily leaving the others below, we climb a flight of stairs that takes us to a patio on the second floor. Then we walk a steep sidewalk that passes through some hedges.

"Where are we going?"

"You should see this. It will explain things." We reach a clearing past the hedges, a view of the hillsides above Montreux. "The view isn't quite as good, but maybe you should know about it."

She points. I see a steep field, not planted with vineyards or built up with hotels, but massively covered with what appear to be graves. Hundreds of them, little white crosses.

They look like war dead. Too many wiped out all at

once to build a proper memorial in the dirt. But they look too recent to have derived from the barmy fever. Given the beatific first impression of Lake Geneva, I now wonder whose nightmare we've blundered into.

CHAPTER 34

Simone explains bitterly,

"Two years ago. Lac Leman District 10 had a population of 8,000. Now it's 5,000. The last epidemic took the rest. Those crosses, you see them there? They have no names. They are symbolic. We burned the bodies, way back in the hills. It took us three months to dispose of them all. Men, women, and children, not just the old. Everyone was involved. No way to properly mark the graves. Now do you see why we are careful?"

"Yes. I'm sorry, what was the disease?"

"Never identified. Fast-moving. It caused a violent reaction, agitation, followed by high fever that was impossible to control. We had no anti-viral medications, you understand."

"You won't take Harry, right? He was just being protective of Gwen."

She hesitates. "No, as long as he stays subdued. Otherwise, he will have to be managed, like the offender we saw by the lake. He will have to be kept in the stockade."

"Stockade?" I ask, unable to hide my disbelief in the dubious need for archaic prisons in this tiny place.

"Where else do you suggest we put dangerous criminals?"

"He's neither dangerous nor criminal. Most men aren't."

She shrugs. "Suit yourself."

I think about the castle, the one Byron wrote about, not far down the lake.

"Why don't we stay at the Chateau de Chillon? That would be a display of true hospitality." ***Rather than this rough treatment you've given us so far, I think.***

She gives me a withering look. "Chillon isn't a spa. It's mostly used for medical research."

"Research in what?"

"Vaccines."

"A vaccine? Isn't that rather grand."

"Why do you say that? Don't disrespect us."

"A vaccine is impossibly complex to design and test, safely, even with the technology and experts that existed before the barmy fever. How can you properly make a vaccine, if you don't even know what the pathogen is? Further, pathogens keep mutating; they out-fox the vaccine."

"You seem confident in your contrary opinions."

"I know this from my mother, and her writings."

"Who's your mother?"

"My mother was Emma Blair, and she was an infectious disease scientist. She was brilliant. She knew what she was talking about."

"Ah-h. Stick around, will you?"

Simone peels away from me for the moment to speak with the other men, outside of our earshot. I notice a old lady watching me from under a tree. She wears a tattered purple dress and pushes a two-wheeled cart full of meagre belongings. She gives me a crooked smile and shuffles closer.

"Don't believe that one," she says to me. "Whatever she's telling you."

"What do you mean?"

"She's a sly devil, that lady. You seem like a nice misses. They're looking for guinea pigs. For this shot they're making. They use new people, and old people like me, to test it on. If something goes wrong..." She fixes me with a glare and begins nodding vigorously, "Yes, they blame it on the poor person's age, or somethin' else. They ruin or kill you, then you're to blame! That's right, just watch yerself."

I nod. The lady appears a bit shaky, but what she says confirms my suspicions about Simone.

I go over to Harry, who's standing with Gwen in the middle of the crowded promenade. I put my hand on Gwen's forehead.

"You're quite warm. Tell them to get her to bed, with plenty of water and vitamin C. Zinc, 30 milligrams, vitamin D, 5000 IU, magnesium: 500 mg, if they have some. We have all that stuff at the van."

"What are you going to do?" By instinct, Harry

already knows. His eyes gleam with co-conspiracy.

"I'm going to run, on the count of 20. They want to test some bogus vaccine on us. They can't possibly have the tools or the know-how to make a proper vaccine.

"I'll provide the diversion. If you can, you two melt into the crowd. I'll meet you back at the van. If you can't break away, Jason and I will come for you. I'll bring Gwen her medications."

Harry nods soberly. He knows Gwen can't run, but one of us has to. "Be careful, Emma."

"Sure I will."

Simone walks up to me rigidly, with her arms crossed.

I'm just not designed to take orders, give in to ultimatums.

She says: "Miss Winslow, you will..."

I place both hands on her crossed forearms and give her a hard shove, strong enough so that the slim bony lady stumbles backwards. Then I run, towards Vevey along the promenade and sprinting as fast as I can go, arms pumping like a boxer's, dodging in and out of the startled, masked crowds.

Out of the corner of my eye, I see that Simone has gone down on her arse, right in front of the old cackling lady with the push cart.

Two of the men in white uniforms have gone like bats out of hell to catch me. Young men, it seems like they should be able to run, decently.

Fat chance they'll catch me, I think. I tear the mask off my face and carry it at my side. To my left are the flat rocks I dived into the lake off of. I quickly turn right around a hedge row and sprint down the path that goes past the Europa Hotel, retracing our steps from earlier.

I reach the spacious boulevard in Vevey, glance behind me, still see the two guys, up the path, not 30 yards away. I cross the boulevard at full speed and head for the road that goes through the vineyards.

I reach a disused funicular, the track snaking up above Vevey. It's almost hidden by shrubs and a fence. I duck into the thick greenery. Shrouded in leaves and branches, I grip the top frame of the fence and scale it, looking over my shoulder towards the boulevard when I get to the top. The men have hesitated in the middle of the street, dodging bicyclists and stray pedestrians.

I swing a leg over and drop down to the track bed. The landing is hard and I roll into grit and splintered rocks. Back on my feet, the exhaustion washes through me, the fatigue of the pursuit, the loss of a sense of belonging somewhere.

Tears streak down my face, I rub them off, start trudging up the steep tracks. Thank God this funicular doesn't run. At least I don't think it does. The retaining walls look tall on both sides of me. The sun beats down. I trudge at least a quarter mile, till I get to the first station platform. Thirst claws at my throat; sweat mixes with the tears.

Steps lead to the platform, which is empty and closed. I see no one behind me or in the general vicinity. I'm intensely aware that:

I've left Harry and Gwen with Simone's creeps, and don't know whether they've been able to slip away.

I don't have a clue where Jason is.

I don't have a place to stay in Lake Geneva, as I'm

unsure whether I can unlock the van, and not sure I can find it. I might be a bit fucked right now. But at least I don't have some creepy control freak testing her half-assed biochemical cocktail on me.

I'm out on the open road now, plodding upwards. Placid sunlight bakes the long lush rows of vineyards. I've gained hundreds of feet of elevation. The egg-shell blue lake stretches to the horizon like an inland sea.

It's a few miles, I remember, to where we parked the van.

The vineyards convey a windless, blissful silence. I let my guard down for a moment. Then I hear loud, urgent voices on the road, around the bend. Beneath me. I pick up the pace, swabbing sweat off my brow with my shirtsleeves. A stone wall separates the vineyard from the road.

I come upon a swinging gate. I push through it, into the vineyards. I scurry into thick, arid rows of plants with dry, flinty soil and broad green leaves; clusters of maturing grapes the size of my fists. After a minute, hidden amongst the leaves, I seize a handful of the grapes, twisting them off the vine and crushing them into my mouth. They're tart, sour, juicy, but hydrating, the juice running down my cheeks like watery blood.

Climbing through the vineyards, I reach the top of the hillside, high above Vevey and the lake. I crouch down among the vines, feeling tired and alone, listening to the footsteps and voices on the road. The gruff conversation grows louder as I hear men enter the vineyard through the swinging gate.

CHAPTER 35: Emma Blair, Isle Of Skye, October 2026

The kettle shrieked, sounding like a distressed baby. The noise jarred me out of a daze, since I was alone, sitting on steps, watching the sun finish its rise. I was making tea, then oatmeal and potatoes. Felt like I've been alone a long time, but it hadn't been that long; it was the attenuated days with no one else to talk to.

After I ate, I wrote in my diary.

October 29, 2026, Emma Wallace Blair, Isle Of Skye, Scotland.

Partly sunny, bank of dark clouds coming in from the loch. About 50 degrees F. Decent sleep, oats and potatoes for breakfast. Last night's dinner, same thing. Took my supplements. Wounds have healed; band-aids off. No fucking reivers around that I've seen the last three days. Today I go into Portree. Will take the truck and really load up, with everything that I find.

I seek CBD oil, because I'm running out.

Later, I drove the empty road to Portree. The truck motor rattled on, with me pushing on the spongy accelerator and brakes. Some of the road was dirt and gravel; the paved portion was already the worse for wear, for lack of regular maintenance, and like everything else, you could blame the pathogen.

I gazed out windows both sides while I drove, to the adjacent yellow fields and the browning, grassy hillsides. I saw no people, or reivers. A squirrel dashed in front of the truck, survived. In the sky, only wet looking blobs of clouds floated past, and I noticed a conspicuous lack of birds.

It was that time of year: cold mornings, piles of yellow leaves sprayed with a blood red; cool winds and early sunsets.

The gray afternoons and the fast-arriving darkness brought on a hungry, lonesome longing. I looked forward to this "trip to town," to check on Gladys and resume my looting.

I didn't think about the on-coming winter. I didn't think about being alone in the cold; the days that barely last eight hours. No one to talk to; the bloody reivers. Don't be defeatist, I said to myself. Fear is made in your brain; you can teach yourself to avoid it. I think a big-wave surfer said that in a book I read.

Someone who's never heard the awful muttering of reivers, seen the glassy eyes with their deranged vengeance; the rotten teeth. And that smell, that pissy, sour-sweat smell.

I did briefly consider a return to Inverness or Edinburgh in the truck. But Ned said that Inverness was infected, overrun. I couldn't reach my father, thought he might have run away to somewhere else. Best case scenario, that. And Edinburgh...the population was decimated down there.

I thought about Mary and Lennox and wished both of them were with me, but if wishes were silver coins, I'd have riches, with nowhere to blow it.

Driving sets free the mind, which is probably why driving has always been associated with freedom. ***If wishes were horses, beggars would ride.*** I've seen neither horses nor bicycles, but I will grab a bike if I see one, because I think this truck lives on borrowed time.

In the back seat was my small axe and the cricket bat. I found them oddly consoling; a knight that sleeps with her sword and her spear.

A shovel, a crowbar, and a rope rattled and shuffled around in the open-air cargo bed. "I'm going to take so much stuff," I declared out loud, conscious of not wanting to cultivate the habit of talking to myself. Thus laying the path to madness. "It will be Christmas in October."

Shit, Christmas! When was the last time I had a normal one? That was with Will in December 2025.

Damn was that Christmas fun! We were in New York City, it had snowed five inches; Christmas Eve walks on Fifth Avenue, scuffing through the snow, powder swirling in the air; slipping into warm pubs for brandy by candlelight; late mornings, frost on the window, deep in the covers; coffee, books, love-making, not getting too hung up about seeing every family member...God did I love that Christmas!

I sniffed once, twice, misty-eyed, I saw Will's face, bearded, warm smile, holding one of those big-bellied brandy glasses with only the little bottom part by the stem actually containing amber-colored liquid. I looked left, out the window. I saw my reflection, smudged with leftover condensation from my breath.

Through the window, beyond the reflection of *my* face, I saw a pond. A genuine, small pond in a field. Movement. It was a dog.

A dog running after a flock of ducks. By instinct I stamped on the spongy brakes. The truck skidded and swerved into gravel. The dog gave chase to a bunch of ducks lingering on the side of the pond. I watched. The ducks took a few steps, then flew off with loud squawks and wildly beating wings. They were brown, with nice striped patterns on their feathers, like little worsted suits. The dog stopped, nose to the air where the ducks flew, as if admiring her work.

I opened the door, stepped down gingerly because a drainage gully fell at my feet, then I walked and stood in front of the truck. Hands on my hips, listening to the whispering of the field with its wind, riveted on the pond, and the stock-still dog. I cupped my hands over my mouth, and yelled to the border collie who, startled, jerked around to look at me: "Bundy!"

Yelled again: "Bundy!!"

# #

Bundy leapt into the passenger seat like it was her second home, which it was, as this was her truck and Robert J. Hardy's. Rest in peace.

Bundy was black with a wide white stripe around her shoulder and neck; the top of her nose was also white. She came to me, across the field, without a lot of hesitancy. Maybe it was the smells from the truck; being a natural sheep herder and intelligent by reputation, she must have had keen senses. Maybe she truly, by nature, wanted to be with a person. I wouldn't speculate much more than...

Bundy probably smelled, by nature, H7N11, and what it did to a human being, and the scent was unholy to a dog. I don't have it, so thus she came to me. Why?

Why hadn't I caught that thing? I had some kind of immunity that should have been deciphered and isolated. And what better person to do it than, Emma Blair, infectious disease scientist with science degrees from St. Andrew's in Scotland and NYU in New York. It was all in the immunity, and people whose immune systems have been tuned by a variety of strong pathogens.

"It's all in the immunity," I said to Bundy, who looked at the windshield and the road with a panting-dog smile. "Both acquired and inherited..."

Changed the subject: "We're going to go to the Co-Op first in Portree. Loot it, with impunity. Dog food will be one of the first things on the menu."

She turned and looked at me when I spoke, human like. I noticed that roadkill interested her as we drove along. So far, only a skunk. Roadkill, however, was very definitely also on the menu. If I saw a dead deer, I'd stop.

Not that I'd really know how to butcher it. I knew that would have to start with a large knife; the kitchen at the farmhouse had them.

I was taking nothing for granted food-wise. But first we had the Co-Op supermarket on the outskirts of Portree. All of its promised delicacies...

I'll have to see Gladys today, I thought. Looking at Bundy, I hoped Gladys didn't have a cat, or the cat was the type that stayed hidden.

I saw the homes, nice seaside ones, dotting the hillsides. ***It's the abandoned homes that have the most and nicest foods, I thought. Everyone's already looted the markets.*** I didn't know whether that was the voice of reason, or the devil on my shoulder, whispering in my ear.

We roamed the outskirts of town, slowing down the truck. No people or vehicles were around, whatsoever. That eerie calm, silence, and vacancy. They produced a sinister chord in the middle of the day, because of what was missing. Ordinary people going about their business. Young gals pushing strollers and kids playing with footballs and frisbees. Vehicles in their endless varieties: Fiats, Subarus, Renaults, and the snobs you can't take your eyes off in the Range Rovers and Audis and Mercedes. Now nothing, an empty road with stuff blowing across it.

"The Co-Op should be right about there," I said, looking up about a mile ahead. Bundy was already a pleasure. "You're a wonderful conversationalist," I said.

Once again, she turned her head to look at me.

"Did you hear the one about the guy that goes to the pub. Outside, there's a scruffy old gent fishing in a puddle. So the guy, feeling all virtuous and high-minded, says 'Hey old man, come on inside and I'll buy you a drink.' Figures he's doing the guy a huge favor. They sit down at the bar and order two martinis.

"The guy looks at the fella who was fishing in the puddle and says, sort of smart-ass, 'How many did you catch today?' The fella sips his martini and turns to him and says, 'You're my eighth.'"

Then I laughed, ***really*** laughed, tears in my eyes laughter, at my own stupid joke. "Do you get it?!" Bundy looked at me with the dog-smile pant.

We pulled into the Co-Op, stopped. The parking lot was a graveyard of orphaned automobiles. Many of them were sitting on flat tires. "We're looking for fish too," I said off-handedly, thinking also of the waterfront. Fishing vessels and sumptuous fish restaurants, abandoned with possible working freezers.

Couldn't ignore Gladys though. Needed pharmaceuticals as well, such as that CBD and propylene glycol and Tylenol. More vitamins and minerals.

"Bundy is a funny name," I said, hand on the inside door handle. "Like, one you'd give a doll. Must have found you on a Sundy, rather than on a Mondy."

I opened the door partway, thinking of leaving the dog in the truck. Bit of a quandary. Still talking: "Funnier when blokes give their dogs common male names like Doug or Hank. They need to go to naming school."

I had this reflex paranoia that when I returned, Bundy

would be gone. In my state of affairs, there weren't too many Bundys left. You only had a shot at a few of them.

I didn't want to be alone again. There was that fear again, rearing its ugly head. "Are you going to stay with me if I let you out?"

"Are you, Bundy?"

CHAPTER 36

I didn't have a leash. I had my emptied backpack with me. I went around to the other side of the truck, opened the passenger door, let Bundy step down onto the pavement. Instantly, she peed.

I posed the question to her. "Are you going to need a leash?" I looked at her, the tail slowly wagging.

"No."

Started walking, "Here..." She followed me. We reached the entrance to the Co-Op. There was a stack of shopping carts, random Styrofoam and paper litter. The lights in the building were off. I concluded that all the electricity in town was out. The entrance, normally an automatic sliding door, was locked and unbroken, leaving no sign of looters.

"*That's* an inconvenience. We're going to try around back." We walked around to the righthand side of the long, one-story, flat-roofed building, to find a rear entrance. Bundy seemed more bored sticking with me, than compelled to sprint away to seek the sources of all the smells that must have been assaulting her nose. But still, she stuck with me.

I turned the corner of the building and we were met by pungent, rancid odors; rotten eggs, spoiled fruit, sour milk, a dumpster with foul spillage leaking over its edges, moldering in the sun, and thus stinking to high heaven. I pulled the shirt up over my mouth, kept walking. Bundy padded beside me, literally a sidekick. This made me happy and I thought, foretold positive tidings.

I scanned around the empty parking lot and neighborhood; still no people. Back there were empty delivery trucks, also primed for searching. I got to a short flight of steps that went up to a greasy loading dock, then an exit door.

Bundy strayed; I called her away from some trash bags, torn up as if by a raccoon. She came away with a turkey thigh bone in her teeth.

"Alright." She'll find things I won't, I thought.

The door off the loading dock was partly open; I yelled to Bundy, "Follow me!"

It was dark, dank, and sour inside. There were piles of empty cartons that once contained cereal boxes, soup cans, crackers, spam and, given the stickiness of the grimy cement floor, spilled ice cream and orange juice. A slender rectangle of light lay just ahead, and I concluded it must be the way to the supermarket's goods.

The dog's nose to the floor went crazy; I temporarily lost her in the darkness. This time firmness in my voice:

"Bundy, this way!"

She came. All I could hear was the plodding of my own footsteps, the scraping of Bundy's claws, and a relentless ticking from a utility box.

The next door was also slightly ajar; the illumination was from ambient light coming from the outside through windows. We found ourselves emerging behind the former deli counter. The counter itself contained, once more, an awful, mold-coated display of foul, rotted, prepared food. I quickly skirted it and headed for the old refrigerators along the edges of the quiet market.

More spoiled food, but also stuff I could use. Sealed plastic bowls of whipped butter and rectangles of wrapped cheddar. More provolone and Swiss, this time unopened and sliced for sandwiches. I stuck as much of it as I could into the backpack.

Sliced meats still sealed and not too warm; turkey and ham.

Bundy wandered down the aisle. "Stay close, will you dog?" I called out, a flat echo coming off the moldy walls and ceiling. She stopped and stared at one of the shelves, many of which were empty. Total panic buying from weeks ago.

"I know I know. Dog food." Must leave space in my pack, I thought, yet she *can* eat some of my food.

I reached the end of the aisle and copped a few unopened waters and sodas, but I only had so much room in the pack. I needed a cart; I saw one up by the checkout counters. I strode over and grabbed it as Bundy sniffed her way down another aisle. I followed her, pushing the cart and throwing in only the few soup cans I could find, and by the end of the row, several cans of dog food. Even the dog food was all gone, by the time I was through.

People were probably eating dog food, I thought. The few people who could manage, cognitively, to open a can and dish the junk into a bowl. Like me and Gladys.

"Bundy, stay close."

She disappeared around the corner, past that grungy deli counter. She was like a toddler set loose in a supermarket, except her nose was super-charged.

I needed to find the super-vol drinks and the pharmaceuticals aisle, when I heard her bark. Steady, relentless barks, the sounds clanging against the blank, emptied out shelves. "Bundy? Bundy!"

I turned the corner, like a stressed-out Mom. I saw a man with greasy, messy black hair and torn jeans; 40-ish, slouching by some emptied shelves. He was gnawing on a drumstick from a rotten meat package, eyes bugging out of his head in that doltish manner, bare arms all sinew, scratches, bone, and veins. He was white as a ghost, making yum-yum sounds like an infant, and Bundy was 10 feet away, barking at him.

"Bundy, get out of there!" I yelled, a harshness coming into my voice. A fearful tone. A woman wandered up the same aisle from the front of the store, left arm trailing in some boxes where there were still a few old potatoes and beets. She seized one of the beets with her left hand and hurled it at Bundy, missed. Then she hissed at her venomously, like a rabid cat. The dog stepped back, now snarling and barking aggressively.

First time I've seen coordinated, hand-motor action by

reivers, beyond rending and tearing in blind rages. A sort of learned behavior amidst advanced stages of cognitive toxicity.

"Bundy, what the *hell* are you doing! Let's get out of here!" *This isn't accomplishing anything, but agitating them further...stupid dog with her defensive instincts!*

I methodically transferred as much as I could from cart to backpack–meats, drinks, dog food. Entering flee mode, I rushed forward to grab Bundy by the collar. She stubbornly refused to budge; jumping up and tugging against my grip. This little sucker dog is strong, I thought.

The female reiver was rummaging around for another projectile. The guy' gnashing at another rotten drumstick and drooling down his cheek.

An old lady dragging a full trash bag, her soiled dress mopping the floor, scuffed past me, staring at me with glazed astonishment, her chin moving up and down silently. She scuttled over next to drumstick man.

That's three...

I know five is the magic number; possibly four.

I looped the straps of the backpack over both shoulders and seized and yanked Bundy by her collar, as an airborne potato struck her on the left flank, further infuriating her. Now she was straining and fairly foaming at the mouth. She knew what this was; she knows what they are, I thought. Poison. Evil. She smells it.

Dammit Bundy, come!

Three more reivers, young males, appeared from the front of the store. *Where are they coming from, the back? Smashing through the front? I heard nothing like windows breaking. They were in the store the entire time, in some kind of dormant state. Checkout guys...*

The first in the new pack seemed to be in a hurry, dragging his left foot in a pathetic imitation of an old-movie Mummy.

Bundy, we have to go! I pulled her in the direction towards the back. She finally followed me. This street-smart dog knows what's going down.

Past the rotten deli counter, through to the exit, a restroom appeared in front of me, I glanced back around at them. Six.

They were all standing close to each other. They were going at drumstick guy's remaining meat package like a pack of hyenas, and that wouldn't take 20 seconds. Then they lit out after us. Gripping Bundy's collar still; we were going too slow!

I let it go and screamed, "Run Bundy! Run!"

CHAPTER 37

We were out the back, full speed, slipping across the grimy floor, past the wall of empty boxes, aiming for the exit door and loading dock.

Axe and cricket bat were in the back seat of the Ford...I had no real weapon. The backpack slowed me down. I reached the loading dock and jumped the five feet down–no time for stairs–my thighs screamed in pain when I hit the ground, consisting of pavement and gravel, and rolled.

No injuries, I was back on my feet. Backpack felt like lead under these circumstances. I heard the thudding of the rubber-soled shoes on the grimy floor behind us. The lead one was growling and humming and already on top of the stairs.

Bundy stopped and sniffed and investigated. She was looking after me.

"Run Bundy! Keep going!" I went as fast as I could, towards the truck.

I left it unlocked, right?

I heard my own labored breathing, my weighted-down shoes pounding on pavement. I was urging Bundy on; I could sense her chomping on the bit to stop and bark or worse, have it out with these infected creeps.

"Get into the back of the truck!"

I got the sense that she was getting the message, trotting along beside me. By smell, she knows the others aren't human, or are a different, foul breed altogether.

All this happened as seconds ticked by. We reached the old Ford F-150. Bundy leapt and scrambled into the rear truck bed, me giving her hind-quarters a shove on the way in.

I wriggled out of the backpack; in it went. I seized the crowbar, and...

I felt a heavy sloppy hand flop on my shoulder and grip me hard, so much so it hurt.

And another hand clawed a bunch of my sweatshirt around the ribcage. The hand crawled up my torso and got tangled in my hair, tearing at it, ripping at it.

The stench hit me: piss plus ammonia; the sound, the nasal muttering, words that can't form or get out. The godawful breath.

"Arrr-ahhhhhh!"

I ripped myself out of the clutches and swiveled, handling the crowbar like an American baseball bat. I recognized Drumstick just as I connected with his left leg above the knee, fracturing the front of the femur. I heard the crack and a squeal as he collapsed and two more reivers, including Beet Hurler, arrived at the same time but...meandered and staggered about, wishy-washy and indecisive.

They'd split from the group by running too fast, now there was only Drumstick groveling in the gravel nearby, and Beet Hurler and one other sidekick slouching around the vehicle, as if waiting for me to tell them what to do.

I was already back around to the driver's side and seizing open the door, slamming it shut behind me, frantically digging into my left waist pocket for the ignition keys. Another newly arrived reiver climbed up on the hood of the truck, as I started the motor, pumped the accelerator, and ground the pavement gravel in reverse to speed out of the Co-Op parking lot.

I slammed the transmission into drive, pinned the accelerator to the floor. The reiver slid off the hood sideways, eyes agape and bony hands grasping at empty air. I saw him in the rearview mirror tumble into the dust of the road, and thank God none of them tried to get into the back with Bundy, who was watching me through a window on the back of the rear seats.

I went about a mile, then stopped the truck and got out. I ran to the back of the vehicle.

Bundy ambled over and I buried my face in her fur. Eyes misty, voice a little shaky. "Oh Bundy, we made it!"

"They didn't get us." More sobs, me bawling into his fur, then daubing my eyes with my sleeves.

I was breathless. "Thanks for following me, thanks for getting into the back of the truck." Bundy exhibited a dog's patience, patiently absorbing and tolerating this human's emotional outburst.

"Okay..." I dug into the backpack and pulled out one of those unopened packets of sliced meat. "If ever we needed this." Then in the backpack I fished around and located my Swiss Army knife.

I held it up. "Shit, I had this the whole time." I gazed up into the cloud-smudged sky with exasperation. "Oh well, this thing worked out in the end and the knife would have made it more messy so..."

I cut open the package and gave Bundy, who poked his nose inside the plastic wrapper, a fistful of sandwich turkey. I took a couple of pieces for myself and chewed them down and dropped the rest in front of her jowls.

She devoured all the turkey in seconds, jaws and muzzle working furiously. "Alright, c'mon, get back in the car..." I opened the passenger door for her, while watching the Co-Op in the distance. Nobody was following, I thought. It all passed like a brief nightmare; it dissipated like that pissy vapor that enveloped them.

I smelled my sleeves, pulled a handful of my sweatshirt to my nose, and I couldn't detect it. I still needed about an hour-long shower.

I started up the truck again and we pulled away. "Maybe Gladys has a shower," I said out loud. "We're going to eat more of this food too. I'm starved."

We moved out onto the main road. I slowed and tried to remember where Gladys lived. "You know, I didn't kill any back there. No reivers. Shit, no notches for the cricket bat." I took a left and worked my way slowly down a side street, seeing her home, gray shingles, a weather vane, the gas station, a block away.

"No kill, no notches. Maybe the one with the snapped

leg counts." I looked at Bundy for her agreement.

I felt like a warrior now, a savage, faintly guilty at this new fierce, untamed attribute. "It's war," I whispered to myself. "Which has broken many a man, and in others bloomed savages like poison flowers."

"Better than you and me being dead," I spoke over to Bundy, who appeared to nod in agreement.

# #

We pulled close to Gladys's driveway. Glancing at the empty petrol station, I realized I'd only put about 12 miles on the F-150 total. Yet, since I last filled up the tank, the gas gauge had retreated a few notches.

"Thing's a gas guzzler, but we're okay for now." I figured Gladys still wasn't hanging around the petrol station because she had no customers, as far as I knew.

We rolled into the parking area of her driveway and stopped. I put the window down a bit. I still needed to rest, take some deep breaths. We waited.

"Gladys!" I yelled at the front of her home. I didn't want to startle her. The silence of the vacated town had a unique sound all its own; the silence of memories, of what used to fill its space–motors, birds, and the cries of children at play.

When I shut off the motor the silence was deafening.

We left the truck and walked up steps to her front door. No one answered my repeated knocks; the door even had an old knocker that I clanked a few times.

"She must be around back." Bundy's ears perked up, as a squirrel darted up a tree. One noticed any movement, when many neighborhoods had become a still-life painting, frozen in a perpetual state of disruption.

I wandered back to the truck and fetched a jar of peanut butter grabbed from the Co-Op. I was going to offer it as a kind of house gift. We'll eat gobs of P.B. and chit-chat, I thought; maybe Gladys has real sliced bread. Bundy followed me around the back of the house.

"She's going to be surprised that I found you," I said to her, imagining the news I can share, including my latest skirmish with the infected hordes. Someone had to relate to that, someone else had to hear me out about my experiences.

The backyard had a small, waist-high fence around a garden. I saw a trellis, where beans were grown in the garden in summer. "Gladys?"

Bundy stopped and sniffed the air. There was a small second-story deck in back, with wooden steps leading up it. I headed for the steps, clutching the peanut butter in my right hand. I'd left the weapons in the truck, not thinking I needed them. I smelled the sea in the wind, the thick brine, and it lifted my spirits.

This *is* a social call, right? I thought. I'd needed to bring a gift. And I'm not used to social calls lately. I climbed the stairs to enter the home from the back.

"Hey Gladys, I..." Out of the corner of my eye, I spotted a woman in blue jeans and a buttoned-down sweater, lying on her side in the garden.

"Oh no." I turned, walked down the steps, Bundy following me. I went over to the garden to make sure it was Gladys. I knelt down, placed my hand on her shoulder, gave her a gentle shake. Her eyes were closed; I picked up her frail, knotty, veiny right wrist. With two fingers I checked her pulse, detecting nothing but cold, bluish skin.

The breeze picked up, bringing with it October's chill. I shivered and ran a sleeve over my wet nose. I checked her carotid artery; her neck was wooden and lifeless. I stood up, glanced at Bundy.

"Must have been a stroke or a heart attack. This wasn't reivers. There isn't a mark on her. Just came outside for some fresh air in the garden and...that was it. Poor Gladys. Poor poor Gladys."

The wind cracked a partially open door at the stop of the stairs.

"Let's go in anyways." I walked up past the deck and into what appeared to be Gladys's living room. Watered, potted plants, pillows arranged on a couch, a table with flowers and what looked like a picture book. Everything neat as a pin. ***Waiting for her husband to come back,*** I thought. I felt a sickening mixture of sorrow and guilt, about not visiting her sooner.

I thought of when my own mother died, which was sudden, and unexpected. She died of heart failure one night in Inverness. It happened Before Carnage, back in the old world, the one that formed me before a pathogen appeared, like a nuclear bomb. It wasn't sadness that hit me first, when I'd found out my mother had died, it was regret and guilt, because I had canceled a trip the weekend before to go visit her. Out of convenience. Death is forever, and that's how long you have to think about your failings with that person.

Just in case, I called out, "Anyone home!" I went into Gladys's kitchen. I still had the peanut butter jar in my right hand. I pulled out the same chair I had sat in before, and slumped down into it. Bundy wandered off to other parts of the house. "Don't go far," I called out.

I stuck the same two fingers I had used to check a pulse into the light-brown, gooey P.B., and spooned it into my mouth. I got up to fetch a real soup spoon. I looked around for Gladys's tea supplies. She had a technique of making tea; perhaps a working stove top. I suddenly felt like I was looting again, taking advantage, but it was *Gladys's misfortune* now, not that of unknown others, that had left me with supplies.

Taking her stuff seemed heartless and a sacrilege, but realistic. That's what I am, I thought, a cold realist. When the parameters of my existence permit me, I'll seek to achieve grace and well-roundedness. But not now, not with the wounds inflicted on me, and the odor of the greasy infected ghouls still on my clothes.

CHAPTER 38

I called Bundy back into the kitchen. A pause, then I heard the click-clack of her paws. She entered the room and instantly took an intense interest in the peanut butter, poking her nose into the crook of my arm and then gently lunging toward the jar. I placed a gob into my own mouth with the soup spoon, then let her lick off a dollop from two fingers. She sucked and chomped on the P.B. comically, as if it was badly stuck on the roof of her mouth.

Which it was.

I spooned another dollop of the tasty condiment into my own mouth.

It had been a long day.

I leaned my elbows on the table and massaged my temples. "I was actually looking forward to talking to Gladys. Hearing another human voice."

Bundy sat on the floor and awaited another spoonful of SunPat "Original Smooth" peanut butter.

I gave her some more on my finger. "I prefer Jif peanut butter, but this will do just fine. You know Bundy," I took a deep breath. "We can't just leave Gladys lying out there."

An awful sensation swept through me, born from the notion of having no one to talk to but a dog, for years.

I thought out loud. "The right thing to do would be to bring her inside. Set her up on this couch, with a blanket and flowers. A kind of tribute. But that won't do because, she'll decompose." Then I looked at Bundy, gave her another finger full. She reminded me of a clown, awkwardly chewing it. I wondered if peanut butter was good for dogs.

"No, we have to bury her. In the garden." I was a little punchy by then. "In the garden she goes, with the onion and the garlic."

I stood up and went outside through the back deck. The backyard was dominated by the presence of her body, as if Gladys had stood up and demanded that I put things into order, concerning her untimely death and the disposition of her body.

I got the shovel out of the back of the truck. The P.B. helped, but I still felt weary of the day's ordeals. Then I carried the shovel to the garden and started digging a hole near Gladys's body. It was only just past noon, I guessed.

I set the shovel down and rechecked her vitals. I picked the tool up again and got working. The ground was hard from recent cold mornings. The digging was tough. I figured I could go down six inches max, then just wide enough for her frame. The only sound was the metal shovel-head biting into the dirt. Almost done, I took a break, hand on a hip and scanning the road.

Bundy following, I went up the steps, through the living room, to Gladys's bathroom. A shelf had neatly folded purple towels. She had running water. At the sink, I washed all the dirt and shitty spit off my arms, hands, face, anywhere I thought they touched me.

I went back into the kitchen, raided the fridge. She had some near-gone cherry tomatoes, apples, and cheddar cheese, which I gobbled up at the kitchen table. All of it. I craved some nuts, couldn't find any, so another SunPat "Original Smooth" dollop melted in my mouth, before I went outside to finish the job.

I shoveled as far down into the fibrous turf as I could, which wasn't very far, then rolled her body in sideways. I covered Gladys with a wool blanket, hoping it was a favorite one.

The thought leapt to mind that Gladys would have still been alive if her husband was still around. She'd died of loneliness.

I'd found a few sad, family photos in frames, and a stack of old LPs in the living room. I placed them in the grave with her, tucked inside the blanket. The LPs were releases by Sam Cooke and Frank Sinatra.

Those records had to have been 65 years old or more. Then I pondered, what's going to happen to music? Will only birds make the music on earth? Whales serenading each other fathoms beneath the sea? And me and my squeaky pipette, which so far cannot compete with increasingly infrequent, late fall bird songs?

The records were real music, as in *Summer Wind* and *You Send Me*. For a full minute I stood still, and wondered whether I could possibly find a record player. I dropped the shovel. I went back into Gladys's living room, and in the next room over found the old turn-style LP player. I unplugged it, then carried it outside to my truck. Slipped it into the back seat. Followed by three records, including the recovered Sinatra and Cooke. I dropped a fourth and a fifth LP into Gladys's grave, with the framed photos. Those two under the blanket in the grave were also Sinatra; he had a lot of hits.

I covered over everything with dirt, a few loose stones I found nearby, and a handful of withered wildflowers, to which I added a potted cactus I found on the dining room table.

I knelt down by the grave and put my arm around Bundy, sensing the warmth in her fur. The chill wind, under gray skies, rattled the leaves in the trees, fluttered a flag she had flying near the kitchen window.

Even the thwacking of the flag startled me; my head darted around. I was looking over my shoulder for the bloody reivers, all of the time.

I wanted to say a few words over the grave. Nothing fancy or with the proper gravitas came to mind, so I went and fetched my thick *Lord Byron, Selected Poems* book, sitting on the back seat. It was dog-eared and it had also been left out in the rain once. I found this book back in the classroom, at the school. I wouldn't have lent it to anyone, even if I could, because I was always afraid they'd burn it for heat, or for perverse enjoyment. That's how tightly I clung to my paperbacks.

I had a habit, when the morning gifted me some sun, of sitting on the back steps at the farm and reading and just letting my spirit soar, sailing away from the troubles that afflicted this land.

By Gladys's grave, I read a passage from the *Prisoner Of Chillon* that I always liked, because of the way this prisoner can hurl his imagination beyond the prison cell, beyond the chains that shackle him. Maybe the poem was a little over the top, because he talks of befriending his chains. No one in their right mind would do that.

I thought, perhaps we're all prisoners in a way of this catastrophe, which had caused the loss of our people, our communities, our food systems, and all the things that make us feel safe and grounded.

I was a prisoner of my fear and loneliness. Gladys didn't survive her own incarceration.

I sat cross-legged by her grave and read the passage out loud. "It's about a bird the prisoner sees from his cell, which sings and lifts his spirit, but a bit more than that," I told Bundy.

But through the crevice where it came
That bird was perched, as fond and tame,
And tamer than upon the tree;
A lovely bird, with azure wings,
And song that said a thousand things,
And seemed to say them all for me!

I never saw its like before,
I ne'er shall see its likeness more:
It seemed like me to want a mate,

But was not half so desolate,
And it was come to love me when
None lived to love me so again,
And cheering from my dungeon's brink,
Had brought me back to feel and think.

I know not if it late were free,
Or broke its cage to perch on mine,
But knowing well captivity,
Sweet bird! I could not wish for thine!
Or if it were, in winged guise,
A visitant from Paradise.

Me and Bundy sat and listened to the wind for a minute. I had my fill of silence, stood up, and played the opening notes of *Amazing Grace* on my pipette (the only notes of that tune I knew at the moment).

"Alright, Gladys, I know this is a hasty sort of memorial, but I wanted to say something. You were kind to me, right away. You showed such resilience! May you rest in peace, in the same place as your husband. Let's go Bundy."

I left with as much food as I could take from her kitchen. The pumps weren't functioning at the petrol station across the street, so we didn't get any more fuel. I can't say I got everything out of this trip that I expected, but I did come away with life and limbs intact, extra food and water, and Bundy.

When we made it home, I left for a nap. Bundy conducted her own tour of the inside of the farmhouse. She seemed comfortable already, an adaptable lass. When

I woke up, I began designing a sort of maze constructed with rope, an idea I had while driving back from Portree. You would have to work your way through this small maze, like vegetable rows in a garden, but less straightforward, before you could get to my back door.

The reivers are useless, tottering dolts who can't even feed themselves, outside of a group. I should be able to fool them, I thought, and I heard myself saying that out loud. *Fool and confuse the idiots.*

I'll finish the maze, I figured, tomorrow. I had nothing else on my agenda. Except for the usual duties: find wood I can burn for heat, organize food, and collect water. Winter was coming. Gladys was gone. I was on my own, with possibly 12 gallons of petrol left in the truck's tank.

Thank God for Bundy.

CHAPTER 39: Emma Winslow, Above Lake Geneva, 2051

I walk the road next to the field where we rested before, with the orchard of peaches and apples. I cross into the field with its long lush grass and pick an apple and a peach, eat them ravenously, the juice running down my cheeks, toss the pit and the core. I shove two more fruits into my pockets.

The voices I heard, they turned out to be two teenaged boys who worked in the vineyards. They paid little attention to me as I made my way back out into the street.

Walking fast again. The road is empty; I think I've dropped my pursuers. I'm knackered, from the combined experience of the road trip to Lake Geneva itself, and then being corralled by Simone. I feel like an alien in an alien land, even a fugitive.

A cart moves slowly up the road with two big draft horses. The cart contains gray, woven bags full of apples and potatoes. An old man with a white beard, suspenders, and shirtsleeves drives the cart.

"Sir," I say, raising my hand as soon as the heavily muscled horses clop past me.

"*Quel*?" The old fella drops the reins. The horses stop, swatting flies with their long bushy tails. The flies gather in the sunlight, as if it had hatched them.

"Do you know Jason Hunter?"

He shrugs, shakes his head. The reins lie in his lap.

"Do you know Randolph Braden? He has a farm near here. Please."

"Braden?" He scratches his rough bearded chin.

"Yeah."

"*Là*," he says, pointing up the road toward the top of the mountain. The van is somewhere up there too.

"Close, there," he adds. I nod and thank him. He clicks his tongue and flips the reins; the horses nod their head in the hot sun, then pull the wagon up to the next switchback.

I wonder if Simone has real vehicles at her disposal. London has so few of them. If so, I might run into her men up here, or they'll get to the van before I do. I hope Harry's description of its location was purposely wrong, or too vague. I'm sure he hid it when they questioned him, and was scheming.

I walk this winding road up over a few switchbacks, then the paved portion stops. There's a quiet, small hotel with a view. No one's around. The road reverts to a rustic path overgrown with dry grass, burnt in the hot sun. It has wide tire marks in it. I vaguely remember this part of the road, on our way out.

Earlier today. Seems like a week ago.

I limp down the path on the sore ankle I got jumping down to the funicular track bed. I wince with pain and frustration; I'm not mobile enough, not fast enough to get away. I come upon a small patch of woods and field planted with corn and other crops. I can see the lake in the distance, all of its contours and peninsulas, the leftover cities on the shoreline, a blanket of hot haze suspended over it.

I figure I've climbed up at least two thousand feet. I'm too tired to look for the van anymore. I need just a little shut-eye, I think. If I can only just close my eyes, for a short spell.

I hear the rush of water through the trees. Beneath me, in a deep gully, a narrow river flows swiftly down over rocks toward the lake. From where I'm standing, there are moss-covered rocks, then a steep drop-off of about 30-40 feet to the river. I keep walking.

I find a place in the shade by a tree and lie down with my sweatshirt crushed up beneath my face. For some reason, it's not exactly logical, I feel like I'm safe now, and I pass out. I wake up to loud squawks from a raven; I open my eyes and see it flapping its black wings against a white sky.

Who knows how many minutes and hours have past?

I get up sluggishly. The country path through the woods seems more familiar. I'm still thirsty and hungry as hell, but somewhat recovered. I'm glad to be out of

Simone's peculiar, obsessive clutches.

I can still see the lake through the trees, and around a few bends of the path, there's the van! Parked in the grasses off the road. Thank God Harry slipped me the keys. My escape doesn't seem quite so rash anymore.

I suddenly feel awful, staring at the vehicle. I feel violence coming on, like some kind of sinister premonition. I write the emotion off to generally feeling "off," from stress, and the exertions and persecution of being a fugitive. It doesn't feel over, until I find Jason, recover Gwen and Harry, get safe.

I unlock the driver's door and lunge for a water container and my backpack, with the medical kit, on the back seat. Zinc, vitamin D, magnesium, vitamin C; I wash down all the pills and liquids with half a liter of stagnant water from a wine sack we brought. I find leftover road-trip food in a canvas bag; a stale loaf of bread and a jar of caky yellow butter, one inch left.

I'm ravenous and enervated; I chow down the dry food two-handed, washing it down with the water. I find extra clothes and stash them away, after pulling on a cleaner T-shirt. I desperately want to use the van as a resting place, but I don't want to be discovered by Simone's paramilitary goons.

I don't have much of a choice. The sun dips behind the dark-green, forested peaks, plunging the woods and the fields into shadows. I want to stay out of sight, in these dark woods. No fires for now; no outdoor camping.

This won't be the first time I've slept in an abandoned car. Harry and I did it when we were kids. We hung out in the rusted hulk of a Volkswagen minus its tires, the seats all ripped, shabby, and stained. It sat in an empty lot in London, amongst the weeds and the broken pavement and the piss spots left over from the drunks and the vagrants. It nonetheless was a cherished playroom and refuge for us. We pretended to drive it, sitting propped up in the driver's seat and jerking around the floppy, dead steering wheel.

I think of us in that wreck as I turn the key in the ignition, change gears, then inch the van in reverse, farther back into the woods, hiding the rear two-thirds of the vehicle in clumps of foliage and low-lying branches.

I make a nest in the back seat out of blankets and clothes, sinking down into it on my back. Moonlight leaks into the vehicle's interior. I only hear the wind, like a train that begins at the lake, plows through the trees, subsides to stillness, only to begin again like the plangency of ocean waves.

I imagine Harry, 14 y.o., laughing and pumping the squeaky clutch and the greasy accelerator of the rusted Volkswagen; me, five y.o., holding a soldier doll in the back seat and staring out the window at empty buildings guarding the Thames. That was my neighborhood, not a kilometer from my home near St. Paul's Cathedral. I pass out thinking of it, remembering it fondly.

# #

I'm splayed out on my back, on a wet pier on Lake Geneva, like a hooked carp drug out of the water. Standing above me are Simone and one of her goons, both wearing sunglasses, and they're throwing a net over me, and I can't move, and I wake up with a jerk of my right arm, then I unsteadily move to a sitting position.

Morning; a pink sunrise through trees. I work my ankle around and it's sore, on second thought, it doesn't feel *too* bad, considering what it's been through.

I open the door, lightly step down on the ground. Everything's quiet; the tree branches move in barely perceptible whispers. The scent is of sweet wet grass; the sun is promising, the lake a darker blue, and as empty as the sky.

Day 2 on Lac Leman. *Find Jason. This has gone on long enough. The days on the road from London, then locking horns with "the authorities."* I drink more water, take more vitamins and minerals, feeling recovered, compared with yesterday. I sense a vagrant, single-minded purpose, a faintly bubbling energy.

I need to pee. I walk down the country lane through the grass. I hear the implacable water rushing through the woods below. Where does it come from? I think. Are there complex warrens of underground chambers, full of water? Only the tallest mountains have melting snow. *Remember to fill your water bottles from that water down there.*

I have the cricket bat with me, the Swiss knife folded up in a side pocket of my trousers. I walk through some moist mossy woods by the road and do my business, then re-emerge onto the path.

I see a black Land Rover parked on the road, brake lights on. They go out. A man in a starched white uniform, navy cap, and armed with one of those ugly nightsticks, steps out.

I duck back into the woods.

CHAPTER 40

He takes his hat off and wipes sweat off his brow. He has a black crew cut and a small, fierce face.

I crouch down on my haunches, watching. I hear the river. The wind shakes the leaves, with angled sunlight casting thin shadows at my feet. He looks both ways up the path, then walks toward where I parked the van. I forgot to lock it, shit. *Shit shit.* Almost everything that I need and cherish is in the van. I come out of the woods and creep along, without a clue what I'm going to do.

I ***know*** he's looking for me. If he gets the van, all I can do is flee into the woods with the key, but they can still ransack and search it.

The guy finds the van, slides back the side-panel door. He pulls out the blankets I slept with, my sweatshirt, the bottles I drank from, litters the nearby ground with this stuff. He's going through our maps, one of Harry's satchel bags. He strews things around the ground like a foraging animal would, a hungry dog.

I see him steal my own and my Mom's diary. He tucks them under an arm, slides and slams the vehicle's door. Stops and looks around. I'm crouched behind a tree. ***My Mom's diary.*** He has it, tucked into an armpit. My fists clench and unclench.

My face feels red and hot. He walks down the road toward me. He's short, broad-shouldered, has a pug's face, the truculent look of a Marseille wharf rat. This mean little face, never pleased, always seeking revenge. I recognize it, from the road, those late-night hooligans on the main French highway. Harry firing the gun into the starlight. The voice inside says, ***he cannot be reasoned with.***

I unfold the Swiss knife; I've got that in my right hand and the bat in my left. I'm a righty. Harry always says, "You think you're ambidextrous, but you're a rightly girl, if I saw one."

I step out from behind the tree.

"You've taken my things from the van." He looks up at me beady-eyed, stops walking. "Put them back please."

"Who are you?"

"Emma. Who are you?"

"Jacques Boucher. Emma who?"

"None of your business."

I don't say anything more. He stares at me with a vacuous smile. "Oh I know. You're Winslow," he says, with the trace of a French accent. I didn't like hearing the name my father gave me come out of his mouth. My grip on the knife tightens.

"Give me those books. They're not yours. Those are special personal documents. They're my personal property."

He laughs insolently.

"You're wanted. By the authorities. Come with me Winslow. You have to get in the vehicle. Get over there."

"Put those books on the ground. Those are important to me. You have no use for them. They come from London." I sense my voice constrict, going up an octave. "Then go away in your car."

"No more nonsense, beech. Get your ass in this vehicle."

"The fuck I will."

His laughs acidly while walking towards me, giving off an air of menace.

"Now *you're* trying to give the orders." I walk away from him, around the back of the Rover.

When he gets to the Rover, he reaches down to take out the taser from where it's tucked into a holster. It has a black grip and a yellow barrel. I swing around the vehicle, back toward its front, and I can't believe I'm doing this. I plunge the knife into the thick, right front tire of the truck. I hear the hiss of escaping air.

Those cruel eyes go narrow and beady. "*Merde*!" he yells. I run, still clutching the bat, around its middle, like a spear. I see him drop the diaries onto the ground.

Emma Winslow, Vevey, Switzerland, June 21, 2051

Thank God I got back both of our diaries, including my Mom's priceless record of her experience, and the one

I write in now. My Mom's diary is the only record I have of her, period. In London, at least to me, the book might as well be the Koran or the Bible. I've always used it as a touchstone to keep me going through life's miseries and hazards.

So I had to do anything to protect it.

Eventful day. I woke up yesterday, went to pee, and when I came back, one of the Lac Leman goons was rummaging through our stuff in the van. Apparently, he moonlights as a highwayman, because we'd had a run-in with him. I confronted "Jacques." He'd stolen and was leaving with my diaries.

Mind you, I'm not a violent person by nature or outlook. I can't even get myself to evict a daddy long-legs from the tub, for fear one of his legs will break off. In fact, I will assist a drowning daddy long-legs spider in the tub. So confronting this vicious man, armed with a taser, was indescribably scary and painful.

To prevent him from leaving with me and the diaries, I punctured his tire with my jack knife! Violent act #1, not proud of it. Oh, maybe you could count earlier in the day when I shoved Simone! This stocky little man with beady eyes and crooked teeth went after me, but before he could engage that taser, I swung the cricket bat with all my might (almost nine stone or 126 pounds of me), smacking him in the upper arm or shoulder, which at least slowed him down. Then I blinded him with a handful of loose dirt thrown in his face, and ran.

I ran along the edge of this ravine, sore ankle and everything. A river ran over rocks way down there. Thought I could lose him in the woods. He seemed like a dumb, one-dimensional mammal, no finesse, all rage and attack. Half blind from the dirt, he blundered along behind me, keeping up pretty well. I was bloody bloody bloody scared, thought he'd throttle me if he caught me.

Imagine it. I'm hopping over roots and slippery leaves and rocks on a sore ankle, just the sort of wild aggro run I'd do with my mates or Harry in the City of London.

He slipped and lost his footing trying to stay with me. He tumbled all the way down onto the rocks and river. When I looked over, he was face down and not moving.

That was not my fault or my doing, but I suppose I have to take some of the blame since I had enraged him, but I was undoubtedly taking evasive action from him, the aggressor. Violent act #2, he drowns. I didn't do it either by accident or premeditation, case closed.

So my fugitive status, on merely Day 2 in Lake Geneva, is emphatic. I feel like I have no future here, an awful sensation. This is a spectacularly beautiful place, but authoritarian and control-freaky Lac Leman District 10 is not for me.

I gathered all my things from the van, including the diaries, locked it, and went back down the country lane to search out those nearby farm fields. I looked down into the gully, and this Jacques bloke was gone. Gone!

He lived after all, rolled out of the stream, dragged his arse somewhere else! I looked around and didn't see him. I figured he was hurt, licking his wounds somewhere. I must admit I'm partly glad he lived, so I don't have that on my conscience. Violent act #2.

But now he's still after my arse.

I thought for a moment and told myself, stay on task.

Protect myself and #1 find Jason, #2 make sure Harry and Gwen are free, and doing okay. Change of plans. I went back to the van, stealthily, aware that crazy wrathful Jacques will stagger out of the woods like a reanimated Frankenstein, to wreak his revenge on me.

I got back into the van and started it up. Now I planned to move the van to a secluded, more hidden locale. I figured this unpaved road led only to one place, a dead end at the top of the mountain, so I maneuvered in a seven-point turn and got going in the other direction.

By driving slowly in low gear, through the scrubby overgrowth on the roadside, I got around the disabled Rover, with my knife still sticking out of the right-front tire. I stopped the van, got out, recovered the knife. I drove back to the paved part of the road, the one that goes down to the lake.

Still no sign of Jacques. The roads were empty.

There are small, potentially uninhabited chalets on this road. I planned to park my vehicle in a back lot and hole up in one of those chalets, until I could find Jason.

I started down the road, very steep with switchbacks going back and forth. It seemed even steeper going downhill; the van was tippy swerving into the first hairpin turn, so I decided to slow down, descend at a crawl, just to be safe, but that tactic induced me to ride the brakes. Bad idea.

The brakes got spongy and loose. When's the last time these brakes have been checked? I thought, but one road trip too late. On the next turn the brake lever went all the way down to the floor. They were gone. I went hurtling down the next straightaway, screaming at the top of my lungs, like some brat on a roller coaster, but this was for real.

CHAPTER 41

The van picks up speed, my heart is in my throat, I pump the brakes wildly. I don't bother to try to make the turn, flying into the opposite lane as I approach the next switchback. I'm lucky that no cars, horses, or bicycles come up the hill at that precise moment, or I would have creamed 'em.

I throw on the emergency brake as the van smashes into the curb by the roadside, raising a cloud of dust inside the sooty vehicle, which bounds over the curb with a crash of hard tires on concrete and continues on out of control, slamming through a hedgerow. I scream bloody murder and the van careens downhill on grass, its speed arrested only slightly by the emergency brake.

I barrel down into a gully full of trees, and as far as I know, I'm heading for a cliff. This is a mountain road. The probability of a soft landing is nil. Thoughts crowding my mind in a five-second span: stay with the van and count on the trees stopping it, or take the chance and open the driver door and eject. I go for the latter. Even with the emergency brake on, the van has all the feel of a large metal coffin.

The front grill crushes a barbed wire fence and the van picks up more speed as now I'm on a slope akin to a moderate ski piste. Images of fiery crashes and rolling vehicles and burning bodies flood my mind. I hesitate for one second, the door partially open, then leap out on my strong ankle, landing awkwardly, rolling, on a tilled field of sheep tracks and dung and rutty, hard-dried mud. I strike something–a root–with the side of my head, and that's the last of what I remember of the wildest, shortest drive in all my oh so brief history as a car driver.

I was out cold, June 21, 2051, roughly 1,500 feet above Vevey, Lake Geneva, and 800 feet below where we'd parked the van.

# #

I wake up in a bed. A duvet covers me, on a cushy mattress. The room is small, with wooden walls, an open porcelain basin, a window that cranks open and has a view of the lake. Old Europe from pictures, I think. I'm still in the clothes I drove in, vivid mud-stains on the right side of my trousers. I have a patch on my head; I touch it delicately.

I don't have the prototypical pounding, blinding headache. I have a woozy dizziness. My head goes back on the pillow, a nice soft down-filled one. There's a painting of lakes and mountains across the room. *Shit, I'm alive!* I move my legs up and down; fine. I clench and unclench my fists.

That reminds me of fighting with Jacques, and I think, *where are the diaries, of all things? Which I put my life on the line for?* Just how badly did I fuck up?

Where is the van? And what day is it?

I have distant memories of rolling over several times, soft pillows, comfortable duvet, darkness; putting myself back to sleep. Trying to get up, give up. Go back to sleep. It's the next day, it's June 22.

I think of Jason. I think, whoever did this for me, is one more person in my life for whom I'm grateful.

I still have to find Jason, but first, the, no doubt, *wreckage* of the van, and my backpack and diaries.

I burst out into tears, just as the door opens. I wonder if it's going to be one of Simone's people, a goon squad member, Lac Leman District 10. But she's a kind-looking, older woman in a long plain dress, carrying a plastic tray.

"Oh no, do you feel okay? Are you sad?" She sets the tray down on a nearby table.

I wipe the tears away. "No, I'm okay. Where am I?"

"You're at a farm, dear, Domaine de Crevie. You had an accident, dear. One of the farm hands found you, brought you here. We had a doctor look at you. He'll be in here in a second. Would you like some soup and tea? I brought it."

"Very much so. Thanks so much. Is the van...?"

"A tractor is towing the vehicle out. It has a few big dents, but hasn't been completely ruined, I don't think. No, it can be fixed. Don't you worry about the van, dear."

"Okay. What day is it, Mum?"

She thinks for a moment. "It's Thursday, June 22." She laughs softly. "You slept for a day."

"Oh. You've been so kind."

"I hope you feel better." She smiles, turns, goes out the door, shuts it softly. I feel like I'm in a hospital, circa nineteenth century.

I pick up the soup bowl and take small, determined sips. I feel out-of-it to the point where if I got up and walked quickly, I'd puke. I sip the tea. So now I've got a sore ankle, the aftermath of a head blow, and who knows what else. My first instinct is to recover my things and go back to London.

Cry, take my toys, and go home.

I hear footsteps outside. The door opens, a tall man with thinning gray hair and a pleasant expression enters. He carries a satchel.

"I'm Dr. Braden. How are you feeling?"

"Okay I guess. Thank you." Ah, so this is the Dr. Randolph Braden I've been hearing about. A mixed bag. Grace, the nurse, told me he has a bad reputation for concocting bogus herbal remedies. But Jason works for him...I won't tell him I know Jason, yet, I think. It doesn't feel like the right time.

"We found you in the field. You'd had a concussion. Do you have a headache?"

"No, I'm a little dizzy."

"You should stay put for a little while, don't move. Where did you come from?"

I take a deep breath. I want my vitamins and minerals! "I came from London a few days ago, with friends. We're emigrating, at least for a short time, to the Lake Geneva region. Hasn't gone that well so far..."

He chuckles, seems like a good lot. Is it always fair to go by the reputations that follow people around, that shadow them, or by instincts and first or second impressions?

"How's the food going down?" he asks.

"Good so far. It's delicious."

"That's a good sign. The dizziness is normal. If you don't have a headache or nausea, then maybe the concussion wasn't so bad." ***I know,*** I feel like telling him. I was a nurse. I am, a nurse.

"I think I'll stay a little while longer," I say.

"That's wise."

"They towed our van?"

"Yes. It seems to be in one piece. Not sure how drivable without some work. What happened?"

"The brakes went. So at least brakes have to be added to the repair list." He chuckles again.

"In that case, you were lucky."

"Can I ask you something?"

"Of course. What do I call you, by the way?"

"Emma."

"Pretty name. Emma from London."

"Could someone fetch my backpack from the vehicle and bring it here?"

"I don't see why not. So, let's see. You don't have nausea, but clearly you have a head blow. I can give you something for the dizziness, it's a mixture of herbs, Ancient Chinese Medicine."

"No thanks, I think I just need more rest. And I'm a bit concerned about my possessions."

"Also, we have a tricky virus going around. Did they tell you about that already? It's serious business, and if and when you're up and about going down into the towns, you have to wear a mask and keep your distance from people."

"They did tell me about that. I do have a mask."

"Brilliant. Okay Emma, rest up, relax, and we'll get you that backpack."

"Thank you." He smiles again, then he too opens the door, leaves, closes it gingerly. Not a bad bloke, good bedside manner. I still need Jason, someone who knows me, to give me a hug. I still have that inclination to find them all, including Harry, and flee home to London. Home.

June 22, 2051, I spend it in bed, drinking soup and tea, then getting up and trying my legs and testing my ankle and looking out the window. The whirling stops after a while. All day, I recover. They bring me my backpack, delivering bliss. I wash down my vitamins and minerals with tea.

I sleep, savor their generous breakfast, then I open the door and step out into the fields and vineyards again, eager to get on with the rest of my life.

CHAPTER 42

Emma Winslow, June 23, 2051, above Vevey and Lake Geneva.

I gathered all my things and left the little farmhouse. They gave me a big breakfast of scrambled eggs and fruit and real local cheese, I needed it. Then I caught a ride back up the mountain on a horse and wagon. Dr. Braden's main farmhouse, as part of Domaine de Crevie, is not far from the hairpin mountain road where I had my perilous ride.

I never told them or mentioned anything about the creep Jacques. Apparently, he's alive. Haven't thought about him much. That chapter is over. I hope that chapter is over.

I saw a road, connected to the hairpin turns, leading into one of the farm fields. The tractor driver told me the doctor lives up here. That is where I hoped to find Jason, or someone who knows him.

It was a nice, temperate, sunny day. I kept on going down the road to the house. I saw a woman in a country dress. She was carrying two heavy grocery bags with handles up the road. She walked slowly, almost languidly. A small boy came toward her up the lane, from the opposite direction. She said something to him, gesturing to one of the bags. He shook his head "no." She appeared to upbraid him for ignoring her request, but kept going. She'd apparently bought groceries somewhere. Here, they have to do a lot of walking, I thought. It makes them stronger.

The boy sauntered toward me. When he got close, I said "Hey kid. Whose farm is this?" He shrugged.

"I'm Emma. What's your name?"

"Willie."

"Hello Willie. Do you live here?"

"Oui." He spoke French, and at least understood English.

"Where's your Mom?" He shrugged again, but this time in a lighter way. He looked away.

"Elle est morte."

"Oh no, I'm so sorry." Now I wished I never asked. "Is the farm this way?"

"Yes."

"Okay. I'm glad I met you Willie. Sorry I don't know much French. They don't speak it where I'm from."

"Where?"

"Old London. England."

"The London Eye," he said.

"That's right! The London Eye." He dug around in his back pocket and pulled out a crumpled postcard. It showed the special ferris wheel that used to, so long ago, give giddy tourists high views of the River Thames. He held it out to me. I turned it over in my hands.

It had Jason's handwriting on the back.

Is your father named Jason? I asked Willie, with a too demanding, frantic tone.

"Oui. Yes." I asked where Jason was. "La," he pointed toward the woods above us.

"Where in the woods, exactly?" I said, staring up into the thick forest, which covered the hillside and kept on going up into the mountains.

"Up there, cutting wood."

"Can you show me?" I said. He led me up a footpath. I could see more than one farm building in the distance. A black dog, with splashes of white, ran through a field nearby and over a hill. It was either harassing or herding a scattered flock of fat gray sheep.

The boy watched and smiled as we walked. He expertly whistled for the dog with two fingers placed in his mouth. He had Jason's sandy red hair, and I detected a certain swagger in his carefree manner. Coming face to face with Willie, I couldn't hide it, I was jealous. Resentful. I'd come all this way and had seriously hostile confrontations to deal with as a consequence (I wanted to start over in Lake Geneva). I could never be as close to this child as Jason. He was the walking-talking embodiment of Jason's other life, the one he hid from me for so long.

I was jittery, antsy, holding my forehead as I walked.

I had my own agenda, more important than this dog that ran toward us over the field.

"Can we find Jason now? Please?"

"Quel?" the boy said, as though he was now pretending to be cheeky and not speak English. I was so close to Jason I felt like I could touch him, smell his breath, bury my nose in his thick, reddish hair. It hadn't been weeks since I'd seen his note.

I was getting cross with Willie, couldn't help it: "Your dad, I have to find him. Now!"

I felt alone, isolated, preyed upon. Jason's my only friend, outside of Harry and his girl, in this strange, beautiful land, with its lake like an inland sea and its dark, labyrinthine forests. The forests where a new people struggle to survive; the trees where bad men like Jacques go to hide.

They'll try to pin that rat Jacque's injuries on me, I thought. We continued along what's like a sheep's track, as the dog sprinted right up to us and past, as though it had suddenly changed its mind.

A man came out from the edge of the woods, wearing work clothes, covered head to toe in wood chips and mud.

Coveralls, muddy boots, a yellow scarf holding back a full head of curly, reddish-blond hair. He stood in the field in the sunlight and looked at me quietly. I broke out into a run, gimpy ankle and all.

Jason.

CHAPTER 43

"Emma!"

I stagger into his rough embrace and kiss. A big sloppy one, then he holds me out in front of him, so he can get a good look. We hardly did this in London, when we weren't drunk or high. He's shocked, giddily happy.

"I thought I wouldn't see you," he says emphatically. "I thought it might be months, or never!" I crush my face into his sweatshirt where it bunches up on his shoulder. I smell an earthy mixture of wood smoke and weed.

It goes on like that for...I don't know how long. The earth rotates too fast for my feet. I sway in his arms. I finally found him again.

"Whatever you're smoking, give me some of that!" I say.

"Serious?"

"Yes!"

"What's happened to you?" My eyes fill with angry tears.

"They're all after me here, this crazy place. Some lady named Simone, she wants to use us as guinea pigs. She sent one of her goon squad guys up here to get me."

"Jesus Emma, calm down. You're alright. You're with me now." I wipe the tears with my sleeve; take some deep breaths. I see the kid petting the dog behind us. A farm tractor rides up from below.

More composed, I say, "*You* seem good. I met Willie. He seems like a good kid. Is his mother really gone?"

"Yes." Jason's hands drop to his sides. "Amelia passed before I got here. Willie was staying with another lady, but now he's up at the farm with me and the others, Dr. Braden."

"Dr. Randolph Braden, right? Yes, I've met him. To make a long story short..." I touch the bandage on my head.

"What happened to you?"

"I crashed our van when the brakes failed. I think it's going to be alright."

"What about you?"

"I'll be fine. Got a small concussion. A kind lady looked after me for a couple of days, and your Dr. Braden patched me up. I appreciate that."

"He's a good bloke, when you get to know 'im."

"You know he was shamed and banished from London for trying to make rogue, untested medicines?"

"Who told you that?"

"My friend Grace. She's a nurse."

"Well, at the moment, he pays good wages. He's my

employer. We're making dairy products and wine up here in the hills. He does a little doctoring. Not much talk about medicine. I don't know about that." I feel I'm raining on his parade, his new gambit.

We walk slowly back toward the farmhouse. "What did Amelia die of? She was quite young, eh?"

"Unknown. There's something deadly going around. Everyone has to wear masks down below, in crowds. You should know that."

"Believe me, I do. I came with Harry and his girlfriend Gwen. The so-called authorities might still be holding them in Vevey. They're like the customs officials from hell. I have no problems with masks, but some bogus vaccine they're making...there are no labs here, equipped to make a proper one. We don't even know what the pathogen is."

"What?"

"I know. You must not know what I'm talking about. I've read the books and papers, the ones my mother had. They had some kind of a plague catastrophe here, so they're jumping the gun on solutions...that's dangerous."

He has no response. He doesn't want to talk about it.

I swallow hard, holding the bandage firmly on my head. "Jason, I don't want to stay in this place. I don't even think they'll have me. We can go with Willie to some place else in the countryside. Another lake, another mountain."

"Emma, I just got here. I have work, and it's better than London. Trust me. Let's go back to the farmhouse, relax. Willie likes it here too," he adds.

"Jason, now that we're together...I'm sorry, but this

place has been nothing but trouble. We can find another one. This here is a whole region of mountains and lakes. The Alps." My hand sweeps the view of Lake Geneva and mountains, as far as we can see. It's a landscape of limitless opportunities, the terrain of our future.

"Emma, you should hear yourself. This was Willie's and his Mom's home. I don't think I should take it away from him. I think that would be cruel."

Jason is stubborn, and I'm in no mood, nor do I have the energy, to mount the Great Debate of Our Future in the here and now.

We walkup the dirt road where I originally saw the woman and her groceries. Another wagon makes its way up the main mountain road, then stops. I see two people step down from the wooden platform, the second, a woman, weakly and unsteadily.

"Harry!" I yell excitedly, then turning to Jason, "It's Harry and Gwen!"

Harry looks only slightly more put together than I do. He wears an irritated grimace, seems emboldened and preoccupied.

"Gwen needs a doctor," he calls over. "She's really not doing good. We hid out for a couple of days on a boat. Where've you been?"

"Around. It's a long story. Where's the boat? Jason, maybe we can take this boat out of here." If Jason can make plans based solely on his own instincts, then I can.

"Yeah, we slipped away when you ran," Harry says. "Then a fisherman down there was nice enough to have us on his boat. He fishes, and cleans up the floating wood debris on the shoreline. I gave the bloke some of my

Euros. Then we came up to check out you and the van. I figured you made it back. I knew you would."

"Have you seen Simone since we had it out with her?"

"No. We wore our masks and kept out of sight."

"Let's get Gwen to the farmhouse...I'll tell you about the van later."

"What happened to your head?"

"About the van..." My voice trails off. Jason and Harry end up taking each one of Gwen's arms, and we walk slowly toward two farm buildings across the fields. Responsive, but fuzzy and lethargic, Gwen's running a high fever.

This isn't opiates withdrawal, I think. *It's a virus, brought over from London. It was probably already present here.*

I'm still carrying the folded up knife. I'm still wary of the slim chance that the enemies I've already made in this area will catch up to me.

Jason seems more shocked than overjoyed to see me. Maybe I startled him. Maybe he doesn't truly want me here. Doubts begin to plague me. *He did write that letter to me. Maybe it's only a fleeting mood, but this version seems like a different Jason than the one who poured his emotions and devotion into that note.*

Maybe he's met somebody else. He's always been dynamic that way. He can't be alone, not for a moment.

I've always known Jason was volatile, carrying significant baggage. Everyone did then; we young Londoners are a society of orphans. The original state of abandonment and loneliness is branded in our souls, so we spend the rest of our lives looking for someone who can heal that.

As nearly a toddler, Jason had to weather some painful blows, before he was equipped to deal with them. He doesn't talk about it. I got his background secondhand, because there's always some snotty-nosed kid in the London ruins who knows the history of his mates.

Jason had two intact parents for a moment in time, unlike me. He had a brother Ralph, two years younger, who he resented for the attention he lost when Ralph was born. The brother died, the cause was thought to be botulism, a loss which drove Jason's Mom mad and unstable with grief. She resented the rebellious and pugnacious Jason, despite his arresting blue eyes, fair mop of hair, and strong chin, because he wasn't the saintly Ralph. She kicked him out of the house.

He was on the street, with Harry's gang for a while, before another couple, over 50 and veterans of the plague that killed their own kids, took him in.

He made an attempt to mend ties with his real parents. Who would have the gumption to do that, at such a young age, when a typical child, harshly rejected once, has the natural inclination to only submerge himself in his mates? But his real parents caught the barmy fever and died. He actually saw them, crossing a Thames bridge with an infected, demented herd, having lost their minds and their souls. He was 12.

These experiences molded his psyche for the future, as they do for everyone. He became independent, valiant, bitter and intense.

Jealousy and indecision flood my mind as we all enter

the main house: me, Jason, Willie, Gwen, and Harry. Up close, the building can hardly be called a farmhouse, a description that is not grand enough. Domaine de Crevie is more like a small castle. It has at least three floors and an attic, round, stained-glass windows, several dormers and tall, brick chimneys.

The spacious grounds, with its hedges and slopes and grapevines, seem unkempt, as if the groundskeepers had all fled its lazy owner.

The interior smells like wood smoke and a delicious stew. Jason tells me they have an "attached pub" around the back of the building, but that "they don't call them pubs here." I'm impressed and relieved, it feels like we're checking into a grand hotel.

We take off shoes and shed the muddy outer layers in the front hall. I tell Jason I have to wash my clothes and maybe borrow some, until I can get into the van again. He shrugs; this kind of stuff isn't his domaine. I'll have to find some for myself.

"There must be maids here?"

"Yes, there are girls who work here." I can get some clothes from them, I think. My trousers are still stained with long-dried sheep dung and mud, my shirtsleeves spotted with dried blood from my crash injury. Willie might be the only clean one among us. He disappears somewhere in the house, with the dog.

Gwen has declined over the days I haven't seen her. The first order of business is getting her to bed, and some treatment. I offer her several rounds of my supplement store; she needs the zinc, vitamin C and D, and magnesium; large doses.

I study her pallid face; white with a tinge of blue. Harry tells me that she's been back and forth with a high fever. They gave her lots of water and fish on the boat. She needs sunshine too; rest and predictability, just like I do.

I think of that sick lad on the Blackfriars Bridge. Something's spreading. It's not addiction to medications or junky opiates. She has caught the Blackfriars boy's plague.

CHAPTER 44

Jason takes me up a winding flight of stairs, then around back to the room where he's staying. The first thing I notice is a big-bellied porcelain tub placed almost in the center of the room.

"I could do with some of that," I say, walking over to the tub. I switch on the water and a thick stream splashes on the clean scrubbed bottom. I let it run over my hand; he also has a dormer window, and a view of foliage, green slopes, and an empty sky. It seems a solemn university quad could lie below, like where I used to hang out in King's College, the unused campus on St. Thomas St., London.

"You have hot water!"

"It's in short supply," Jason says. "We're allowed one wash per day." I turn off the water, pad over to the window.

"This is your home now? They've given you this nice room, your very own?" His digs are better than they were in London, emphatically a step above. They're better than my old place.

"For the time being." I see the lake and mountains, too. I move over to the big bed, which has thick pillows, blankets, room for at least two, and a wooden headboard. I sit on it and test its bounciness. "So comfy...I could crash out, right now."

"You can sleep here, with me." His invitation seems matter-of-fact, and I have this thought, *we're finally together, perhaps for good.*

"But we can eat first down at the kitchen. The food is more varied than a pub, and involves more than just getting monged on pints."

We didn't truly have the pubs of old in London anymore, but we brewed beers and actively consumed them. Lake Geneva is wine country.

The room has a shelf full of old, hardcover books. I love everything about this bedroom.

Jason helps me change the bandage on my head; I didn't need stitches but still have to keep an eye on the tender, walnut-sized lump just below the hairline, which has gone from purple to yellow.

The afternoon and evening go by. In the atmosphere of the big house, run by "the good doctor," I sense a palpable pause, like the darkening horizon before a storm.

We put Gwen to bed, after she devours my supplements with water. Then for her, it's mint tea with honey and lemon, a visit with Dr. Braden, and sleep.

I feel safe, for once, behind the walls of the vineyards. Jacques and Simone seem miles away.

We go down to "the pub," passing through a main room that has thick rugs, oil paintings of the mountains and a former king and queen, a stuffed stag's head, a large chessboard. A deep fireplace with easy chairs in front of it reinforces the impression of a traditional hunting lodge.

The kitchen or serving area is also wood-paneled, with lamps that cast a soft yellow glow. We sit on sturdy wood benches covered with sheep skins, eating rabbit stew with onions, carrots, garlic, and fresh bread loaves embedded with olives. Real butter melts on the bread, washed down with the local white wine and cold water.

I devour it greedily.

One glass of wine does it for me. I sense an internal glow, just short of dizziness. After all, I'm just coming off a head injury and a terrifying van accident.

We got word that the van was towed. It awaits us on a gravel clearing where they park wagons and trucks nearby the house. A girl who works in the kitchen gave me a flannel nighty that fits well enough on my increasingly gaunt frame.

I can't let myself drop below eight stone or 112 pounds. Eat, when you have the opportunity!

The girl, whose name is Jessica, is my age. She came from somewhere in the former Germany, with her brother and mother, but they were assaulted by bandits on the northern road. Her brother was killed. Her mother was the lady lugging the groceries that I saw before. The mother wants to go back to her own home ground, which is the border of Italy and Switzerland, a stretch of shoreline along a large lake called Lago Maggiore.

Going there would do me good, too, I think.

Jessica gives me a beige cloth robe that wraps around the nighty. I thank her and she closes the door. I hear muffled voices through walls and floors. Jason is gabbing and joking with the lads he works with, and Harry, while they're having more pints. They're typically not wine drinkers. I hear one muffled voice telling a story, usually Harry, then they all burst out laughing. It's as close as Jason's going to get to a merry pub scene.

If they're too loud and rowdy, the bloody Brits!–we'll get kicked out of this polite, calm house.

I push the faint, deep-throated voices and laughter to the edges, as the sun goes down for the evening and envelopes the room in darkness. I pull the blankets over my head and pass out.

Jason keeps his window open a crack, providing a cool breeze that I sense only on my face, when I sporadically peak out from beneath the covers. It's the middle of the night; the moonlight leaks through the window, where the curtain is partially drawn. I hear crickets. I sense Jason's weight under the blankets, his thick, sun-lightened hair on the pillow, crushed up against his face.

I imagine semi-tropical lake shores, swimming in the sunshine of the lake, the warm sun on my face. I fall quickly back into dreams that for once aren't ominous or threatening.

# #

I lay under the covers for a while, watching daylight grow stronger through the window. The sleep was deep, restorative. Jason didn't go for me last night, in bed. I wondered about that, him drinking pints and all. At least last night, we weren't ready for the heavy petting and everything that comes after it. He let me sleep, I let him.

I gaze at the tub, the big-bellied inviting tub.

I don't know what I would have done if he started caressing me under the covers. Yes, I do, of course I would've given into it. He pushes my buttons. In London, it was all heavy petting. I hadn't let him shag me yet. I'm a virgin, lily white Emma at 22 years of age. Of course, I'm curious about what he'd feel like; I'm a flower all too ready to be pollinated. But I don't want to get pregnant, until I absolutely do.

I think of all these things as I sit on the edge of the bed and Jason, tied up in the covers, quietly snores. It'll happen, soon. I remember my mother's stories about pregnancy, and the assumed pregnancy with her New York boyfriend Will, which never came to be, despite a dramatic build-up.

I don't want mine to be quite so dramatic.

What's important is the alchemy of the two of us together, almost the entire reason for me leaving London, other than seeking adventure. Which I got in spades.

I move over to the tub, turn it on, push the socket plug into its hole. I watch the water splatter on the porcelain, hold my hand out, feel its warmth. I walk over and shut the window all the way. There's a glass bottle with a rubber stopper sitting on a small wooden stand near the tub. It contains liquid soap. I pick it up, unstopper it, as the sound of the water deepens, filling the tub. The soap is lavender. I drop the nightly, sensing my ribs, a bit gaunt, goose bumps on my breasts.

The cool air is unpleasant, so I escape it by stepping into the water, now hot. The water's halfway up my shins; it's been perhaps two weeks since I've had a complete bath, a good deep scrub. I turn on the cold tap to even out the temperature. I sense Jason stirring in bed, then I lower myself into the water. Hmmmm...

I pour some of the lavender soap into the water; it forms a kind of slick on top, then bubbles. I wash all up and down my arms, lift a leg out of the water, wash behind the knee.

I look up and I see Jason standing, disheveled, by the bed, only in boxers. Behind the boxers is a rather obvious tumescence. He's half asleep and his boxers protrude dumbly, somewhat like seeing an animal's erection in a farmyard. But I'm feeling all kinds of tingles inside.

"So you like the bath, huh?" he mumbles.

"Come here, Jase," I say. "Join me."

"Kind of a small tub for two."

"There's room enough."

"Okay, so..." He pads over, wrestles down his boxers. His loins are ready; I sense a control over him, he could never help it. I pull back in the tub to make room for him. He scrunches down into the water, and the tired, impassive face breaks into a smile.

"Nice?"

"Smashing," he says. "Ta. Smells good."

Right away he strokes my leg, slippery with soap. Our legs are all tangled up. I smile at him, lift my torso and breasts out of the water. His eyes go wide. I'm in control, so much so that I giggle.

"Does that door lock?" I ask.

"Not really."

"Well, no one's really up but us."

"Guess not."

I stand up in the tub, proffering him the first look at my wet, matted pubic hair. Then I plop down into the water, straddling him. It's a wonderful, sneaky surprise as I get part of him in me; it's like two doors with a space between them. He'd made it through the first door. I feel as horny as a male and I push down all of him inside me.

"Oh!" he says, moving his hips against the weight of me. I've got a hand on each of the sides of the tub, steadying myself, as his face is almost pushed underwater. I'm in control, almost deviously, like Simone. I've got him at the end of a rope; that's the sensation, and a tremendous fullness and heat.

It's been worth the wait.

Not sure I better be getting myself pregnant now. But I am most assuredly deflowered.

"You tell me when you're about done."

He makes a noise of almost strangling.

"Now...Already."

I get off him and he says, "Oh. Oh. Oh. Aahn." Some of the stuff floats to the top of the water; it seems like glue, or a kind of soap.

# #

I pad across the wooden floor. I have a change of clothes, only one. A pair of trousers and a clean T-shirt. When I dress, I think of my clothes piled neatly on that rock near Lake Geneva. I think of keeping an eye on it during the blissful swim, just prior to Simone's stormy intrusion.

Jason has toweled himself off and crawled back into bed. Maybe it was with Grace, but I remember a chat about the post-coital time; men get tired and women get perky.

Like the voices I heard through the brick, stone, and wood of the sprawling house last night, the smell of breakfast seeps through the walls. Salty bacon, frying eggs; coffee. Jason pulls the covers over his head.

I finish dressing and head out the room, hungry as a lioness after the hunt and the kill.

I wonder who's at breakfast. I wonder who I'm going to find, and whether I'm going to run into the man of the house, the doctor. How's Gwen doing? I think.

The door shuts behind me with a soft click. No one's out in the hall. No one's on the wide staircase that I descend. I think I'm going to tell Gwen what happened with me and Jase. I have to tell someone. I have to tell another lady. Jase better not tell Harry. This is a test of his tactfulness. No kissing, then telling the boys. It's a test of his respect for me, and of his tactfulness toward what goes on between us.

CHAPTER 45

I hear soft, morning voices behind a partially open door, clinks of metal on plates. A cook in a white apron prepares breakfast behind a counter. I pause, take a seat. A young woman, not Jessica, drifts over, and I ask for some scrambled eggs, bacon, fruit, and coffee. She brings me the coffee; I sit and nurse it, gazing out a window. I see chickens fidget by on the grass of the lawn, that black-and-white dog from the day before sits by a fence, ignoring them.

The waitress sees me looking at the dog. She stands and wipes her hands with a small blue towel. "His name is Winston. Dr. Braden's wife named him after Winston Churchill, who named his cats after lords."

I laugh softly. "I'm Emma, by the way."

"Gretchen." She smiles and moves quickly away toward the kitchen.

If I move the curtain farther to the right, I see another five acres or so of vineyards, pale green leaves trembling in the sunlight. Beyond, the lake reflects the sun's rays flaring through a valley. I take pleasure in *this* moment: lake, vineyard, sun. Coffee. A plate arrives piled with breakfast, including hash, and cut-up apples. I didn't order the hash, but I'll take it.

"Ta. That's brilliant, thank you."

"Where did you come from, Emma?"

"London."

"Oh, I can't imagine a city that big."

"It used to be enormous. Only ten thousand people at most there now. I grew up there, with Jason."

"With Jason?" she says, with renewed interest.

"Yeah, Jason Hunter, the same guy who lives in this house. You must have seen him. Then again, he's only been here a few weeks."

"I know him," she says.

"Oh?"

"It's only small villages here. Everyone knows everyone." She shrugs.

"He's been here nary a month."

"We went down to the lake with some friends, once."

"Oh. Once?"

"We have parties, you know? We light bonfires at night. Nude swimming sometimes." She shrugs blithely, laughs.

"With Jason." A little drum starts beating inside me, war tom-toms.

"Yuh. He was there. Lots of people. You should try it some time. Listen, I have to go wait on some other people. It was nice meeting you."

"Ta." I glare and eat the toast, chewing with agitation.

I silently finish the rest of breakfast, then make my way back upstairs. Jason is probably still asleep. I think I really should check in on Gwen. She's had a tough trip, and Harry was down there quaffing pints with the lads.

Her room is two doors down from mine. I knock once, say her name, I don't hear anything. I turn the door knob, the lock clicks open. I slip into the room, not wanting to interrupt whatever might be going on.

When I step inside, my mouth drops. Gwen stands by the window without a shred of clothes on. Her feverish skin has the ashen pallor of a prisoner's in solitary confinement. She turns to me, with an empty glare, then she pads across the room like a bored cat and stands in front of a full-length mirror. She appears dizzy and unsteady, like she's going to pitch forward flat on her face. Her bed is a jumble of unmade covers; clothes are strewn on the floor.

"Gwen!" I shut the door behind me. "What are you doing? How are you feeling, dear?" She needs that doctor badly, I think. I wish I had the tools that I have in the London clinic; my various potions, made up of rosemary, saffron, turmeric, and essential oils like frankincense.

Gwen doesn't speak. Her chin moves up and down, but nothing comes out. Her hair appears matted and snarled, the blond beauty of a week ago has become drawn and waxen.

"Gwen, let's get you under the covers, okay? Let's get some clothes on." Not that I'm a prude or against nudity. Nothing wrong with "naked in the morning sun." I just swam *dénudé* in the lake, and it was divine. It's the warped nature of her nudity, however, that makes it different. She reminds me of the buck naked sods streaking through Southwark in London.

Her nakedness is more like a *symptom* than the healthy state I'd felt just hours ago.

Jessica enters the room. "Oh, I found her in the hallway, completely without clothes! I brought her in here and went to fetch some clean ones."

"Where's the doctor?"

"He's coming." Gwen still stands awkwardly by the mirror, then she turns and hisses, "I want to go to the Millennium Bridge. Remember? I want to go back to the city. I want to look down into the muddy river...and...and...I want to stare into that muddy river!" She seems crazed, possessed, but this place, as far as I know, doesn't have any dangerous opiates.

"Gwen," I say insistently, in a coaxing manner. "We have to put this on first."

Between me and Jessica, we approach her tentatively. She stares down at the nighty like it's a wicked, unappetizing plate of food we're forcing her to eat.

Jessica stands holding the nighty, reluctant to get closer. I go to the sink, wet a face cloth, return with it, gently pass it over Gwen's forehead, then wipe away her tears. She's crying, but it seems to be the old Gwen, trying to get out of this armor of madness that encases her. She submits to the wet cloth passively.

We lift the cotton nighty up and drop it over her head. I collect the rest of her clothes and pile them on a chair. The room has a stale, pissy odor, like some hospital wards.

"Isn't it contagious?" Jessica asks, wide-eyed, backing away, wearing her surgical mask. "Whatever she has, we should have our masks on all the time! We should take her down to the clinic by the lake!"

"Hand-washing is important, too," I mutter. "You won't need to go near her again. Go do that now. Wash your hands, thoroughly," I say, mildly irritated. I have to play the take-charge nurse again.

The morning, before, had such blissful detachment.

Jessica strides across the room to the open basin and splashes water on her hands and face, dries herself off.

"Are we in trouble? Will we get sick?" she asks over her shoulder, toweling off her face and nervously examining her eyes in the mirror.

"To be honest, I came all the way over here from London with Gwen. She wasn't feeling well, from the beginning. She's been a bit sickly, but I didn't suspect anything serious. I'd be sick by now if it was all that contagious." This reassures Jessica, for at least the moment.

I think of my mother, Emma Blair, and her unique resistance to H7N11. A resistance based partly on her consumption of cannabis in its different forms. But she was always convinced that her immunity was tuned from childhood.

We inherit our mom's innate immunity when we pass through the birth canal, we know that much. It's an initiation rite for the newborn babe, which, despite the profound and torturous passage (especially for the mum) confers more strength for the future than immediate peril. If we make it through in one piece, then we're stronger coming out the other side.

Your mother, your grandmother, her mother, and so on, have fought the battles with microbial foes that you don't have to fight (other than new ones arising in your lifetime).

For that, we owe a debt to our maternal forebears.

Now I'm convinced that Gwen has London's new pathogen, the one I thought I left behind. I think I should toss aside my reticence and discuss it with Braden. Harry should be here, instead of sleeping off his pints. I go out in the hallway to look for him. I tell Jessica to keep Gwen in her room. We lock the window, shut the door. I hear a moaning afterward, from the other side of the door.

It takes me two rooms to find Harry. I guess he's lucky he didn't sleep with Gwen. He's comatose, under the covers, wearing only a pair of boxer shorts. When I come through the door, he rips the covers off and stares, like I've jarred him out of a dream. I tell him Gwen's not doing well, he should look in on her. He pulls the covers back over and mutters from beneath the pillow. The bed smells like stale grog. He was monged last night.

I use his white porcelain basin to wash up thoroughly, feeling nursey again. Zinc, vitamin D, vitamin K, vitamin C, magnesium, higher doses, for me, Gwen, all of us. I go back to my own room, to Jason. He's in bed, but he turns over when I come in.

"Gwen's in bad shape. I think she has the London virus. You know, the sweats, the fevers, the jumping off of bridges..."

"Shit," he mumbles.

"Who's Gretchen?"

"Gretchen?" Still talking from beneath the covers. I smell beer again; I walk across the room and open the window. The water has already drained from the tub, passing away like time.

"Yeah, Gretchen, down in the kitchen."

"A kitchen worker, a maid."

"How does she know you?" I'm now rifling through a bureau of drawers, still frustrated by Gwen's sickness. I don't want to be a full-time nurse again, not yet. I had stuffed what clothes and underwear I'd had in these drawers.

Jase merely grunts, still spent from our sex.

Then I find some unfamiliar items. My eyes glaze over; I sense a bit of nausea. I remove a pink pair of panties and a bra. Not mine.

"Whose are these?" I hold them out, one in each hand. Didn't think I was the jealous type; never had time for it in London. Now I realize I am.

"Whose are these?"

He goes up on one elbow, shirtless, eyes slits, hair flopping over on a crushed pillow.

"How would I know? Yours?"

"I said they're not mine! Are they Gretchen's?"

"Pffft!"

"This is your room! Why would you have some girl's knickers in the drawer?"

"Knickers and a tit sling," he mumbles.

"That isn't funny! By the way, Gwen, remember her? She's out of her head next door."

I throw them down onto the floor, something surges up against my will and tugs down at the corners of my mouth. Tears well up. I run out of the bedroom. Down the stairs; Harry's in the hallway, trousers haphazardly yanked on and still unbuckled.

"What's the rush, Emma?"

Yelling over my shoulder, "Tell yah later." Trying to control my voice so as not to convey my skewed emotions, but failing. I stride straight through the foyer with its grave decor and stag's head and chessboard, open the ponderous oaken front door, and I'm out into fresh air.

I don't want to talk to Jason anymore, not now. I don't even want to see him right now. I walk quickly through the gravel parking area. The old man who drives the wagon is sitting on a stool, smoking a pipe. He smiles and takes the pipe out of his mouth, gesturing to me. I smile back, but it comes out more as a toothy grimace.

Jason and me in the tub, this morning. First time. First time, for me at least!

I'm on the sheep's beaten track back to the main road. I need some space. My ankle's sore, my head hurts, it's like a different day all of a sudden, than the one the sun came up on. I don't need Jason in my face, with his tendency to be both raw and honest and insistent. He'll be concocting a story on the fly about how the knickers got into his clothes drawer, and it could be marginally true. In any event, he doesn't deserve extra points right now; I can still picture Gretchen's sly smirk, and her Winston Churchill anecdotes, about cats, whatever.

If I have to, I'll walk and run all the way to the lake, all the way to the Chateau de Chillon, before I decide what to do with the rest of my life. What would Byron do? He'd banish the offending lover (man or woman), then drink, swim, write poetry.

It feels like I've crossed a desperate continent–it was 900 kilometers but might as well have been 10,000–to get out of London, to change my life, to be with Jason. To come all the way here to deal with the fascist Simone, her wicked lackey Jacques, crashing the van. Now this.

I'm on the main road; I turn and cut through the vineyards. Long dry rows with fist-sized clumps of Chardonnay and Sauvignon grapes, nestled and bunched in the sunlit leaves, like a man's balls.

I make my way through five acres of vineyards, I feel better already. In the near distance is that gorge, and the river that winds down to the lake. I hear the gushing of water, feel a faint breeze come up from the deep gully. It carries a scent of copper. The path I'm on merges with another paved road that snakes down, mainly following the path of the water-filled ravine.

It's only me, for a few minutes, but a few blocks away a woman walks her bicycle. She's dismounted because the grade is too steep and treacherous to ride down.

Beyond the vineyard I just crossed, is a lush green field. I see two figures running across the field; it's far away, the distance plays tricks with my eyes. I think they're children. They're pale white in the sun, naked children. No! They are two emaciated males, streaking for no apparent reason across the field, toward the road, toward the woman.

Buck naked sods.

"Hey you!" I yell out to the lady. I begin waving my arms. "Watch out!" She stops, looks at me, I'm still yelling, beckoning her on, "Watch out! Run! Come up here!"

The two men get to her, faster than I can believe. One is on to her, like a rabid dog, tearing at her hair and toppling her. She screams. My hand's on my mouth, "No!" More tears. The second naked man rips at her skirt and she's kicking and screaming. I take the knife out of my pocket. I open it up to the blade. I stride faster.

Two motorbikes bomb down the road past me. The drivers are men dressed in black leather, fake leather, with helmets. They park the bikes on the side of the road, dismount, briskly take out two tasers, march forward, all purposeful and unhesitant. They aim the tasers, and jolt both naked sods. It's like flash bulbs going off; I can almost smell the burning. The whole thing–attack, arrival, tasing–doesn't take three minutes.

I stop and watch. They help the woman to her feet. She rubs the tears away and brushes herself off. The two shaven-head, white naked sods lie by the side of the road like two bodies pulled out of a crematorium.

The men put on surgical masks, and methodically pull the bodies farther off the road. The lady wipes her face with a kerchief, nods at the men, picks up her bicycle. She's off down the hill, slowly.

I think the men are going to roll the bodies into the gully. But they don't. One of them talks into a hand-held device. I've seen these; they're radio operated. It's one of the highest tech things we have in London. He talks into it, then they both get on their motorcycles, start them up, and leave.

The bodies lie there like trash. One of them moves a leg, an arm. The other infected man pushes up on an elbow. I look away.

If he moves again, I'll run.

CHAPTER 46

That man on Blackfriars Bridge in London, he hadn't regressed to the stage of degeneration presented by these two naked victims.

I walk over closer to the side of the gorge. A rising spray comes off the stream below. The water really is going hard down in the gorge. I hear a motor.

I look behind me; it's a black Range Rover, slowly passing me on the road.

The vehicle pulls up to the two men lying by the side of the road, sick and out of their heads. A man gets out of the passenger side, dressed in white starched clothing, wearing a fancy surgical mask that seems to contain a charcoal filter. He summarily tasers both men, until they are again, inert.

A second masked man, dressed the same, opens up the back of the Rover, removes a litter, and together they lift both bodies into the back of the vehicle. They slam shut the hatch door, get into the still running vehicle, and leave. It's all very efficient, like taking out the trash.

I watch the proceedings with a scandalous fascination.

Another black motorbike pulls up behind me and stops. I turn around. The man parks the bike on a stand, dismounts, removes his helmet. Only a black stubble on his head. His eyes light up, like a black cat's at night. It's Jacques.

# #

The same close-shaven stubble, the same pug nose and pock-marked, fierce face. He comes after me, expressionlessly, wordlessly, thumping down the road. He has no tact, he doesn't even call out my name. The implied rage and hostility in his hunched shoulders, the rabid, narrow eyes, suggests he's been waiting too long to do this.

With the deep gully on one side, and a steep grade rising in another direction, I can only plod on my bad foot down the long winding street. *He's going to catch me, I think, frantically running through the options. I take the knife out of my trousers again, the same blade I'd plunged into Jacques's tire.*

My ankle starts to give out, and within half a minute I'm limping along, tasting the salt from my tears. So much for my ability to outrun my pursuers.

The water cascades deep down in the gorge off to my right, with a great rushing noise and a mist rising up into the forest canopy. I stop, quickly turn, brandishing the small Swiss Army knife, still gripped tightly in my right hand.

"It's you again, eh?" Jacques mutters coldly, slowing to a cocky walk. He brandishes the black nightstick, but now he reaches with his left hand to unbuckle and display a black and yellow taser.

"Why are you following me? Leave me alone!" I face him, then nervously look over my shoulder. My hand shakes. Deep in the gorge, the run-off water flows in waves and torrents, funneling hard to the lake.

"You think I forget? You slashed my tire. You run. You leave me to die. Listen, beech...you think I have no memory of these events? Eh? We've got a score to settle. *Maintenant ou jamais, eh.*" He has a small, bitter voice; the volume goes up as he moves closer, as if I'm hard of hearing. I'm in the ready position, holding the knife, edging away from the gully.

"You're going to drop that knife, beech? Or use it?"

"You bet I'm gonna use it."

He's the Marseille wharf rat with a score to settle, a score to settle with life, I think. He smiles slyly, showing yellow eyes and a row of black-capped teeth, a few of them missing.

He's like a feral dog; he's going to go for my throat.

I pray that another vehicle comes down the road, something to distract him. I'll kick him where it hurts the most. Whoever's driving the vehicle could help. The road remains empty.

When I look over my shoulder to the road behind me, he lunges forward and the nightstick smashes the knife out of my hand. I scream, clinging to my bruised hand, the knife clattering to the roadside. Then he's on me, gripping my hair and tearing me down, a brutal, muscular grip fueled by fury and wrath. He drags me to the side of the road, right up to the edge of the gorge.

I stick my hand plumb into his face, thumbing an eye. *Bite! I think, my mind desperate and panicked. Scratch and gouge!*

He growls and punches away my arm and seizes me by the throat and pins me down on my back, shoving a knee in my stomach.

I flail away with my legs and knees, vainly seeking his groin. The word *help* escapes my throat as a faint gargle. *He wants to throw me into the gorge,* my eyes are wide open, staring at the sky, avoiding his ghastly, sweating, odorous grimace; still kicking, still punching at those yellow eyes and ugly black stubble, still trying to detach his dirty fist from my throat.

Dust, soot, blood, in my mouth, in my eyes; vision going black, I hear the raging waters below.

Amidst the grime and the pain and the fists flying, a heavy boot sweeps in an arc through my peripheral view. It connects bluntly with Jacques's head. He grunts; the weight lets go.

"Emma!"

Jason's face is close to mine; a mop of hair, freckles, dark blue furious alarmed eyes. "Are you okay?"

Spitting blood and a cracked tooth, Jacques is still half on me. He fumbles for his taser. Jason grips two handfuls of excess faux-leather coat bunching around Jacques's shoulders, and he lifts Jacques half off the ground and hurls him toward the defile. Head over black boots, speedily over Jacques goes, with a tight grip on one of Jason's trouser legs.

Jason goes over, too.

They both topple over the edge, out of sight, "No!" I scream.

I hear a sequence of faint thuds and two splashes. I crawl to the edge of the gorge, listening for Jason's familiar, reassuring voice, telling me *I'm alright. No worries.*

The first thing I think is, Jacques is dead. Or dying. That was not survivable. That was also self-defense. And I know Jason has somehow survived; that he's clinging to the wall somewhere, the river's edge. *All I have to do is find help.*

If Jason is hurt badly, or worse, it's all my fault: for picking this fight with Jacques, for coming to Lac Leman in the first place, to claim Jason as only mine.

The dog, the black and white border collie, runs down the road, toward me. I'm sore as hell and pathetically splayed out by the side of the silent road, the incessant water rushing like the refrain of an orchestra. I've got no spit left; I wave, the dog trots over. He noses all the way up my grimy body, then he licks my sore throat and wet cheeks.

"Jason," I whisper, "Find out if Jason's alive down there."

The dog stands on the edge of the precipice, pauses, paws the ground, looks at me, barks three times down into the defile. He thinks it's a game. I listen to his barks echo dully against the granite walls.

CHAPTER 47: Two Years Later: Emma Winslow, Quinten, September 2053

Vineyards blanket dry slopes, baking under a hot sky. The leaves rustle in a wind from the lake. They are hiding tight bunches of not-quite-mature white and red grapes. The vineyards descend all the way down to the shore, where there are homes and the moorings for small boats. The boats carry crates of wine to the opposite shoreline.

Above the village are 6,000 foot cliffs, where eagles live.

A footpath wends above the village and then goes nine more miles to another town at the end of the lake. There is no way to drive a vehicle to this village, and there never has been. You can walk, ride a bike, or take a horse. But most people get back and forth by the boats.

In the early morning, I take my breakfast outside,

sitting on a polished, wooden stump in the sun. There is always someone sailing, tacking in the wind, but the lake never gets crowded. Breakfast is coffee, two eggs, apples, Asiago cheese, and a doughy blob of baked bread we generously call a pastry or croissant. Some people use the old German word *gipfeli*.

I watch black-and-white Arctic Terns and Alpine Swifts soar and dart above the water; where Black-Headed Gulls perch on the piers. Occasionally, Golden Eagles appear from the crags hundreds of feet above, gracefully riding the thermal wind currents.

A black cat, Marcus, makes its way amongst the flowers and bushes, hunting for mice and moles. Here is where I eat, read, gaze absently, often write in my diary.

Monique sleeps past my breakfast. She's my daughter, two y.o. She's looked after by me and Evelyn and Layla, two of the clutch of older ladies that help care for the infants and toddlers. For all of us women, and men, spend a lot of time in the vineyards. The village has a grand total of 87 citizens, with everyone focused on harvesting grapes, and making and bottling the wine.

When Monique gets old enough, that's what she'll do.

After breakfast, I walk down a narrow path to where I work in the vineyards, but first I stop at a church. It's the tiniest chapel you ever will see, which in the early morning makes it easy to pretend it's a personal shrine. From a steep gravel walking path that goes down to the water, I open a heavy oaken door. It has a stained glass window that depicts a knight. It's almost never locked. I sit down in the quiet shadows, and it makes me feel good, and whole, and grateful for what we have.

A modest set of wooden and metal piers, down from the church, are where the boats come in and out. The marina sits in the middle of the 12-mile-long lake bordered by cliffs and a few other small villages, in what used to be called northeastern Switzerland.

I sit in shafts of light inside the tiny church, giving blessings to whatever angel spared us from the disease, and the depredations of the thugs from Lac Leman District 10. I think a lot about St. Paul's Cathedral, where I took care of many people. I was born there, but who wants to think about the specific circumstances of their own birth? I think about my mother's courage, without which, including her wisdom, I would merely have been another infant who couldn't survive 2028.

We are all faced with stark choices, forks in the road. Each fork chosen over another alters the direction of life forever. I could have run back to London from Lake Geneva, alone, Jason gone. Harry mourning poor Gwen by the lake. I'd be back in the hospital in St. Paul's Cathedral, nursing the injured and the sick and all of my regrets.

I think of all these things, sitting alone in the tiny Medieval church next to the lake, carpeted in lush vineyards.

I chose a different life, beside the water and under the shadows of tall cliffs. I don't have any regrets, not seeing London again. I've sent a note to my friend Grace, by way of a tradesman who was passing through with his London cargo of coffee. I hope she gets it, reads it, and visits me here sometime.

I can barely wrap my head around two years ago, before Monique was born. She's almost talking now. To recall that momentous time, I read from my diary, June, 2051.

Against my best instincts, I'm forced to conclude that Jason Hunter, my lover and soulmate, has perished in the gorge. When I looked down in there, the border collie Winston standing beside me, I saw nothing but weeds, rocks, and rapids. I stared down there for what seemed like forever. I contemplated jumping myself.

All my fault, I'd concluded.

Jason and Jacques had each other by their throats and went tumbling over the side, but from this height I can't see bodies. Nothing like bodies. I've looked and called out for a long time. About three feet of water hoses over rocks down to the lake.

I spent forever staring down into the gorge. It mesmerized me, when I didn't feel abject despair and emptiness. It would have been easy to follow through and tumble in myself. The thought, the temptation, tormented and swirled through my mind. It was my fault Jason fell into the gorge. If I hadn't lost it and run from Domain de Crevie, he'd be alive. He died saving my life, and I set the stage for his death with a callow act of selfishness.

I thought, if I could just move about four more feet, and send it from the cliff's edge, out into the abyss, I could stop the flow of these unbearable thoughts forever.

If Winston wasn't standing beside me, patiently, with this "What's she gonna do next?" dog look on his face, I don't know what I would have done. We don't know, do we, what might happen to us and our loved ones, second by second and day by day?

A voice, reassuring, urging me on; some voice rising out of the ether of my past, not the mist from the gorge, the tempting and wicked abyss. 'You've got this,' the voice said. 'This is just another bump in the road. There will be more, perhaps worse than this. Are you going to kill yourself then, too?'

I stood up, brushed my trousers off, felt around my face where I took a punch from Jacques.

Little did I know that I was carrying Monique, merely the tiniest stages of her. I kept reading:

I wiped away the tears with my sleeve. Feeling zombified by sadness, guilt, and physical assault, I wandered down the road, with Winston at my side. I kept looking down into the gorge by the side of the road, hoping to see something. I must have worn a pitiable scowl, along with my bruises, because a woman stopped me on the road. She asked me what was wrong in French.

I told her a bandit had beat me up. She gasped, went "tch tch," and she handed me a kerchief to wipe my face. She offered to give me a ride in her tiny van to a doctor she knew in town, but I told her that I would be grateful for a lift, including Winston, back up to the farm.

I got to Braden's farm and no one was in the farmhouse, but I was able to go back into my room and wash my face at the basin, and patch up some of my wounds. I appeared attacked by a vicious cat, but it was only the psychotic Jacques, and now he probably lay dead, somewhere near Jason, soggy, dead, and shattered in the torrent at the bottom of the gorge.

I packed up all my things. It was dark. I ate some leftover food we had in a canvas bag in the room: apples, hard cheese, the stale end of a baguette. I sat on the edge of the bed, gazed at the tub Jase and I had shared, then I took a shot of some whisky that Jase kept around in a flask. That, of course, intensified my despair. I thought of going to the dining area or returning to the gorge, but the sun had already gone down. I went through our clothes and books and weapons (my cricket bat) and papers, and all of it reminded me of Jase.

I didn't want to see Gretchen, Dr. Braden, anybody, only Harry. He'll understand. I wanted out of this place; it's been a nightmare. Possibly worse, because don't we wake up from nightmares, constantly getting our temporary reprieves? Maybe I can get over it in London, I thought. I lay down and slept only fitfully until the light filled the window.

I finished packing and after a while took my things outside. I saw some orchard workers milling about; I asked them if they'd seen Harry, and they pointed me to some trees near the sheep pasture. I found Harry sitting under one of the trees, with his elbows on his knees.

When he saw me, he picked up a stick, and lightly tossed it into the grass. His eyes were red, misted, and teared-up, like he'd been slicing onions. He grimaced a few times; I know Harry. He doesn't like outward emotional displays. This was bad.

Jesus, what else? I thought.

He said that Gwen had died the night before. She'd run a terrible fever, and they couldn't control it, bring it down.

He wanted to go back to London, too, and surprisingly, like me, wouldn't wait to fix the van. He said we could start the trip from a ferry he knew about from the boatman on the lake. So it's me and Harry again, forever.

Me and Harry in St. Paul's Cathedral, me with goo all over me and still with the umbilical attached, and him calling Max a wanker for thinking I was a boy.

We found only tragedy here, and it's utterly whacked what kind of week we had, and how we wholly failed to make it work in Lake Geneva. What an epic, fucking life we've had!

Me and Harry...

When I told him what had happened to Jase, his eyes went wide with disbelief. He stood up, picked up a larger stick, and smashed it on the ground. He said, get this, down by the lake where the river pours into a small bay, the run-off had coughed up two bodies. Fishermen found them.

# #

Harry and I left as quickly as we could, and that's how it began, how Monique and I made it to our present home. The route went by water, about 25 miles overland in a horse-drawn wagon, then by lake again.

Harry left for London a year ago, with an 18 y.o. woman named Alyssa, who was also bored with only working in a tiny vineyard by a lake. I was sad to see him go, but knew that two things were inevitable: he would find a replacement for Gwen, and that he would get sick of living here.

I, of course, was pregnant with Monique, which I only discovered a few months after leaving Domaine de Crevie and Lake Geneva.

When I gave birth to Monique, I had plenty of help from the women of Quinten, unlike my poor mother, who only had Harry, Max, and Jack. Then I was busy as hell, taking care of the child and myself, our new home. The first year went by eventfully and quickly.

CHAPTER 48: Emma Blair, Isle of Skye, Late October 2026

Taking the LP phonograph from Gladys's was pure wishful inspiration. I didn't have a generator, making it unlikely that silver-tongued Sinatra or Sam Cooke would ever grace these parts with their silky sounds. The turntable was, alas, an antique well before the pandemic hit.

Sitting under an old Sycamore, the lone prominent tree in the backyard of the Skye farmhouse, I gamely played a rough version of ***You Send Me*** on my pipette, learning chords along the way. The notes I did manage to get right resonated wistfully amidst the grassy, windswept fields. The bulky headlands sat in the distance, like a silent, respectful audience.

I added Gladys's supplies to my own food stores,

organizing my kitchen shelves the morning after I buried her. For once, the weather offered unblemished blue sky in Skye. I sat on the back wooden step, reading William Blake's brief, enigmatic poems–*Auguries of Innocence* and *The Garden Of Love.* The latter piece reminded me of the garden where I hastily decided to bury Gladys; "tomb-stones where flowers should be," indeed.

I had found that book in the abandoned schoolhouse. I'd go back there to hunt around some more, I thought, if the route itself wasn't a minefield of reivers.

The morning air was chilly, but my creamy Scottish skin was so sun deprived that I rolled up my trousers and sleeves and took off my knit cap, trying to soak it all in. On the back steps, out of the wind, the sun was nourishing.

Not much vitamin D in an early winter sun, but the sun has other benefits.

"Bundy, stay close! Okay?" I called out. The dog ran around on the grass in the back, literally following her nose. She probably smelled reivers that had plodded past at night, like ravaged boats adrift on the sea. If you want the unvarnished truth, they are unmoored, wandering ghouls, inhabiting a vague netherworld between the "normal life" they once led, and the boneyard.

I looked around the empty countryside and realized how easy it was during the day to spot anything sizable moving about, like reivers or ruminant animals. I thought I'd have to be a lot more savvy about food stores now that Bundy was around. I was going to have to hunt for meat and bones.

"I said, don't go far!" I yelled at the dog, cradling the

Blake paperback in my lap. Her wanderings had taken her past a copse of skeletal hardwoods and beech trees, and down into a nearby gully that was stuffed with moldering leaves. She loved to root around in leaves. She seemed content, and I wondered if Bundy missed Robert J. Hardy at all?

With some dogs, you couldn't tell. Given their boundless and distracted energy and curiosity, you could easily imagine a quick fade of certain humans from their memories. The speed with which they dispensed of us, however, was more than made up for by their unhesitant loyalty when we were together.

"Come over here, Bundy," I said more conversationally, less demanding. "You've hardly gotten to know me." I figured it was about 10 a.m., but I no longer paid much attention to time, especially after finding Gladys dead. Who cares? I thought, dismissing all alarm clocks and watches from my consciousness. I have no one to meet, no deadlines to keep.

Bundy came over this time, settling down next to me on the wooden steps. Doubtless, she figured she would be fed. I scratched her behind the ears and stroked her along the knobby backbone, and gradually, the death, mayhem, and narrow escape of the day before, all the dark mojo, began to evaporate.

"I'll trap some squirrels for you, that's what I'll do. Hate to do it, but you need fresh meat, not the crap I've been feeding you. SunPat Original Smooth peanut butter and Ritz Crackers. Come on with me."

I stood up, and headed for the kitchen, where I had a dozen dog-food cans lined up on a shelf. I'd kept them around for me, too, if it ever got to that acutely desperate stage. The pinkish mush actually smelled kind of good, when I jimmied the can open with the opener tool of the knife. It smelled like salty meat loaf, despite the unappetizing gelatin jiggling on top.

I globbed it onto a plate and placed it in front of Bundy, who dived in with relish, then eagerly looked up for more.

"Don't get greedy now." I picked up three empty plastic gallon containers; we were going to go down to the river to fill them. Bundy would find out where the river is, whenever she needed a drink, and a wash or a swim. I'd see how well she fished.

We headed outside, where a pale sun leaked through thin, waxen clouds.

Bundy now filled what seemed an empty chamber in my life, which I almost hadn't known existed before I had her. She had a way of flinching when I got down close to her, and I wondered if Robert J. Hardy had ever beat her. Poor Robert J., if he did beat Bundy, then he got what he deserved.

We went all the way down to the river, Bundy wading in up to the tops of her legs. She drank comically, by taking bites out of the current flowing in front of her nose. I filled the bottles by holding them under water. I stood up and looked around; silent, breezy, bucolic. I felt lucky, for still having health, heartbeats, and a river that will flow throughout the winter. It was a small river; it reminded me of the Water Of Leith in Edinburgh. I didn't get the impression that it would dry up, or completely freeze over.

When I finished, I capped the water bottles and we walked up from the shoreline. The water was cold and I thought about adding a wee Scotch to it. Bundy stopped in the grass and went rigid, lifting a paw.

I looked up and saw five or six gray sheep in the distance, distributed almost like statues, porcelain figurines on the side of a hill. Bundy took off like a shot towards them.

"No! No, Bundy! Come back!" She was in full sprint mode, ignoring me. The tiny sheep arrayed along the hills raised their heads. Bundy was quickly reduced to a black and white figure bounding through the tall grasses. I heard her barking; she was a border collie. It was all driven by instinct, by her breed, but she didn't know these parts particularly well.

I put the bottles down. I strode out past a tree next to the river, cupping my hands over my mouth and yelling, "Bundy! Here girl! Come back here! Come back Bundy!" Over and over again.

The sheep turned and dumbly began trotting away from the chasing Bundy, up the hill.

"Bundy, fucking come back! Don't leave me, dammit!"

I remembered where I put the bottles and I followed the dog's determined path. I didn't usually stray this far from the farmhouse without weapons, but I didn't want to lose her, and my desire to get her back felt like it would drive me out of mind. The sheep disappeared over the tops of the hills, and so did Bundy.

Shit!

When I got to the top of the first hill, after some

pretty hard running and climbing, I could see a few sheep and I could see Bundy, a moving, black-and-white dot, running over another hillside. I cupped my hands over my mouth again, and cried out for her departing figure, putting all of my heart into it.

The sheep and the dog reached the top of the slope, then disappeared over its crest. They must have been two miles away or more.

I stood in the wind at the top of the hill with my hands on my hips. The silence of the countryside was now a heavy blanket, settling over me. I gazed hungrily back at the farmhouse and its cluster of trees; it seemed tiny and meager. A lonely, isolated refuge. I started weeping, sopping up the tears with my sleeve, then stopped as quickly as I began.

She'll come back, I know she will. She'll remember where she was fed.

I plodded downhill to where I'd left the bottles, fetched them, returned to the farmhouse. A palpable maw expanded in my gut; it was that space that Bundy had filled. I kept looking up to where she disappeared over those hills. How could she run away so quickly? She didn't even look back, when I was calling her. She didn't look back *once*, just went right towards the sheep, like she wanted to hunt one. But she wasn't going to; it was only a stupid herding instinct! Hers was a "good riddance" departure.

She didn't stop and look back once.

The sun appeared to sink faster toward the headlands. I thought of the darkness, the loneliness. When I got back to the farmhouse, I went into the kitchen and poured a

Scotch into that cold river water. I took it out to the steps for the last light. I called for Bundy many more times, for at least an hour, but I wasn't keeping track of time.

I took out my pipette, and I played what I'd learned of *You Send Me*, over and over again, until I thought I might attract reivers. Like Sirens, drawing the demons out of their dark crevices with irresistible sounds. But the dog might hear it, too, I thought. I stood up, went inside, poured more water and Scotch, fetched the album cover, which I remembered included the lyrics. I took a candle, and I put it outside on the steps, and lit it, watching the flame waver in a gentle breeze that came and went.

I sang *You Send Me,* sure that Bundy would hear it. "...Honest you do, honest you do, honest you do..." Stars began to pepper the velvet cloak above me.

Six months to my 27th birthday, April 1, I thought. It was going to be a long winter, it was going to be a long haul, me here in the house, but at least I have my birthday to look forward to: my books and my Scotch and my music and my diary. I kept wishing and hoping that I would find Bundy again.

I sat with my Scotch and pipette and let the starry night drop over me. It's remarkable how being alone can heighten your senses. Finally, I went inside and burrowed under the covers and thought of how I'd find Bundy waiting for me, tail wagging apologetically, by the same back door in the morning. Wishing, hoping, thinking positive, I slept.

Determined to reject the notion, I refused to think of myself as eternally alone.

CHAPTER 49: Emma Winslow, Quinten, September 2053

Ladies often compare their life to their Mom's at the same age.

I will turn 25 y.o. in January, almost my mother's age when she fled New York and was marooned by the pandemic in Scotland. With Monique, I'm a mom. Emma Blair wasn't; she was merely a single scientist, her lover having already succumbed to the disease. My life is wholly more predictable and less action-packed than hers was at 26.

Emma Blair didn't live long enough to settle comfortably into maternity, but I learned a lot from her. Somewhat like adopting the lessons of a saint from reading a sacred text, or maybe simply taut narratives from the King James Bible. As in: have a thick hide, think for yourself, be kind to others, handle disappointments gracefully, take each day as it comes. Also, defend yourself gallantly, without hesitation, if the need arises.

Today begins like many others: wake up, heat coffee, take breakfast outside, if it's nice; get ready to drop two y.o. Monique off with Evelyn or her sister Layla. I think, Monique needs a father. I don't truly want her to only grow up with me as a parent; as in my own orphaned childhood, learning random stuff from Max, Harry, and Jack, only when they were in the mood to pass something on.

We have men here in Quinten, but I haven't found one who is quite right for me, not close. It's not London, where I had Jason, bless his heart, and before him, Harry's cheeky friends and any number of cute, rambunctious lads. Here in the village, they're either gruff, shy, and backward, or too old. Lots of gray beards, baggy pants, and suspenders. Lots of blokes who know nothing beyond vineyard work, fishing, and timbering, whereas I came here with a background in medicine, books, and anything else I could dabble in.

The young ones here don't know how to approach me; I'm a fetching lass, glamorous by my own right, as Evelyn puts it. All the guys here are gawky and tongue-tied around me, and the older men, well, eew!

The only handsome one here ever was 19 y.o. Stefan. He used to grin at me shyly through the vineyards. I think of him, after I drop Monique off with Evelyn, who will take her down to the lake where there's a small beach for the kids.

It's a shame I didn't get to know Stefan, I think as I

enter the little chapel and sit down. He was very young, however, and tragic. He tried to climb the 100-foot waterfall here, it's called Seerenbach Falls, and fell to his death. Rumors had it that he was trying to impress me. Rubbish! I thought that the suffocating parochial limits of this otherwise beautiful place drove him to seek adventure and take risks.

Young men are risk-takers and nomads, like Jason. It's in their blood.

After my rumination in the chapel, I step out of the interior shadows, onto the sun-splashed gravel of the steep road. They have a generator that can run a sound system here. They softly pipe music through the vineyards–it doesn't blare loudly–so that the day can go by faster for us workers. It's quite lovely. It's one of the few modern things about Quinten, and they play any music they can get, including lots of pop from England, not just the Chopin, Beethoven, and Alpine oom-pah-pah stuff. They get music that was stored on LPs and discs, and they have a player and speakers.

This morning, I hear the end of a beautiful song by Roy Orbison, an American from about 100 years ago, called *Crying*. I stop and listen. I've got hours ahead of me in the sun, pulling grapes from vines and dropping them into a sack, sorting them out at the end. I look down the road toward the lake.

Monique is shy. She won't let older men go near her; she runs to me and clings to my legs, when they appear. I think her DNA contains the trauma of my own.

So I'm shocked when I see her coming up the path holding hands with a man.

He's young, but walks with a cane. He appears otherwise lanky and vigorous; he has a tanned face, a broad smile. He looks up at me; I get a good look at his road-weary but rakish expression. My Lord! I think, it's Jason! It's Jason Hunter, and he's alive! How can that be true?

This isn't quite real, and I wonder if it's some kind of sweet concocted day dream I've left the chapel with. Just then a new song begins in the vineyard, notes pealing out over the lake. *You-hoo Send Me...Dar-ling you-hoo send me...Honest you do, Honest you do...*

I run down steeply through the shadows cast on the gravelly path, to reach my daughter and her father.

Emma Hunter, October 10, 2053, Quinten, Switzerland

Jason appears to have found us, only by steadfast persistence and a huge stroke of good luck. He didn't even know I was pregnant. He didn't have a clue where I'd ended up. I thought he was dead. He'd thought I'd fled to London, and anything can happen to a young lady motoring through that 900-kilometer wilderness.

After we finished hugs, kisses, and expressions of disbelief, the story spilled out of him. It's true that fishermen hauled two bodies from the river, but Jason happened to still be alive, Jacques wasn't. Jason had a concussion and a broken right femur, but he was able to keep himself floating on the water's surface for about a quarter mile downstream, barely conscious and going into shock. He was rescued from the small estuary where the river met the lake, and he lay in bed with his leg set for weeks. It still isn't quite right.

He then went about asking everyone, discreetly mind you, because I was an escapee, where I had gone. The last he had seen of me, I was being brutally assaulted by Jacques. The only thing he could find out was that I had taken a boat with Harry and gone east.

Knowing my love for home, he'd concluded that I'd gone back to London (despite the direction I'd taken). Only a few people had asked about Jacques, and everyone thought the death had been an accident. Jason kept working in Lac Leman, feeling an obligation after they had spent so long tending to his injuries. Several months went by. He ignored Gretchen's moves on him, out of guilt (he tells me). She'd nursed him part of the time, when he was all beaten and broken. He focused on making himself useful and taking care of his son Willie, who'd come so close to being an orphan himself.

Then who shows up in Lac Leman District 10 but Harry, on his way back to London. It was a pure stroke of luck that Jason runs into him, in a cafe that pours pints of beer in Vevey!

First, you see, Harry thought Jason was dead, and Harry'd had a couple of pints already, so seeing Jason thoroughly freaked him out. He rubbed his eyes and gasped, swaying a little on his feet, repeating "fuck no it's you," over and over again, like it was someone else's mouth and he had no control over it. Harry goes on to tell Jason that I'm in a lake village east of there, called Quinten. I have a daughter, Monique.

And guess what? Harry says. The daughter Monique

*is yours. Now Jason's the freaked-out one, standing there with his half-empty pint and his eyes bugging out. "No, you bloody bugger, that's shyte, that is! I *have* a son, that's all!"*

"No, you have a daughter too, you silly sod," and it goes back and forth like that.

So that's how Jason found us. He took Willie, no longer Willie Fairfield, but Willie Hunter, packed up their things, and they sailed off in a boat bound for not-too-distant lands.

Thankfully, Jason's own trip was uneventful; it didn't involve bandits, reivers, or buck naked sods. He didn't try to send a message or a missive along ahead first, because he wasn't confident it would ever get to me. Besides, momentous events that have positive outcomes are so rare in life, why ruin them by rushing the news?

Life has calmed down for us. Keeping a family, working in the wine business. Simple is good. The grapes ripen on the vines, and so do my children. Willie even helps in the vineyard now. We're known as the Hunters, ever since me and Jason had a little marriage ceremony in the tiny chapel.

But before I agreed to marry, we had some unresolved issues to work out. When you have something vexing on your mind, it's going to germinate and grow, like a rotten seed, if you don't talk it out. So I asked him, Gretchen? The knickers and the bra, did you really sleep with her, at the same time I almost killed myself getting to you?

That doesn't matter now, he replied. It happened long ago, and there's the saying, Let sleeping dogs lie.

I grabbed him firmly by the collar, Did you sleep with

her, you daft bastard, yes or no?

No! We played around a bit, those weren't her knickers anyways! She offered, she wanted to, but...I was afraid of getting her pregnant. Okay?

Ah! I scowled, then quietly smiled.

So we had our ceremony, lots of flowers, wine, and choice music: Sam Cooke and Roy Orbison. I'm Emma Blair Winslow Hunter now, I have a family of four, and for once, in the year of our Lord 2053, I feel I can breathe. Easier. My mind is clear. Everything is good.

CHAPTER 50: Emma Hunter, Quinten, April 2054

I have my 25th birthday in January 2054. Winter arrives, but snow only piles up in the high mountains, far above the village. I read the part of my Mom's diary where she spends the winter alone, 2026-27. A depopulated island, and her dog Bundy runs away. She only sees her once again, on the edge of a distant wood. She calls out for her and leaves the dog food, to no avail.

Emma Blair didn't pretend to understand why Bundy didn't come back. She thought this Robert J. Hardy might have tainted Bundy's spirit, left her poisoned with distrust. For my Mom, it was another heartbreak, and one more nail in the coffin that was winter 2026-27.

It would have been months before she meets my father by accident; frigid, wet weeks of hardscrabble, lone survival.

I feel a vague, persistent regret for the life this woman had to lead, this lady who's a stranger to me. The regret thickens as I get older, like wet oatmeal left out on the wooden breakfast table. I have a close record of her experiences, however, from her diary. Lots of stories of overcoming adversity, of courage, resiliency, and coping with danger and loneliness. This prevents me from ever falling into complacency.

I know how vulnerable we are, this young family of four–including Willie and Monique. I take things one day at a time. I know the tranquility of many days here by the lake is not an eternal state; it is to be enjoyed for what it is, a moment by moment joy.

I maintain a state of readiness, a constant one, like a beating heart. I never stop looking over my shoulder; I never stop looking at things twice. I hold Monique close to me, tighter than I should sometimes. She looks up at me with puzzled eyes, which melts my heart even more.

One morning, an unfamiliar boat floats up to our shores. It's a long boat made of wood and painted white; it has an ornament of a crown attached to the prow. A team of two men work the oars; two more stand up near the prow. I wrote in my diary later:

Emma Hunter, April 1, 2054 Quinten, Switzerland

Late morning today, I was planting onions and turnips in a garden by the lake, where the soil gets a lot of sun, when I saw a boat approaching our piers. Two guys were standing up in the boat, somewhat self-

importantly, while two other guys were rowing. I vaguely recognized the vessel, by the crown ornament, then remembered that I'd see them on Lake Geneva, collecting wood that would float in the lake after a storm.

I didn't know the men though. Up the steep gravelly drive from our piers, I knew that Jake was working in the vineyards. He's a friend of Willie's, and Jason's. He is tall and strapping, even though barely 15 y.o.

The men tied off the boat, then climbed up onto the wooden pier. I stopped what I was doing. I stood up to watch. One of the men was short, dark-haired, with a blue scarf and a jean coat; the other taller with an unkempt mop of hair. Strapped to the second man's shoulder was a leather scabbard, with the grip of a sword protruding from it.

I saw nothing to sell or trade on their boat. Standing on the pier, they talked to Freddie, the old man who helps with the fishing boats. Freddie turned, scanned the shoreline for a moment, then gestured to me.

The short one looked up at me from a distance, unsmiling. I didn't like this one bit. They walked toward me. Jason was not in the village at the moment; he was above the lake cutting timber. The two men just kept walking; they didn't hail me at all.

When he got close enough, the one with the blue scarf said, 'Emma Winslow.'

'Emma Hunter,' I said.

'I've been looking for you, for a long time. For you and that boyfriend.'

'I don't know you,' I said. 'I've never seen you. I have no business with you.' I looked up the gravelly path, and

yelled out, Jake!

'Oh, we have a tight kind of connection,' he sneered, in a fractured French accent. I looked up the path and it was empty. I was breathing faster, sweating, my body shaking with the sense of bad omens.

There was something about his smile that I remembered. It was cold, contemptuous.

'I have no business with you,' I said. 'I have to go back to work.'

'Oh right you do, Madame, have business with me. My name is Francois Boucher. My brother was Jacques Boucher.'

'I don't know him, whoever he is. Now if you'll excuse me, I have to leave and tend to my garden.' I turned to go and he grabbed me by the sleeve.

'Let go of that!' I said. I wrenched my arm away from his. The gravel path above me was empty. 'You're not welcome here!'

He laughed in a dismissive way, then he said with a corrupt bonhomie, 'I'm glad I found you. Because now you can tell me where that boyfriend is, or else...' He looked at the water, the flat water reflecting sunlight. His silent, dumbly compliant companion moved forward slightly, wearing an imitative sneer.

'Stay there, Leo,' Francois said, snapping off the order, as if to a dog. I moved away until I stood up to my calves in the water. The two men smelled pissy, like fermented sweat and clinging cigarette-smoke residues.

'My older brother Jacques...He was a hard-working man. He was butchered by this Jason,' he said.

Butchered?

Now I knew exactly who he was; a nightmare that had come back to life and returned.

'My brother was thrown off a cliff, left to die. Justice will be done, that's right. With that boyfriend first.'

Leo had crept over to my other side, standing on the beach, blocking my path if I tried to run. My mouth had gone dry, I couldn't scream. I fished around in the side pocket for the small knife that I normally carried; I'd left it in the house.

I saw Monique, coming down the gravel path. 'Mommie! I want to swim!'

'Monique, Mommie's busy right now! Where's Layla?'

'Monique, ah!" Boucher said, pretending to be warm and friendly. 'Come on over here and let me have a look at you. My, you are the spitting image of your mother!'

'Don't go near him, Monique!' I screamed. She ran up to me, into the water. I took her by the hand; now we both stood up to my knees in the lake. I picked her up. 'Time to leave now,' I warned. I was shaking, but it wasn't from cold water.

'Tch tch, now now,' Boucher said. 'Merely tell me where that Jason is, and you can go. Where is he?'

'I don't know.' Leo slowly pulled the sword from its scabbard; I watched the shiny blade emerge. I hugged Monique tightly; our backs were to the lake. I slowly backed up.

Boucher appeared to lose patience. He scowled. 'How about I give Monique a swimming lesson?'

I fell back into the water and pushed off, still holding onto Monique. I kicked furiously in the strong sun. Quickly, I'd put 10 yards between the two men and us.

'Go get them, Allez!' I heard Boucher yell.

'Non,' Leo said. 'I don't swim.' I was kicking so hard and swimming so hard with 27 pounds of Monique on me, my head was going under. I held my breath. The top of the water was warm, then it cooled where my legs kicked deeper. I was able to reach back with one arm and push more water behind us. It reminded me of swimming in Lake Geneva nude; the murky blue-green underwater color.

I heard 'merde!' and Boucher was in the water, swimming toward us. It occurred to me, if he caught us he would try to separate me from Monique, who didn't swim well in deep water. I kicked more furiously, and watched the horizon move as we swam farther out into the lake.

I stopped for a few seconds and looked up. Freddie, and one other man, had a boat out nearby. The boat maneuvered alongside the swimming Boucher. Freddy had a long pole with a metal hook on the end; it was used to move fishing nets. He hooked Boucher with it; the stranger thrashed around in the water like a frantic fish, but he couldn't free himself. The tool was hooked onto his clothes, or a belt. The boat dragged him toward the shore, with Freddie holding onto the pole.

I treaded water with Monique. On the shore, a group of men that included Jake, carrying axes and other heavy, sharp tools they used for timbering and the vineyards, had taken the sword and scabbard away from Leo. They were leading him back to Boucher's boat; one of the guys with Jake had a sharp pike pointing at Leo's back. Boucher was trying to pull himself up on the pier, still with the hook gripping the belt on his soggy pants. He fell back a couple of times into the water, and the men started laughing.

I treaded water some more, then kicked back to shore with Monique. The swimming was pleasurable now, relaxing. When the water was shallow, I let go of Monique, then I stood up and watched what the men were doing on the pier. Boucher and Leo got back into their own boat, and they shoved off with the two others. They left in the same direction in which they had come; everyone stood on the pier until they were gone, and Jake still had Leo's confiscated sword.

'Were those men bad?,' Monique asked quietly.

'Yes.' We walked out of the lake. I was soaked through, but happier. The shimmering water was beautiful in the sunlight. I told her: 'But we'll always be safe with Jake, and your father and the other men in the village. You don't have to worry.' Willie was still only 7 years old, but I meant him, too.

Some men are born with black hearts, or acquired them because of vile things that happened early in their lives. It wasn't only the pathogens that produced the dread ills that tormented mens' souls.

Epilogue: Quinten, 2054, And Beyond

I returned to being a nurse again, which was, after all, my calling. We worked partly in the vineyards, me and Monique, but ultimately, the village needed a working medical clinic. People got injuries and flu's, women had babies, there were old people and the typical ailments, but all year and for months after, I saw nothing like the infections I'd witnessed in London, or beside Lake Geneva.

I worked out of a little, solid wood building that had a wide patio or veranda. The open-air veranda had a canvas roof over it. As many patients as possible lay in the open air, and in direct sunlight. I pumped up everyone with vitamins and minerals. We obtained these supplements over the trade routes and from pilfered pharmacies, but I gradually learned, with the villagers who were better gardeners than me, how to cultivate these substances ourselves.

For example, we made vitamin-C rich pine-needle tea. We planted a whole acre of cannabis plants. We pushed people to eat a lot of the fresh fish and plants; and quality cheeses some of the old women knew how to make.

The village began to grow. I got pregnant again, but decided that this was going to be it. People began to call me "Doctor Emma," and I called my building, the Emma Wallace Blair Clinic. Travelers came to it; the clinic was growing a bit too fast, like Monique was.

Once in a while I would think, with mixed feelings, about Monique's life when *she* was 25 y.o., in 2076. Who knows what men, and the earth, would have in store for us, or for her, then. I wanted all of us to still be around to protect her, but more importantly, I wanted her to learn to be strong, and a survivor.

THE END

Printed in Great Britain
by Amazon

25628098R00182